A GOOD SCENT
FROM A
STRANGE MOUNTAIN

A GOOD
SCENT
FROM A
STRANGE
MOUNTAIN

STORIES BY

ROBERT
OLEN
BUTLER

GROVE PRESS
New York

First published in 1992 by
Henry Holt and Company, Inc., New York

This Grove Press edition includes two stories—"Salem" and
"Missing"—not included in the original collection.

Published simultaneously in Canada
Printed in the United States of America

Library of Congress Cataloging-in-Publication Data

Butler, Robert Olen.
A good scent from a strange mountain : stories / by Robert Olen
Butler.
p. cm.
ISBN-13: 978-0-8021-3798-2
1. Vietnamese Americans—Fiction. 2. Vietnamese Conflict,
1961–1975—Fiction. 3. Louisiana—Social life and
customs—Fiction. I. Title.

PS3552.U8278 G66 2001
813'.54—dc21   00-066310

Grove Press
an imprint of Grove/Atlantic, Inc.
154 West 14th Street
New York, NY 10011

Distributed by Publishers Group West

www.groveatlantic.com

13 14 15   16 15 14 13 12

FOR JOHN WOOD

The stories in this book have appeared in the following places: "Open Arms," *The Missouri Review*; "Mr. Green," *The Hudson Review*; "The Trip Back," *The Southern Review*, reprinted in the 1991 edition of *The Best American Short Stories*; "Fairy Tale," *The Virginia Quarterly Review*; "Crickets," syndicated by P.E.N. and broadcast on National Public Radio's "NPR Playhouse"; "Letters from My Father," *Cimarron Review*; "Love," *Writer's Forum*; "Mid-Autumn," *Hawaii Review*; "In the Clearing," *Icarus*; "A Ghost Story," *Colorado Review*; "Snow," *The New Orleans Review*; "Relic," *The Gettysburg Review*, reprinted in *New Stories from the South, The Year's Best 1991*; "Preparation," *The Sewanee Review*; "A Good Scent from a Strange Mountain," *New England Review*, reprinted in the 1992 edition of *The Best American Short Stories* and in *New Stories from the South, The Year's Best 1992*; "Salem," *Mississippi Review*, reprinted in the 1996 edition of *The Best American Short Stories*; "Missing," *Gentleman's Quarterly*.

CONTENTS

CONTENTS

A   GOOD   SCENT

FROM   A

STRANGE   MOUNTAIN

O P E N   A R M S

I have no hatred in me. I'm almost certain of that. I fought for my country long enough to lose my wife to another man, a cripple. This was because even though I was alive, I was dead to her, being far away. Perhaps it bothers me a little that his deformity was something he was born with and not earned in the war. But even that doesn't matter. In the end, my country itself was lost and I am no longer there and the two of them are surely suffering, from what I read in the papers about life in a unified Vietnam. They mean nothing to me, really. It seems strange even to mention them like this, and it is stranger still to speak of them before I speak of the man who suffered the most complicated feeling I could imagine. It is he who makes me feel sometimes that I am sitting with my legs crossed in an attitude of peace and with an acceptance of all that I've been taught about the suffering that comes from desire.

There are others I could hate. But I feel sorry for my enemies and the enemies of my country. I live on South Mary Poppins Drive in Gretna, Louisiana, and since I speak perfect English, I am influential with the others who live here, the Westbank Vietnamese. We are all of us from South Vietnam. If you go across the bridge and into New Orleans and you take the interstate north and then turn on a highway named after a chef, you will come to the place called Versailles. There you will find the Vietnamese who are originally from the North. They are Catholics in Versailles. I am a Buddhist. But what I know now about things, I learned from a communist one dark evening in the province of Phước Tuy in the Republic of South Vietnam.

I was working as an interpreter for the Australians in their base camp near Núi Đất. The Australians were different from the Americans when they made a camp. The Americans cleared the land, cut it and plowed it and leveled it and strung their barbed wire and put up their tin hootches. The Australians put up tents. They lived under canvas with wooden floors and they didn't cut down the trees. They raised their tents under the trees and you could hear the birds above you when you woke in the morning, and I could think of home that way. My village was far away, up-country, near Pleiku, but my wife was still my wife at that time. I could lie in a tent under the trees and think of her and that would last until I was in the mess hall and I was faced with eggs and curried sausages and beans for breakfast.

The Australians made a good camp, but I could not understand their food, especially at the start of the day. The morning I met Đặng Văn Thập, I first saw him across the mess hall staring at a tray full of this food. He had the commanding officer at one elbow and the executive officer at his other, so I knew he was important, and I looked at Thập closely. His skin was dark, basic peasant blood like me, and he wore a sport shirt of green and blue plaid. He could be anybody on a motor scooter in Saigon or hustling for xích-lô fares in Vũng Tàu. But I knew there was something special about him right away.

His hair was wildly fanned on his head, the product of VC field-barbering, but there was something else about him that gave him away. He sat between these two Australian officers who were nearly a head taller, and he was hunched forward a little bit. But he seemed enormous, somehow. The people in our village believe in ghosts. Many people in Vietnam have this belief. And sometimes a ghost will appear in human form and then vanish. When that happens and you think back on the encounter, you realize that all along you felt like you were near something enormous, like if you came upon a mountain in the dark and could not see it but knew it was there. I had something of that feeling as I looked at Thập for the first time. Not that I believed he was a ghost. But I knew he was much bigger than the body he was in as he stared at the curried sausages.

Then there was a stir to my left, someone sitting down, but I didn't look right away because Thập held me. "You'll have your chance with him, mate," a voice said in a loud whisper, very near my ear. I turned and it was Captain Townsend, the intelligence officer. His mustache, waxed and twirled to two sharp points, twitched as it usually did when he and I were in the midst of an interrogation and he was getting especially interested in what he heard. But it was Thập now causing the twitch. Townsend's eyes had slid away from me and back across the mess hall, and I followed his gaze. Another Vietnamese was arriving with a tray, an ARVN major, and the C.O. slid over and let the new man sit next to Thập. The major said a few words to Thập and Thập made some sort of answer and the major spoke to the C.O.

"He's our new bushman scout," Townsend said. "The major there is heading back to division after breakfast and then we can talk to him."

I'd heard that a new scout was coming in, but he would be working mostly with the units out interdicting the infiltration routes and so I hadn't given him much thought. Townsend was fumbling around for something and I glanced over. He was pulling a slip of paper out of his pocket. He read a name off the paper, but he butchered the tones and I had no idea what he was saying. I took the paper from him and read Thập's name. Townsend said, "They tell me he's a real smart little bastard. Political cadre. Before that he was a sapper. Brains and a killer, too. Hope this conversion of his is for real."

I looked up and it was the ARVN major who was doing all the talking. He was in fatigues that were so starched and crisp they could sit there all by themselves, and his hair was slicked into careful shape and rose over his forehead in a pompadour the shape of the front fender on the elegant old Citroën sedans you saw around Saigon. Thập had sat back in his chair now and he was watching the major talk, and if I was the major I'd feel very nervous, because the man beside him had the mountain shadow and the steady look of the ghost of somebody his grandfather had cheated or cuckolded or murdered fifty years ago and he was back to take him.

It wasn't until the next day that Captain Townsend dropped Thập's file into the center of my desk. The desk was spread with a dozen photographs, different angles on two dead woodcutters that an Australian patrol had shot yesterday. The woodcutters had been in a restricted area, and when they ran, they were killed. The photos were taken after the two had been laid out in their cart, their arms sprawled, their legs angled like they were leaping up and clicking their heels. The fall of Thập's file scattered the photos, fluttered them away. Townsend said, "Look this over right away, mate. We'll have him here in an hour."

The government program that allowed a longtime, hard-core Viet Cong like Thập to switch sides so easily had a stiff name in Vietnamese but it came to be known as "Open Arms." An hour later, when Thập came through the door with Townsend, he filled the room and looked at me once, knowing everything about me that he wished, and the idea of our opening our arms to him, exposing our chests, our hearts, truly frightened me. In my village you ran from a ghost because if he wants you, he can reach into that chest of yours and pull out not only your heart but your soul as well.

I knew the facts about Thập from the file, but I wondered what he would say about some of these things I'd just read. The things about his life, about the terrible act that turned him away from the cause he'd been fighting for. But Townsend grilled him, through me, for an hour first. He asked him all the things an intelligence captain would be expected to ask, even though the file already had the answers to these questions as well. The division interrogation had already learned all that Thập knew about the locations and strengths of the VC units in our area, the names of shadow government cadre in the villages, things like that. But Thập patiently repeated his answers, smoking one Chesterfield cigarette after another, careful about keeping his ash from falling on the floor, never really looking at either of us, not in the eye, only occasionally at our hands, a quick glance, like he expected us to suddenly be holding a weapon, and he seemed very small now, no less smart and skilled in killing, but a man, at last, in my eyes.

So when Captain Townsend was through, he gave me a nod and, as we'd arranged, he stepped out for me to chat with Thập informally. Townsend figured that Thập might feel more comfortable talking with his countryman one on one. I had my doubts about that. Still, I was interested in this man, though not for the reasons Townsend was. At that moment I didn't care about the tactical intelligence my boss wanted, and so even before he was out of the room I intended to ignore it. But I felt no guilt. He had all he needed already.

As soon as the Australian was gone, Thập lifted his face high for the first time and blew a puff of smoke toward the ceiling. This stopped me cold, like he'd just sprung an ambush from the undergrowth where he'd been crouching very low. He did not look at me.

He watched the smoke rise and he waited, his face placid. Finally I felt my voice would come out steady and I said, "We are from the same region. I am from Pleiku Province." The file said that Thập was from Kontum, the next province north, bordering both Cambodia and Laos. He said nothing, though he lowered his face a little. He looked straight ahead and took another drag on his cigarette, a long one, the ash lengthening visibly, doubling in size, as he drew the smoke in.

I knew from the file the sadness he was bearing, but I wanted to make him show it to me, speak of it. I knew I should talk with him indirectly, at least for a time. But I could only think of the crude approach, and to my shame, I took it. I said, "Do you have family there?"

His face turned to me now, and I could not draw a breath. I thought for a moment that my first impression of him had been correct. He was a ghost and this was the moment he would carry me away with him. My breath was gone, never to return. But he did not dissolve into the air. His eyes fixed me and then they went down to the file on the desk, as if to say that I asked what I already knew. He had been sent to Phước Tuy Province to indoctrinate the villagers. He was a master, our other sources said, of explaining the communist vision of the world to the woodcutters and fishermen and rice farmers. And meanwhile, in Kontum, the tactics had changed, as they always do, and three months ago the VC made a lesson out of a little village that had a chief with a taste for American consumer goods and information to trade for them. This time the lesson was severe and the ones who did not run were all killed. Thập's wife and two children expected to be safe because someone was supposed to know whose family they were. They stayed and they were murdered by the VC and Thập made a choice.

His eyes were still on the file and my breath had come back to me and I said, "Yes, I know."

He turned away again and he stared at the cigarette, watched the curl of smoke without drawing it into him. I said, "But isn't that just the war? I thought you were a believer."

"I still am," he said and then he looked at me and smiled faintly, but the smile was only for himself, like he knew what I was thinking. And he did. "This is nothing new," he said. "I confessed to the same thing at your division headquarters. I believe in the government caring for all the people, the poor before the rich. I believe in the state of personal purity that makes this possible. But I finally came to believe that the government these men from the north want to set up can't be controlled by the very people it's supposed to serve."

"And what do you think of these people you've joined to fight with now?" I said.

He took a last drag on his cigarette and then leaned forward to stub it out in an ashtray at the corner of my desk. He sat back and folded his hands in his lap and his face grew still, his mouth drew down in placid seriousness. "I understand them," he said. "The Americans, too. I learned about their history. What they believe is good."

I admit that my first impulse at this was to challenge him. He didn't know anything about the history of Western democracy until after he'd left the communists. They killed his wife and his children and he wanted to get them. But I knew that what he said was also true. He was a believer. I could see his Buddhist upbringing in him. The communists could appeal to that. They couldn't touch the Catholics, but the Buddhists who didn't believe in all the mysticism were well prepared for communism. The communists were full of right views, right intentions, right speech, and all that. And Buddha's second Truth, about the thirst of the passions being the big trap, the communists were real strict about that, real prudes. If a VC got caught by his superiors with a pinup, just a girl in a bathing suit even, he'd be in very deep trouble.

That thing Thập said about personal purity. After it sank in a little bit, it pissed me off. But this is a weakness of my own, I guess, though at times I can't quite see it as a weakness. I'm not that good a Buddhist. I live in America and things just don't look the way my mother and my grandmother explained them to me. But Thập suddenly seemed a little too smug. And I wasn't frightened by him anymore. He was a communist prude and I even had trouble figuring out how he'd brought himself to make a couple of kids. Then, to my shame, I said, "You miss being with your wife, do you?" What I almost said was, "Do you miss sleeping with your wife?" but I wasn't quite that heartless, even with this smug true believer who until very recently had been a bitter enemy of my country.

Changing my question as I did, even as I spoke it, I thought I would never get the answer to what I really wanted to know. As soon as the words were out of my mouth, I felt a flush spread from under my chin and up my face. It was only a minor attack of shame until I saw what was happening before me. I suppose it was the suddenness of this question, its unexpectedness, that caught him off guard. It's an old interrogation trick. But Thập's hands rose gently from his lap and I knew they were remembering her. It all happened in a few seconds and the hands simply lifted up briefly, but I knew without any doubt that his palms, his fingertips, were stunned by the memory of touching her. Then the hands returned to his lap and he said in a low voice, "Of course I miss her."

I asked him no more questions, and after he was gone, my own hands, lying on the desktop, grew restless, rose and then hid in my lap and burned with their own soft memories. I still had a wife and she had not been my wife for long before I'd had to leave her. I knew that Thập was no ghost but a man and he loved his wife and desired her as I loved and desired mine and that was within the bounds of his purity. He was a man, but I wished from then on only to stay far away from him. The infantry guys had their own interpreter and I wouldn't have to deal with Thập and I was very glad for that.

Less than a week later, however, I saw him again. It was on a Sunday. Early that morning there'd been some contact out in the Long Khánh Mountains just to the east of us. First there was the popping of small arms for a few minutes and then a long roar, the mini-guns on the Cobras as they swooped in, and then there was silence.

In the afternoon the enlisted men played cricket and I sat beneath a tree with my eyes on them but not really following this strange game, just feeling the press of the tree's shade and listening to the thunk of the ball on the bat and the smatterings of applause, and I let the breeze bring me a vision of my wife wearing her aó dài, the long silk panels fluttering, as if lifted by this very breeze, as if she was nearby, waiting for me. And a few times as I sat there, I thought of Thập. Maybe it was my wife who brought him to me, the link of our yearning hands. But it wasn't until the evening that I actually saw him.

It was in the officers' club. Sometimes they had a film to show and this was one of the nights. Captain Townsend got me there early to help him move the wicker chairs around to face the big bed sheet they'd put up at one end for a screen. Townsend wouldn't tell me what the film was. When I asked him, he just winked and said, "You'll like it, mate," and I figured it was another of the Norman Wisdom films. This little man, Wisdom, was forever being knocked down and tormented by a world of people bigger than him. Townsend knew I didn't like these films, and so I decided that was what the wink was all about.

Thập came in with a couple of the infantry officers and I was sorry to see that their interpreter wasn't with them. I couldn't understand why they had him here. I guess they were trying to make him feel welcome, a part of their world. I still think that. They just didn't understand what sort of man he was. They clapped him on the back and pointed to the screen and the projector, and they tried their own few words of Vietnamese with him and some of that baby talk, the pidgin English that sounded so ridiculous to me, even with English being my second language. I didn't think Thập would like Norman Wisdom either. Thập and I were both little men.

But when he came in, the thing I was most concerned about was that since I was the only other Vietnamese in the club, Thập would seek me out for help. But he didn't. He glanced at me once and that was it. The two infantry officers took him up to the front row and sat him between them, and when Thập was settled, my attention shifted enough that I finally realized that something was going on here out of the ordinary. The Aussies were unusually boisterous, poking at one another and laughing, and one of them yelled to Townsend, "You intelligence boys have to smuggle this stuff in?"

Townsend laughed and said, "It was too bloody hot even for us, mate."

I didn't know what he was talking about and I was evidently staring at Captain Townsend with my confusion clear on my face. He looked at me and then put his arm around my shoulders. "You'll see," he said. "It's for all us boys who are missing our little ladies." He nodded me toward the chairs and I went and sat a couple of rows behind Thập and a little to his left. I could see only the back of his head, the spray of his hair, his deep brown neck, the collar of his plaid shirt. He raised his face to the screen and the lights went out and the films began.

There were nine of them, each lasting about twenty minutes. The first began without any credits. A man was walking along a country path. He was a large, blond-haired man, Swedish I later learned, though at the time it simply struck me that this wasn't the sort of man who would be in a Norman Wisdom movie. He was dressed in tight blue jeans and a flannel shirt that was unbuttoned, exposing his bare chest. I had never seen an Englishman dressed like that. Or an Australian either. And Wisdom's movies were all in black and white. This one was in grainy color and the camera was quaking just a little bit and then I realized that all I was hearing were the sounds of the projector clicking away and the men beginning to laugh. There was no soundtrack on this film. Someone shouted something that I didn't catch, then someone else. I thought at first that there'd been a mistake. This was the wrong film and the men were telling Townsend to stop the show, put on little Norman. But then the camera turned to a young woman standing by a fence with cows in the background and she was wearing shorts that were cut high up into her crotch and she shook her long hair and the Australians whooped. The camera returned to the man and he was clearly agitated and the club filled with cries that I could understand now: Go for her, mate; put it to her, mate; get on with it.

I glanced at Thập and his face was lifted to the screen, but of course he did not know what was about to happen. I looked up, too, and the man and woman were talking with each other and then they kissed. Not for long. The woman pulled back and knelt down before the man and she unsnapped and unzipped his blue jeans and she pulled them down and he still had his underpants on. I discovered, a little to my surprise, that I could not breathe very well and I felt weak in my arms. I had never seen a film like this, though I'd heard things about them. But there was a moment, when the man remained clad in his underpants, that I thought there was still some boundary here, that this was not a true example of the films I'd heard about.

But the woman squeezed at him there, playfully, smiling, like this was wonderful fun for her, and then she stripped off his underpants. His body was ready for her and that was very clear there, right on the screen, and she seemed truly happy about this and she brought her face near to this part of him and I drew in a sudden breath as she did a thing that I had never even asked my wife to do, though seeing it now made me weak with desire for her.

And then I looked at Thập. It was simply a reflex. I still had not put together what was happening in this club and what Thập was and what had happened to him in his life and what he believed. I looked to him and his face was still lifted; he was watching, and I glanced up and the woman's eyes lifted, too; she looked at the man even as she did this for him, and I returned to Thập and now his face was coming down, very slowly. His head bowed low and it remained bowed and I watched him for as long as I could.

I must admit, to my shame, that it was not very long. I was distracted. I said before, speaking of Thập's "personal purity," that an indifference to this notion is a weakness of mine. I have never remarried, and I must admit that it pleases me to look at the pictures in some of the magazines easily available in America. The women are so naked I feel I know them very well and the looks on their faces are usually so pleasant that they seem somehow willing for me to know them this way—me personally. It's a childish fantasy, I realize, hardly the right intentions, and I suppose someday this little desire will lead to unhappiness. But I am susceptible to that. And on that dark night, in that Australian tent in the province of Phước Tuy, I was filled with desire, and I watched all nine films, desiring my wife— mostly her, I think—but at times, too, briefly desiring one of these long-haired women who took such pleasure in the passing farmer, the sailor on the town, the delivery man, even the elderly and rather small doctor.

Three more times I looked at Thập. The first time, his head was still bowed. The second time, he was, to my surprise, looking at the screen. He was watching as the camera settled on the face of a dark-haired woman who was being made love to in the only way I had ever known to do it, and for a time all we could see was her face, turned a little to the side, jarred again and again, her eyes closed. But on her face was a smile, quiet, full of love, but a little sad, like she knew her man would soon have to leave her. I know I was reading this into her from my own life. She was a Swedish prostitute making a pornographic movie, and the smile was nothing of this sort. It was fake. And I know that it's the same with all the smiles in the magazines. The smiles of these naked women are the smiles of money, of fame, of a hope to break into movies or buy some cocaine or whatever. But on that night in the Australian tent, Thập and I looked at this woman's face and I know what I felt and something told me that Thập was feeling that, too. He watched for a long time, his face lifted, his hands, I know, yearning.

He was still watching as I turned my own face back to the screen. There were two more films after that, and I viewed them carefully. But my mind was now on Thập. I knew that a few rows in front of me he was suffering. This man had been my sworn enemy till a week ago. The others in this room had been my friends. But Thập was my countryman in some deeper way. And it had nothing to do with his being Vietnamese, either. I knew what was happening inside him. He was desiring his wife, just as I was desiring mine. Except on that night I thought I would one day be with my wife again, and his was newly dead.

But if that was all of it, I don't think he would have made this impression on me that does not leave. These films he saw sucked at his desire, brought the feel of his wife to him, made his hands rise before him. He was a man, after all. I watched the films till there were no more and I felt bad for Thập, his wanting a woman, wanting his wife, his being drawn by that very yearning to a vision of her body as ashes now and bits of bone. The third time I looked at him, his head was bowed again and it probably remained bowed. It was bowed still when the lights went on and Captain Townsend was called to the front of the room and was hailed for his show with wild applause and cheers.

And as we all shuffled out of the tent I saw Thập's face briefly, between his two Australian mates, the two infantry officers who had made him feel like he was really part of the gang. Thập's face told me how it would all end. His eyes were wildly restless, like he'd been on a sapper mission and a flare had just gone off and he suddenly found himself here in the midst of his enemy.

That night he went to a tent and killed one of the two infantry officers, the one, no doubt, who had insisted on his coming to the club. Then Thập killed himself, a bullet in his brain. It was lucky for Townsend that Thập didn't understand the cheers at the end or the captain might have been chosen instead of the infantry officer. Thập's desire for his wife had made him very unhappy. But it alone did not drive him to his final act. That was a result of a history lesson. Thập was a true believer, and that night he felt that he had suddenly understood the democracies he was trying to believe in. He felt that the communists whom he had rightly broken with, who had killed his wife and shown him their own fatal flaw, nevertheless had been right about all the rest of us. The fact that the impurity of the West had touched Thập directly, had made him feel something strongly for his dead wife, had only made things worse. He'd had no choice.

And as for myself, I live my life in the United States of America. I work in a bank. I have my own apartment with my own furniture and I have saved more money than I expect ever to need, if I can keep my job. And there's no worry about that. It's a big bank and they like me there. I can talk to the Vietnamese customers, and they think I'm a good worker beyond that. I read the newspapers. I subscribe to several magazines, and in one of them beautiful women smile at me each month. I no longer think of my wife. I go to the movies. I own a VCR and at last I saw the movie "Mary Poppins." The street I live on is one of four named after Mary Poppins in our neighborhood. This is true. You can look it up on any street map.

The Vietnamese on the Westbank do not like the Vietnamese in Versailles. The ones on the Westbank point out that for the ones in Versailles, freedom only means the freedom to make money. They are cold people, driving people, Northerners. The Southerners say that for them, freedom means the freedom to think, to enjoy life. The Vietnamese in Versailles do not like the Southerners. We are lazy people, to them. Unfocused. Greedy but not capable of working hard together for what we want. They say that they are the ones who understand America and how to succeed here. There are many on the Westbank and in Versailles who are full of hatred.

I say that desire can lead to unhappiness, and so can a strong belief. I can sit for long hours from the late afternoon and into the darkness of night and I do not feel compelled to watch anything or hear anything or do anything. I can think about Thập and I can fold my hands together and at those times there is no hatred at all within me.

MR. GREEN

I am a Catholic, the daughter of a Catholic mother and father, and
I do not believe in the worship of my ancestors, especially in the
form of a parrot. My father's parents died when he was very young
and he became a Catholic in an orphanage run by nuns in Hanoi. My
mother's mother was a Catholic but her father was not and, like
many Vietnamese, he was a believer in what Confucius taught about
ancestors. I remember him taking me by the hand while my parents
and my grandmother were sitting under a banana tree in the yard
and he said, "Let's go talk with Mr. Green." He led me into the
house and he touched his lips with his forefinger to tell me that this
was a secret. Mr. Green was my grandfather's parrot and I loved
talking to him, but we passed Mr. Green's roost in the front room.
Mr. Green said, "Hello, kind sir," but we didn't even answer him.

My grandfather took me to the back of his house, to a room that
my mother had said was private, that she had yanked me away from
when I once had tried to look. It had a bead curtain at the door and
we passed through it and the beads rustled like tall grass. The room
was dim, lit by candles, and it smelled of incense, and my grandfather

stood me before a little shrine with flowers and a smoking incense bowl and two brass candlesticks and between them a photo of a man in a Chinese mandarin hat. "That's my father," he said, nodding toward the photo. "He lives here." Then he let go of my hand and touched my shoulder. "Say a prayer for my father." The face in the photo was tilted a little to the side and was smiling faintly, like he'd asked me a question and he was waiting for an answer that he expected to like. I knelt before the shrine as I did at Mass and I said the only prayer I knew by heart, The Lord's Prayer.

But as I prayed, I was conscious of my grandfather. I even peeked at him as he stepped to the door and parted the beads and looked toward the front of the house. Then he returned and stood beside me and I finished my prayer as I listened to the beads rustling into silence behind us. When I said "Amen" aloud, my grandfather knelt beside me and leaned near and whispered, "Your father is doing a terrible thing. If he must be a Catholic, that's one thing. But he has left the spirits of his ancestors to wander for eternity in loneliness." It was hard for me to believe that my father was doing something as terrible as this, but it was harder for me to believe that my grandfather, who was even older than my father, could be wrong.

My grandfather explained about the spirit world, how the souls of our ancestors continue to need love and attention and devotion. Given these things, they will share in our lives and they will bless us and even warn us about disasters in our dreams. But if we neglect the souls of our ancestors, they will become lost and lonely and will wander around in the kingdom of the dead no better off than a warrior killed by his enemy and left unburied in a rice paddy to be eaten by black birds of prey.

When my grandfather told me about the birds plucking out the eyes of the dead and about the possibility of our own ancestors, our own family, suffering just like that if we ignore them, I said, "Don't worry, Grandfather, I will always say prayers for you and make offerings for you, even if I'm a Catholic."

I thought this would please my grandfather, but he just shook his head sharply, like he was mad at me, and he said, "Not possible." "I can," I said.

Then he looked at me and I guess he realized that he'd spoken harshly. He tilted his head slightly and smiled a little smile—just like his father in the picture—but what he said wasn't something to smile about. "You are a girl," he said. "So it's not possible for you to do it alone. Only a son can oversee the worship of his ancestors."

I felt a strange thing inside me, a recoiling, like I'd stepped barefoot on a slug, but how can you recoil from your own body? And so I began to cry. My grandfather patted me and kissed me and said it was all right, but it wasn't all right for me. I wanted to protect my grandfather's soul, but it wasn't in my power. I was a girl. We waited together before the shrine and when I'd stopped crying, we went back to the front room and my grandfather bowed to his parrot and said, "Hello, kind sir," and Mr. Green said, "Hello, kind sir," and even though I loved the parrot, I would not speak to him that day because he was a boy and I wasn't.

This was in our town, which was on the bank of the Red River just south of Hanoi. We left that town not long after. I was seven years old and I remember hearing my grandfather arguing with my parents. I was sleeping on a mat at the back of our house and I woke up and I heard voices and my grandfather said, "Not possible." The words chilled me, but then I listened more closely and I knew they were discussing the trip we were about to go on. Everyone was very frightened and excited. There were many families in our little town who were planning to leave. They had even taken the bell out of the church tower to carry with them. We were all Catholics. But Grandfather did not have the concerns of the Catholics. He was concerned

about the spirits of his ancestors. This was the place where they were
born and died and were buried. He was afraid that they would not
make the trip. "What then?" he cried. And later he spoke of the
people of the South and how they would hate us, being from the
North. "What then?" he said.

Mr. Green says that, too. "What then?" he has cried to me a
thousand times, ten thousand times, in the past sixteen years. Parrots
can live for a hundred years. And though I could not protect my
dead grandfather's soul, I could take care of his parrot. When my
grandfather died in Saigon in 1972, he made sure that Mr. Green
came to me. I was twenty-four then and newly married and I still
loved Mr. Green. He would sit on my shoulder and take the top of
my ear in his beak, a beak that could crush the hardest shell, and he
would hold my ear with the greatest gentleness and touch me with
his tongue.

I have brought Mr. Green with me to the United States of America,
and in the long summers here in New Orleans and in the warm
springs and falls and even in many days of our mild winters, he sits
on my screened-in back porch, near the door, and he speaks in the
voice of my grandfather. When he wants to get onto my shoulder
and go with me into the community garden, he says, "What then?"
And when I first come to him in the morning, he says, "Hello,
kind sir."

He loves me. That is, I am the only person who can go near him
without his attempting to draw blood. But he loved my grandfather
before me, and there are times when he seems to hold the spirit of
my grandfather and all his knowledge. Mr. Green sits on my shoulder
and presses close to my head and he repeats the words that he has
heard from my husband and my children. My children even teach
him English words. He says all these things, but without any feeling.
The Vietnamese words of my grandfather, however, come out pow-

erfully, like someone very strong is inside him. And whenever he speaks with my grandfather's voice, Mr. Green's eyes dilate and contract over and over, which is a parrot's display of happiness. Yesterday I tried to give him some drops that the veterinarian prescribed for him and Mr. Green said, "Not possible," and even though he is sick, his eyes showed how pleased he was to defy me.

When we all lived in Saigon at last, my grandfather discovered the bird market on Hàm Nghi Street and he would take me there. Actually, in the street market of Hàm Nghi there were animals of all kinds—dogs and monkeys and rabbits and turtles and even wildcats. But when my grandfather took my hand and said to me, "Come, little one," and we walked down Trần Hưng Đạo, where our house was, and we came to Hàm Nghi, he always took me to the place with the birds.

The canaries were the most loved by everyone who came to the market, and my grandfather sang with them. They all hopped to the side of their cages that was closest to my grandfather and he whistled and hummed and even sang words, songs from the North that he sang quite low, so that only the birds could hear. He did not want the people of Saigon to realize he was from the North. And the canaries all opened their mouths and the air filled with their sounds, their throats ruffling and puffing, and I looked at my grandfather's throat to see if it moved the way the throats of these birds moved. It did not move at all. His skin was slack there, and in all the times I saw him charm the birds, I never saw his throat move, like he didn't really mean the sounds he made. The people all laughed when they saw what he could do and they said that my grandfather was a wizard, but he would just ignore them.

The canaries seemed to be his favorite birds on Hàm Nghi, though he spent time with them all. The dark-plumed ones—the magpies and the blackbirds—were always singing on their own, especially the blackbirds with their orange beaks. My grandfather came near the blackbirds and they were gabbling among themselves and he frowned at them, like they were fools to be content only with their own company. They did not need him to prompt their songs. He growled at them, "You're just a bunch of old women," and we moved on to the doves that were big-eyed and quiet and he cooed at them and he told them how pretty they were and we looked at the moorhens, pecking at the bottoms of their cages like chickens, and the cranes with their wonderful necks curling and stretching.

We visited all the birds and my grandfather loved them, and the first time we went to Hàm Nghi, we ended up at the cages crowded with sparrows. He bent near their chattering and I liked these birds very much. They were small and their eyes were bright, and even though the birds were crowded, they were always in motion, hopping and fluffing up and shaking themselves like my vain friends. I was a quiet little girl, but I, too, would sometimes look at myself in a mirror and primp and puff myself up, even as in public I tried to hold myself apart a little bit from the other girls.

I was surprised and delighted that first day when my grandfather motioned to the birdseller and began to point at sparrows and the merchant reached into the cage and caught one bird after another and he put them all into a cardboard box. My grandfather bought twelve birds and they did not fly as they sat in the box. "Why aren't they flying?" I asked.

"Their wings are clipped," my grandfather said.

This was all right with me. They clearly weren't in any pain and they could still hop and they would never fly away from me. I wouldn't even need a cage for my vain little friends.

I'm sure that my grandfather knew what I was thinking. But he said nothing. When we got home, he gave me the box and told me to take the birds to show my mother. I found her on the back stoop slicing vegetables. I showed her the box and she said that Grandfather was wonderful. She set the box down and told me to stay with her, I could help her. I crouched beside her and waited and I could hear the chattering of the sparrows from the box.

We had always kept chickens and ducks and geese. Some of them were pecking around near us even as I crouched there with my mother. I knew that we ate those animals, but for some reason Hàm Nghi seemed like a different place altogether and the sparrows could only be for song and friendship. But finally my mother finished cutting the vegetables and she reached into the box and drew out a sparrow, its feet dangling from the bottom of her fist and its head poking out of the top. I looked at its face and I knew it was a girl and my mother said, "This is the way it's done," and she fisted her other hand around the sparrow's head and she twisted.

I don't remember how long it took me to get used to this. But I would always drift away when my grandfather went to the sparrow cages on Hàm Nghi. I did not like his face when he bought them. It seemed the same as when he cooed at the doves or sang with the canaries. But I must have decided that it was all part of growing up, of becoming a woman like my mother, for it was she who killed them, after all. And she taught me to do this thing and I wanted to be just like her and I twisted the necks of the sparrows and I plucked their feathers and we roasted them and ate them and my grandfather would take a deep breath after the meal and his eyes would close in pleasure.

There were parrots, too, on Hàm Nghi. They all looked very much like Mr. Green. They were the color of breadfruit leaves with a little yellow on the throat. My grandfather chose one bird each time and cocked his head at it, copying the angle of the bird's head, and my grandfather said, "Hello," or "What's your name?"—things he never said to Mr. Green. The parrots on Hàm Nghi did not talk to my grandfather, though once one of them made a sound like the horns of the little cream and blue taxis that rushed past in the streets. But they never spoke any words, and my grandfather took care to explain to me that these parrots were too recently captured to have learned anything. He said that they were probably not as smart as Mr. Green either, but one day they would speak. Once after explaining this, he leaned near me and motioned to a parrot that was digging for mites under his wing and said, "That bird will still be alive and speaking to someone when you have grown to be an old woman and have died and are buried in the ground."

I am forty-one years old now. I go each day to the garden on the bank of the bayou that runs through this place they call Versailles. It is part of New Orleans, but it is far from the center of the town and it is full of Vietnamese who once came from the North. My grandfather never saw the United States. I don't know what he would think. But I come to this garden each day and I crouch in the rich earth and I wear my straw hat and my black pantaloons and I grow lettuce and collards and turnip greens and mint, and my feet, which were once quite beautiful, grow coarse. My family likes the things I bring to the table.

Sometimes Mr. Green comes with me to this garden. He rides on my shoulder and he stays there for a long time, often imitating the cardinals, the sharp ricochet sound they make. Then finally Mr. Green climbs down my arm and drops to the ground and he waddles about in the garden, and when he starts to bite off the stalk of a plant, I cry, "Not possible" to him and he looks at me like he is angry, like I've dared to use his own words, his and his first master's, against him. I always bring twigs with me and I throw him one to chew on so that neither of us has to back down. I have always tried to preserve his dignity. He is at least fifty years older than me. My grandfather was eighteen when he himself caught Mr. Green on a trip to the highlands with his father.

So Mr. Green is quite old and old people sometimes lose their understanding of the things around them. It is not strange, then, that a few weeks ago Mr. Green began to pluck his feathers out. I went to the veterinarian when it became clear what was happening. A great bare spot had appeared on Mr. Green's chest and I had been finding his feathers at the foot of his perch, so I watched him one afternoon through the kitchen window. He sat there on his perch beside the door of the back porch and he pulled twelve feathers from his chest, one at a time, and felt each with his tongue and then dropped it to the floor. I came out onto the porch and he squawked at me, as if he was doing something private and I should have known better than to intrude. I sat down on the porch and he stopped.

I took Mr. Green to the veterinarian and he said that when parrots do this, it may be because they lack a certain vitamin or mineral. But more often the reason is that the bird is bored. I tried to convince myself that this is what it meant when Mr. Green stopped plucking his feathers as soon as I appeared on the porch. Keep him busy, the doctor said. So I got Mr. Green a new climbing tree with lots of fresh bark to peel and I spent more time with him. I took him to the garden even when he didn't ask to go and I brought my sewing and even some of my cooking—the preparation of the foods—out onto the porch, and while I did these household things, I talked to him. It was just idle chatter but there were plenty of words, and often Mr. Green looked at me sharply as I spoke and I could hear how I sounded, chattering away like a blackbird.

But I felt driven to do something for him. He was old and he was sick and I felt I had to do something. My grandfather took six months to die and he lay in a bed on the top floor of our house and Mr. Green was always on a perch beside him. I remember a wind chime at the window. It was made of brass and I've never had a wind chime in my home because when I hear one, another sound always comes with it, the deep rattling cough of my grandfather. I would visit him in his room with my mother and once he called me back as we were about to leave. I came to him and my mother had gone on out the door and I could hear her talking rapidly with my grandmother. My grandfather motioned me to come very near and he twisted his body in the bed. His face crumpled in pain as he did it, but he forced himself because he wanted to tell me a secret. I leaned close to him. "Do you hear them talking?" he said. He nodded toward the door and he obviously meant my mother and grandmother.

"Yes," I said.

He frowned. "How foolish they sound. Chattering and yammering. All the women sound like that. You don't want to grow up sounding like all these foolish women, do you?"

I did not know how to answer his question. I wanted very much to be like my mother, and when my grandfather said this, I felt the recoiling begin inside me and the tears begin to rise. But my mother called my name at that moment and I did not have to find an answer to my grandfather's question. I turned my back on him and ran across the room without saying a word. As I got to the door, however, Mr. Green cried, "What then?" and it sounded as if he had actually finished my grandfather's thought. You will grow up to be a woman—what then?

And maybe he did finish the thought. Parrots are very smart. Mr. Green in particular. And he knows more than just my grandfather's words. The Buddhists believe in the transmigration of souls, though I suppose it's impossible to transmigrate into some creature that's already alive. But after a few days of angry looks from Mr. Green when I filled the porch with talk that was intended to save his life, he began to cry, "Not possible" over and over until I stopped speaking. Perhaps a male voice would have been acceptable to him, but mine was not, and then Mr. Green began to pluck himself once more, even with me sitting there in the room. I went to him when he began to do this and I said, "Not possible," but he ignored me. He did not even raise his head to look at me but tore away at his feathers, each one making a faint popping sound as it came out. Then the next day he began to cough.

I knew the cough well. But I took Mr. Green to the veterinarian and he told me what I expected, that the cough was not the bird's. This was a sound he was imitating. "Did someone in your household recently have a cold or the flu?" the doctor said.

"It is my grandfather," I said.

On the last visit to my grandfather's room he began to cough. My mother went to him and he waved her away. She backed off and I came forward, wanting to help him. He was sitting up now and hunched over and the cough rattled deep inside his chest and then there was a sudden silence and I drew nearer, thinking that my step forward had actually helped, but my grandfather lifted his face and his eyes were very sad, and I knew he was disappointed. My brothers were not yet born and I held my breath so that this silence would go on, but the sound raked up from his chest and filled the room again.

This morning I went to the back porch and Mr. Green was pulling out a feather and he did not acknowledge me, even to taunt me by calling me "sir." He dropped the feather and began to pluck another from beneath his left wing. His chest was naked now and the skin looked as slack as my grandfather's throat. I stood before him and I offered my arm for him to come and sit on my shoulder. Yesterday he had said, "Not possible," but today he said nothing. He dropped a feather and leaned over and bit me hard on my arm. I bled. But I did not move my arm and he looked at me. His eyes were steady in their sadness, fully dilated, as if he was considering all of this. I pushed my arm to him again and he knew that he had no choice, so he climbed on, but he did not go to my shoulder.

I held my arm aloft and carried Mr. Green outside. The sun had still not burned the fog off the bayou and I went straight into the garden. My feet were bare, like a child's, and the earth was soft and wet and I crouched there and I quickly reached to Mr. Green and grasped him at his chest, lifted him and caught him with my other hand before he could struggle. His wings were pinned and he was bigger in my hands than I had ever imagined. But a Vietnamese woman is experienced in these things and Mr. Green did not have a chance even to make a sound as I laid him on his side, pinned him with my knee, slid my hands up and wrung his neck.

I pray for the soul of my grandfather. I do not bear him any anger. Sometimes I go to Mass during the week. Versailles has a Catholic church just for the Vietnamese and the Mass is celebrated in our language. I sit near the back and I look at the section where all the old women go. They take the Eucharist every day of their lives and they sit together wearing their traditional dresses and with their hair in scarves rolled up on their heads and I wonder if that is where I will finally end up, in the old women's section at Mass each day. No one in my church will likely live as long as a parrot. But our savior lived only thirty-three years, so maybe it's not important. There were women around Jesus when He died, the two Marys. They couldn't do anything for Him. But neither could the men, who had all run away.

THE
TRIP BACK

I am just a businessman, not a poet. It is the poet who is supposed
to see things so clearly and to remember. Perhaps it is only the poets
who can die well. Not the rest of us. I drove from my home in Lake
Charles, Louisiana, to the airport in Houston, Texas, to pick up my
wife's grandfather. And what is it that I experienced on that trip?
What is it that struck me as I got off the interstate highway in
Beaumont, knowing the quick route to the airport as I do? I was
driving through real towns in Texas. One was named China, another
Nome. One was Liberty. If I was a man who believed in symbols and
omens, I would have smiled at this. I was passing through Liberty to
pick up my wife's grandfather, whose own liberty my wife and I and
the man's nephew in San Francisco had finally won, after many years
of trying. He was arriving this very day from the West Coast after
living thirteen years under communist rule in our home country of
Vietnam. Perhaps a poet would think of those things—about Liberty,
Texas, and my wife's grandfather—and write a memorable poem.
Though maybe not. I am ignorant of these matters. Maybe it is only
the bird taking flight or the frog jumping into the pond that the poet
is interested in.

All I know is that for me I drove the two-lane highway across Texas and I just noticed the businesses. The little ones that seemed so Vietnamese to me in how the people always looked for some new angle, some empty corner in the marketplace. I noticed the signs for stump grinding and for house leveling and for mud pumping. The different stands along the way—fireworks, fruit and vegetables, hubcaps and antiques. The Paradise Club had a miniskirt contest and The Bait Barn had a nightcrawler special and Texas Winners had a baseball trophy sale. There was a Donut Delight and a Future Star Twirling Academy and a handpainted sign on a post saying that the finest porch swings were a mile down this dusty road. The Mattress Man said on his sign, right underneath his business name, JESUS IS LORD.

I am a Catholic and I must say that this made me smile. The Lord of the universe, the Man of Sorrows, turned into the Lord of the Mattress, the Mattress Man. But even so, I understood what this owner was trying to do, appealing specially to those of his own kind. This is good business practice, when you know your sales area. I have done very well for myself in Lake Charles in the laundry and dry-cleaning business. It is very simple. People sweat a lot in the climate of southern Louisiana, and there was a place for a very good laundry and dry cleaner. I have two locations in Lake Charles and I will soon open one in Sulphur. So it was this that interested me as I drove through Texas, as it always does. I am a businessman. It is my way.

And if I was a man who believed in symbols and omens, I would have been very interested toward the end of my journey when I came to a low highway bridge that took me across the wide converging of two rivers, for as I entered the bridge, the sign said, LOST AND OLD RIVERS. These two rivers were full of little islands and submerged trees and it was hard to see how the two ran together, for they looked more like one sprawling thing, like perhaps a large lake, something that was bound in and not moving, not flowing. Lost and old.

I had not given much serious thought to Mr. Chinh, my wife's grandfather. I knew this: My wife loved him very much. We are all like that in Vietnam. We honor our families. My four children honor me very much and I honor them. My wife is devoted to me and I am devoted to her. I love her. We were very lucky in that our parents allowed us to marry for love. That is to say, my mother and father and my wife's mother allowed it. Her father was dead. We still have a little shrine in our house and pray for him, which is the way of all Vietnamese, even if they are Catholic. As Catholics we understand this as the communion of saints. But my wife has no clear memory of her father. He died when she was very young. He drowned swimming in the South China Sea. And after that, Mr. Chinh became like a father for my wife.

She wept the night before my trip to the airport. She was very happy to have her grandfather again and very sorry that she'd missed all those years with him. I heard her muffling the sound of her crying in the pillow and I touched her on the shoulder and felt her shaking, and then I switched on the light by the bed. She turned her face sharply away from me, as if I would reproach her for her tears, as if there was some shame in it. I said to her, "Mai, it is all right. I understand your feeling."

"I know," she said, but she did not turn back to me. So I switched the light off once more and in the dark she came to me and I held her.

You must wait to understand why it is important, but at this point I must confess one thing. My wife came to me in the dark and I held her and her crying slowed and stopped and of course I was happy for that. I was happy to hold my wife in the dark in this moment of strong feeling for her and to be of help, but as I lay there, my mind could not focus on this woman that I love. My mind understood that she was feeling these things for a man of her own blood who had been very important to her and who then disappeared from her life for more than a decade and now was coming back into it. But these are merely bloodless words, saying it this way, things of the mind. And that was all they were to me, even lying there in the dark. I made those words run in my head, but what was preoccupying me at that moment was an itching on my heel that I could not scratch and the prices of two different types of paint for the outer shop of the new dry-cleaning store. My wife was a certain pressure, a warmth against me, but there was also a buzz in the electric alarm clock that I was just as conscious of.

Do not misjudge me. I am not a cold man. I drew my wife closer as she grew quieter, but it was a conscious decision, and even saying that, I have to work hard to remember the moment, and the memory that I have is more like a thought than a memory of my senses. And it's not as if the itching on my heel, the buzz of the clock, are any more vivid. I have to work extremely hard to reconstruct this very recent night so that I can even tell you with assurance that there was a clock in the room or that there was a foot at the end of my leg.

But you will see that it is Mr. Chinh who has put me in this present state of agitation. After a time, as I held her in the bed, my wife said, "My tears are mostly happy. Don't worry for me, Khánh. I only wish I was small enough and his back was strong enough that I could ride upon it again."

At the airport gate I looked at the people filing through the door from the jetway. The faces were all white or Spanish and they filed briskly through the door and rushed away and then there were a long few moments when no one appeared. I began to think that Mr. Chinh had missed the plane. I thought of the meal that my wife was preparing at home. She and my children and our best friends in Lake Charles had been working since dawn on the house and on the food for this wonderful reuniting, and when the door to the jetway gaped there with no one coming through, that is the only thought I had, that the food would be ruined. I did not worry about Mr. Chinh or wonder what the matter could really be.

I looked over to the airline agents working behind their computers, checking in the passengers for the next flight. I was ready to seek their help when I glanced back to the door, and there was Mr. Chinh. He was dressed in a red-and-black-plaid sport shirt and chino pants and he was hunched a little bit over a cane, but what surprised me was that he was not alone. A Vietnamese man about my age was holding him up on the side without the cane and bending close and talking into his ear. Then the younger man looked up and saw me and I recognized a cousin of my wife, the son of Mr. Chinh's nephew. He smiled at me and nodded a hello and he jiggled the old man into looking at me as well. Mr. Chinh raised his head and an overhead light flashed in his glasses, making his eyes disappear. He, too, smiled, so I felt that it was all right.

They approached me and I shook Mr. Chinh's hand first. "I am so happy you have come to visit us," I said.

I would have said more—I had a little speech in my head about my wife's love for him and how she is so sorry she is not at the airport and how much his great-grandchildren want to see him— but my wife's cousin cut in before I had a chance. "This is Mr. Khánh," he said to the old man. "The one I told you about who would meet you."

Mr. Chinh nodded and looked at me and repeated my name. He spoke no more and I looked to the cousin, who said, "I'm Hương," and he bowed to me very formally.

"I remember you," I said and I offered my hand. He took it readily, but I knew from his formality that there could be things I did not know about Mr. Chinh. It is the custom of Vietnamese, especially of the old school of manners, not to tell you things that are unpleasant to hear. The world need not be made worse than it is by embracing the difficult things. It is assumed that you wish to hear that all is well, and many people will tell you this no matter what the situation really is. Hương struck me as being of this tradition—as surely his father must, too, for this is how an otherwise practical people learns an attitude such as this.

But I am a blunt man. Business has made me that way, particularly business in America. So I said to Mr. Hương, "Is there something wrong with Mr. Chinh?"

He smiled at me as if I was a child asking about the thunder. "I came with our dear uncle to make sure he traveled safely. He is very old."

I suddenly felt a little uncomfortable talking about the man as if he wasn't there, so I looked at him. He was leaning contentedly on his cane, gazing around the circle of gates. I bent nearer to him and said, "Mr. Chinh, do you like the airport?"

He turned to me at once and said, "This is a fine airport. The best I have seen."

The man's voice was strong, and this reassured me. I liked his appreciation of the airport, which I, too, admired, so I said to Mr. Hương, "Is he a little frail, physically?"

"Yes," said Mr. Hương, happy, I suppose, to have words put in his mouth sufficient to answer my blunt question. I did not like this cousin Hương.

But I was compelled to ask, "Will you be coming to Lake Charles to join us?"

"No. I must decline your gracious invitation. I return by a flight later this day."

I was blunt again. "You came all this way never to leave the airport? Just to return at once?"

Mr. Hương shrugged. "It is my pleasure to make sure our beloved uncle arrives safely. My father said that if you should wish to discuss Uncle Chinh's permanent home after perhaps a week or so, he will await your call."

I didn't know the details of all that, except that I was prepared for my wife's sake and the sake of our country's family tradition to make him part of our household. So I just nodded and took Mr. Chinh by the arm and said a brief good-bye to Mr. Hương, and the old man and I started off for the baggage check.

Mr. Chinh was enchanted with the airport, gawking about as we moved, and his interest was so intent and his pleasure so evident from the little clucks and nods he made that I did not try to speak with him. Twice he asked me a question, once about where they would take the luggage, answered by our arrival at the carousel, which caused him to laugh loud when the bell rang and the silver metal track began to run. Mr. Chinh stood at the opening and he watched each bag emerging through the plastic flaps as closely as a customs inspector. The second question was if I had a car. And when I said yes, he seemed very pleased, lifting his cane before him and tapping it down hard. "Good," he said. "Don't tell me what kind. I will see for myself."

But in the parking garage, he was baffled. He circled the car and touched it gently with the rubber tip of his cane, touched it several places, on a taillight, a hubcap, the front bumper, the name on the grill. "I don't know this car," he said. "I don't know it at all."

"It's an Acura," I said.

He shook the name off as if a mosquito had just buzzed his head. "I thought you would own a French car. A Citroën, I had predicted. A 15CV saloon."

"No, Mr. Chinh. It's an Acura. It's a very good car," and I stopped myself from telling him it was from Japan.

Mr. Chinh lifted his shoulders and let them drop heavily, as if he was greatly disappointed and perhaps even a little scornful. I put his bags in the trunk and opened the door for him and we made it out of the airport and back onto the two-lane highway before any more words were spoken. I was holding my eyes on the road, trying to think of small talk, something I'm not very good at, when Mr. Chinh finally said, "The inside is very nice."

I didn't understand. I glanced over at him and he was running his hand along the dashboard and I realized that he'd been thinking about the car all this time. "Good," I said. "I'm glad you like it."

"Not as nice as many others," he said. "But nice."

There's no car interior short of a Rolls that is nicer than my Acura, but I nodded at the old man and I told myself that there was no need to debate with him or entertain him but just to be cordial with him. Let him carry the conversation, if he wished one. But the trip looked very long ahead of me. We hadn't even gotten out into the country of stump grinders and fruit stands. It was still franchised fast food and clusters of gas stations and mini-malls and car dealerships. There were many miles to go.

Then up ahead I saw the work of a clever man, a car dealer who had dangled a big luxury car from the top of what looked like a seventy-foot crane. I said to Mr. Chinh, "There's something the Citroëns don't do," and I motioned the man's attention to the car in the sky. He bent down and angled his head up to look and his mouth gaped open. He said nothing but quickly shifted to the side window as we passed the car dealership and then he turned around to watch out the back window until the car on the crane was out of sight.

I expected Mr. Chinh to remark on this. Perhaps how no one would ever do such a thing to a French car. There would be no need. Something like that. But he said nothing, and after a time, I decided to appreciate the silence. I just concentrated on covering these miles before the old man would be reunited with the granddaughter he loved. I found that I myself was no longer comfortable with the old ways. Like the extended family. Like other things, too. The Vietnamese indirectness, for instance. The superstition. I was a good American now, and though I wished I could do more for this old man next to me, at least for my wife's sake, it was not an unpleasant thought that I had finally left Vietnam behind.

And I'd left behind more than the customs. I don't suppose that struck me as I was driving home from the airport. But it is clear to me now. I grew up, as did my wife, in Vũng Tàu. Both our families were pretty well off and we lived the year around in this seaside resort on the South China Sea. The French had called it Cap St. Jacques. The sand was white and the sea was the color of jade. But I say these things not from any vivid recollection, but from a thought in my head, as real only as lines from a travel brochure. I'd left behind me the city on the coast and the sea as well.

But you must understand that ultimately this doesn't have anything to do with being a refugee in the United States. When I got to the two rivers again, Old and Lost, I could recognize the look of them, like a lake, but it was only my mind working.

Perhaps that is a bad example. What are those two rivers to me? I mention them now only to delay speaking of the rest of my ride with Mr. Chinh. When we crossed the rivers, I suppose I was reminded of him somehow. Probably because of the earlier thoughts of the rivers as an omen. But now I tried once more to think of small talk. I saw a large curl of rubber on the shoulder of the road and then another a little later on and I said to Mr. Chinh, "Those are retreads from trucks. In Vietnam some enterprising man would have already collected those to make some use of them. Here no one cares."

The old man did not speak, but after a few moments I sensed something beside me and I glanced and found him staring at me. "Do we have far to go?" he asked.

"Perhaps an hour and a half," I said.

"May I roll down the window?"

"Of course," I said. I turned off the air conditioning and as he made faint grabbing motions at the door, I pressed the power button and lowered his window. Mr. Chinh turned his face to me with eyes slightly widened in what looked to me like alarm. "They're power windows," I said. "No handle."

His face did not change. I thought to explain further, but before I could, he turned to the window and leaned slightly forward so that the wind rushed into his face, and his hair—still more black than gray—rose and danced and he was just a little bit scary to me for some reason. So I concentrated again on the road and I was happy to let him stay silent, watching the Texas highway, and this was a terrible mistake.

If I'd forced him into conversation earlier, I would've had more time to prepare for our arrival in Lake Charles. Not that I could have done much, though. As it was, we were only fifteen minutes or so from home. We'd already crossed the Sabine River into Louisiana and I'd pointed it out to Mr. Chinh, the first words spoken in the car for an hour. Even that didn't start the conversation. Some time later the wandering of his own mind finally made him speak. He said, "The air feels good here. It's good when you can feel it on your face as you drive."

I naturally thought he was talking to me, but when I said, "Yes, that's right," he snapped his head around as if he'd forgotten that I was there.

What could I have said to such a reaction? I should have spoken of it to him right away. But I treated it as I would treat Mai waking from a dream and not knowing where she is. I said, "We're less than twenty miles from Lake Charles, Mr. Chinh."

He did not reply, but his face softened, as if he was awake now.

I said, "Mai can't wait to see you. And our children are very excited."

He did not acknowledge this, which I thought was rude for the grandfather who was becoming the elder of our household. Instead, he looked out the window again, and he said, "My favorite car of all was a Hotchkiss. I had a 1934 Hotchkiss. An AM80 tourer. It was a wonderful car. I would drive it from Saigon to Hanoi. A fine car. Just like the car that won the Monte Carlo rally in 1932. I drove many cars to Hanoi over the years. Citroën, Peugeot, Ford, Desoto, Simca. But the Hotchkiss was the best. I would drive to Hanoi at the end of the year and spend ten days and return. It was eighteen hundred kilometers. I drove it in two days. I'd drive in the day and my driver would drive at night. At night it was very nice. We had the top down and the moon was shining and we drove along the beach. Then we'd stop and turn the lights on and rabbits would come out and we'd catch them. Very simple. I can see their eyes shining in the lights. Then we'd make a fire on the beach. The sparks would fly up and we'd sit and eat and listen to the sea. It was very nice, driving. Very nice."

Mr. Chinh stopped speaking. He kept his face to the wind and I was conscious of the hum of my Acura's engine and I felt very strange. This man beside me was rushing along the South China Sea. Right now. He had felt something so strong that he could summon it up and place himself within it and the moment would not fade, the eyes of the rabbits still shone and the sparks still climbed into the sky and he was a happy man.

Then we were passing the oil refineries west of the lake and we rose on the I-10 bridge and Lake Charles was before us and I said to Mr. Chinh, "We are almost home now."

And the old man turned to me and said, "Where is it that we are going?"

"Where?"

"You're the friend of my nephew?"

"I'm the husband of Mai, your granddaughter," I said, and I tried to tell myself he was still caught on some beach on the way to Hanoi.

"Granddaughter?" he said.

"Mai. The daughter of your daughter Chim." I was trying to hold off the feeling in my chest that moved like the old man's hair was moving in the wind.

Mr. Chinh slowly cocked his head and he narrowed his eyes and he thought for a long moment and said, "Chim lost her husband in the sea."

"Yes," I said, and I drew a breath in relief.

But then the old man said, "She had no daughter."

"What do you mean? Of course she had a daughter."

"I think she was childless."

"She had a daughter and a son." I found that I was shouting. Perhaps I should have pulled off to the side of the road at that moment. I should have pulled off and tried to get through to Mr. Chinh. But it would have been futile, and then I would still have been forced to take him to my wife. I couldn't very well just walk him into the lake and drive away. As it was, I had five more minutes as I drove to our house, and I spent every second trying carefully to explain who Mai was. But Mr. Chinh could not remember. Worse than that. He was certain I was wrong.

I stopped at the final stop sign before our house and I tried once more. "Mai is the daughter of Nho and Chim. Nho died in the sea, just as you said. Then you were like a father to Mai . . . you carried her on your back."

"My daughter Chim had no children. She lived in Nha Trang."

"Not in Nha Trang. She never lived in Nha Trang."

Mr. Chinh shook his head no, refuting me with the gentleness of absolute conviction. "She lived on the beach of Nha Trang, a very beautiful beach. And she had no children. She was just a little girl herself. How could she have children?"

I felt weak now. I could barely speak the words, but I said, "She had a daughter. My wife. You love her."

The old man finally just turned his face away from me. He sat with his head in the window as if he was patiently waiting for the wind to start up again.

I felt very bad for my wife. But it wasn't that simple. I've become a blunt man. Not like a Vietnamese at all. It's the way I do business. So I will say this bluntly. I felt bad for Mai, but I was even more concerned for myself. The old man frightened me. And it wasn't in the way you might think, saying to myself, Oh, that could be me over there sitting with my head out the window and forgetting who my closest relatives are. It was different from that, I knew.

I drove the last two blocks to our house on the corner. The long house with the steep roof and the massively gnarled live oak in the front yard. My family heard my car as I turned onto the side street and then into our driveway. They came to the side door and poured out and I got out of the car quickly, intercepting the children. I told my oldest son to take the others into the house and wait, to give their mother some time alone with her grandfather, who she hadn't seen in so many years. I have good children, obedient children, and they disappeared again even as I heard my wife opening the car door for Mr. Chinh.

I turned and looked and the old man was standing beside the car. My wife embraced him and his head was perched on her shoulder and there was nothing on his face at all, no feeling except perhaps the faintest wrinkling of puzzlement. Perhaps I should have stayed at my wife's side as the old man went on to explain to her that she didn't exist. But I could not. I wished to walk briskly away, far from this house, far from the old man and his granddaughter. I wished to walk as fast as I could, to run. But at least I fought that desire. I simply turned away and moved off, along the side of the house to the front yard.

I stopped near the live oak and looked about, trying to see things. Trying to see this tree, for instance. This tree as black as a charcoal cricket and with great lower limbs, as massive themselves as the main trunks of most other trees, shooting straight out and then sagging and rooting again in the ground. A monstrous tree. I leaned against it and as I looked away, the tree faded within me. It was gone and I envied the old man, I knew. I envied him driving his Hotchkiss along the beach half a century ago. Envied him his sparks flying into the air. But my very envy frightened me. Look at the man, I thought. He remembered his car, but he can't remember his granddaughter.

And I demanded of myself: Could I? Even as I stood there? Could I remember this woman who I loved? I'd seen her just moments ago. I'd lived with her for more than twenty years. And certainly if she was standing there beside me, if she spoke, she would have been intensely familiar. But separated from her, I could not picture her clearly. I could construct her face accurately in my mind. But the image did not burn there, did not rush upon me and fill me up with the feelings that I genuinely held for her. I could not put my face into the wind and see her eyes as clearly as Mr. Chinh saw the eyes of the rabbits in his headlights.

Not the eyes of my wife and not my country either. I'd lost a whole country and I didn't give it a thought. Vũng Tàu was a beautiful city, and if I put my face into the wind, I could see nothing of it clearly, not its shaded streets or its white-sand beaches, not the South China Sea lying there beside it. I can speak these words and perhaps you can see these things clearly because you are using your imagination. But I cannot imagine these things because I lived them, and to remember them with the vividness I know they should have is impossible. They are lost to me.

Except perhaps when I am as old as Mr. Chinh. Perhaps he, too, moved through his life as distracted as me. Perhaps only after he forgot his granddaughter did he remember his Hotchkiss. And perhaps that was necessary. Perhaps he had to forget the one to remember the other. Not that I think he'd made that conscious choice. Something deep inside him was sorting out his life as it was about to end. And that is what frightens me the most. I am afraid that deep down I am built on a much smaller scale than the surface of my mind aspires to. When something finally comes back to me with real force, perhaps it will be a luxury car hanging on a crane or the freshly painted wall of a new dry-cleaning store or the faint buzz of the alarm clock beside my bed. Deep down, secretly, I may be prepared to betray all that I think I love the most.

This is what brought me to the slump of grief against the live oak in my front yard. I leaned there and the time passed and then my wife crept up beside me. I turned to her and she was crying quietly, her head bowed and her hand covering her eyes.

"I'm sorry," I said.

"I put him in the guest room," she said. "He thanked me as he would an innkeeper." She sobbed faintly and I wanted to touch her, but my arm was very heavy, as if I was standing at the bottom of the sea. It rose only a few inches from my side. Then she said, "I thought he might remember after he slept."

I could neither reassure her with a lie nor make her face the truth. But I had to do something. I had thought too much about this already. A good businessman knows when to stop thinking and to act instead. I drew close to my wife, but only briefly did my arm rise and hold her. That was the same as all the other forgotten gestures of my life. Suddenly I surprised myself and my wife, too. I stepped in front of her and crouched down and before either of us could think to feel foolish, I had taken Mai onto my back and straightened up and I began to move about the yard, walking at first, down the long drooping lower branch of the oak tree and then faster along the sidewalk and then up the other side of the house, and I was going faster and she only protested for a moment before she was laughing and holding on tighter, clinging with her legs about my waist and her arms around my neck, and I ran with her, ran as fast as I could so that she laughed harder and I felt her clinging against me, pressing against me, and I felt her breath on the side of my face as warm and moist as a breeze off the South China Sea.

FAIRY TALE

I like the way fairy tales start in America. When I learn English for real, I buy books for children and I read, "Once upon a time." I recognize this word "upon" from some GI who buys me Saigon teas and spends some time with me and he is a cowboy from the great state of Texas. He tells me he gets up on the back of a bull and he rides it. I tell him he is joking with Miss Noi (that's my Vietnam name), but he says no, he really gets up on a bull. I make him explain that "up on" so I know I am hearing right. I want to know for true so I can tell this story to all my friends so that they understand, no lie, what this man who stays with me can do. After that, a few years later, I come to America and I read some fairy tales to help me learn more English and I see this word and I ask a man in the place I work on Bourbon Street in New Orleans if this is the same. Up on and upon. He is a nice man who comes late in the evening to clean up after the men who see the show. He says this is a good question and he thinks about it and he says that yes, they are the same. I think this is very nice, how you get up on the back of time and ride and you don't know where it will go or how it will try to throw you off.

Once upon a time I was a dumb Saigon bargirl. If you want to know how dumb some Vietnam bargirl can be, I can give you one example. A man brought me to America in 1974. He says he loves me and I say I love that man. When I meet him in Saigon, he works in the embassy of America. He can bring me to this country even before he marries me. He says he wants to marry me and maybe I think that this idea scares me a little bit. But I say, what the hell. I love him. Then boom. I'm in America and this man is different from in Vietnam, and I guess he thinks I am different, too. How dumb is a Saigon bargirl is this. I hear him talk to a big crowd of important people in Vietnam—businessman, politician, big people like that. I am there, too, and I wear my best aó dài, red like an apple, and my quần, my silk trousers, are white. He speaks in English to these Vietnam people because they are big, so they know English. Also my boyfriend does not speak Vietnam. But at the end of his speech he says something in my language and it is very important to me.

You must understand one thing about the Vietnam language. We use tones to make our words. The sound you say is important, but just as important is what your voice does, if it goes up or down or stays the same or it curls around or it comes from your throat, very tight. These all change the meaning of the word, sometimes very much, and if you say one tone and I hear a certain word, there is no reason for me to think that you mean some other tone and some other word. It was not until everything is too late and I am in America that I realize something is wrong in what I am hearing that day. Even after this man is gone and I am in New Orleans, I have to sit down and try all different tones to know what he wanted to say to those people in Saigon.

He wanted to say in my language, "May Vietnam live for ten thousand years." What he said, very clear, was, "The sunburnt duck is lying down." Now, if I think this man says that Vietnam should

live for ten thousand years, I think he is a certain kind of man. But
when he says that a sunburnt duck is lying down—boom, my heart
melts. We have many tales in Vietnam, some about ducks. I never
hear this tale that he is telling us about, but it sounds like it is very
good. I should ask him that night what this tale is, but we make love
and we talk about me going to America and I think I understand
anyway. The duck is not burned up, destroyed. He is only sunburnt.
Vietnam women don't like the sun. It makes their skin dark, like the
peasants. I understand. And the duck is not crushed on the ground.
He is just lying down and he can get up when he wants to. I love
that man for telling the Vietnam people this true thing. So I come
to America and when I come here I do not know I will be in more
bars. I come thinking I still love that man and I will be a housewife
with a toaster machine and a vacuum cleaner. Then when I think I
don't love him anymore, I try one last time and I ask him in the dark
night to tell me about the sunburnt duck, what is that story. He
thinks I am one crazy Vietnam girl and he says things that can burn
Miss Noi more than the sun.

So boom, I am gone from that man. There is no more South
Vietnam and he gives me all the right papers so I can be American
and he can look like a good man. This is all happening in Atlanta.
Then I hear about New Orleans. I am a Catholic girl and I am a
bargirl, and this city sounds for me like I can be both those things.
I am twenty-five years old and my titties are small, especially in
America, but I am still number-one girl. I can shake it baby, and soon
I am a dancer in a bar on Bourbon Street and everybody likes me to
stay a Vietnam girl. Maybe some men have nice memories of Vietnam
girls.

I have nice memories. In Saigon I work in a bar they call Blossoms.
I am one blossom. Around the corner I have a little apartment. You
have to walk into the alley and then you go up the stairs three floors

and I have a place there where all the shouting and the crying and sometimes the gunfire in the street sounds very far away. I do not mix with the other girls. They do bad things. Take drugs, steal from the men. One girl lives next to me in Saigon and she does bad things. Soon people begin to come in a black car. She goes. She likes that, but I do not talk to her. One day she goes in the black car and does not come back. She leaves everything in her place. Even her Buddha shrine to her parents. Very bad. I live alone in Saigon. I have a double bed with a very nice sheet. Two pillows. A cedar closet with my clothes, which are very nice. Three aó dàis, one apple red, one blue like you see in the eyes of some American man, one black like my hair. I have a glass cabinet with pictures. My father. Some two or three American men who like me very special. My mother. My son.

Yes, I have a son. One American gives me that son, but my boy is living in Vietnam with my mother. My mother says I cannot bring up a child with my life. I say to her that my son should have the best. If Miss Noi is not best for my son, then my son should be someplace different. When the man brings me to America, he does not want a son either, and my mother does not talk to me very much anyway except to say my son is Vietnam boy, not American boy. At least my mother is my blood, though sometimes she is unhappy about that, I think. I do not think they are happy in Vietnam now, but who can say? You have a mother and then you have a son and then boom, you do not have either a mother or a son, though they are alive somewhere, so I do not have to pray for their souls. I do not have to be unhappy.

I pray in my little room in Saigon. I am a Catholic girl and I have a large statue of Mary in my room. That statue is Mary the mother of God, not Mary Magdalene, who was a bargirl one time, too. My statue of Mary the mother of God is very beautiful. She is wearing a blue robe and her bare feet are sticking out of the bottom. Her feet are beautiful like the feet of a Vietnam girl, and I pray to Mary and I paint her toenails and I talk to her. She faces the door and does not see my bed.

I sleep with men in Saigon. This is true. But I sleep with only one at a time. I do not take drugs with any man. I do not steal from any man. I give some man love when he is alone and frightened and he wants something soft to be close to him. I take money for this loving, but I do not ask them to take me to restaurants or to movie shows or to buy me jewelry or any gifts. If a girl does not make money but makes him take her to a restaurant and a movie show and buy her jewelry and then gives him loving, is this different? I would not take a man to my room and love him if I did not want to do that. The others could buy me Saigon tea in the Blossoms bar. The men would water the blossoms with Saigon tea. I talk with them and they put their arm around me and play music on the jukebox, but I do not take them to my room unless I would like them to be there. Then they would give me money, but I ask for nothing else. Only when they love me very much I ask them to get me something. In the place where the GI eats, they have something I cannot get in Saigon. This thing is an apple. I only ask for apples. I buy mangoes and papayas and pineapples and other sweet things to eat in the market, but in South Vietnam, an apple is a special thing. I hold an apple and it fills my hand and it is very smooth and very hard and it is red like my favorite aó dài. So red. I bite it and it is very sweet, like sweet water, like a stream of water from a mountain, and it is not stringy like a pineapple, and it is not mushy like a mango or papaya.

In New Orleans I buy many apples. I eat them in America whenever I want to. But is that memory not better? A GI who loves me brings me an apple and I put it on the table where Mary sits and after that man is sleeping and the room is dark, I walk across the floor and I am naked and the air feels cool on me and I take that apple and go to the window and I watch the dark roofs of Saigon and the moon rising and I eat my apple.

In New Orleans, there are apples in the stores and I buy them and I eat too many. The taste is still good but it is not special anymore. I am sometimes very tired. I take off my clothes on the stage of the club. I am not a blossom in New Orleans. I am a voodoo girl. The manager of the club gives me a necklace of bones to wear and the faces of the men are raised to me and I am naked. Many eyes see me. Many men want to touch Miss Noi, and I sleep with men in New Orleans. I still do not take them to my bed if I am not ready to like them. When they get up in the morning I always make sure they shave right. Many of the men miss a place at the back of their jaw or under their bottom lip. I make sure they have a clean shirt. I am ready to wash their shirt if they want me to. But they pay me money and they go, and they do not let me clean their shirt. Sometimes they go before the night is done. These are the men who have wives. I can see the place on their fingers where the sun has tanned around the ring which they took off to come to the bar. Their finger is dark skinned, but the band of flesh is white and they look naked there, even more naked than I must look to them on the stage. Their ring is in some pocket. I worry about their rings. What if the ring is to fall out on my floor and get kicked under the bed? What do they say to their wife when she sees their naked hand?

How does a life change? You meet some man who says he will take you away across the sea and he will marry you. A blossom and even a voodoo girl gets many men who talk about love and some of them talk about marriage. You are very careful about that. Many girls on Bourbon Street tell stories and laugh very hard about the men who say they want to marry them. I do not tell the story about the embassy man and the sunburnt duck. They would not understand. I dance naked on the stage and one night the announcer makes a big deal about Miss Noi being Vietnam girl. Sometimes he does this, sometimes Miss Noi is just some voodoo girl. But this night he sees some men in the audience with jackets on that says they were in Vietnam, so he says I am from Saigon and I am ready to please.

After I dance and put on my clothes and go and sit at the bar, these men in the jackets do not come near me. But one other man comes and stands beside me and he calls me "Miss." He says, "Miss, may I sit down?" If you want to sit next to a bargirl and hope that she will think you are an okay man, this is a good way to start, with "May I sit down, Miss." I look at this man and he is a tall man with a long neck so that he seems to stretch up as high as he can to see over a fence. His skin is dark, like he's been in the sun too long, and he is wearing a plaid shirt and blue jeans and his hands are rough, but there is no white band where a ring has been taken off. I look at his face and his eyes are black, but very small. His nose is long. Vietnam noses are not long, and though I know many Americans in my life and some French, too, I still lean back just a little when there is a long nose, because it seems to be pointing at me.

This man is not number one for looking at him, but he calls me "Miss" and he stands with his eyes looking down and then he peeks at me and then he lowers his eyes again as he waits for me to say if he can sit down. So I say yes. He seems like a nice man.

"You are very beautiful, Miss Noi," this man says.

This is 1981 and Miss Noi is thirty years old and I am glad to hear some man say it this way. I am not sexy bitch, wiggle it baby, oh boy oh boy it's hot, it feels good. These are okay things, too, for Miss Noi. These men give me money and they love me. But this man says I am beautiful and I say, "Thank you. You buy me a drink, okay?" I say this to all the men who sit next to me at the bar. This is what I am supposed to do. But I want this man to buy me a drink because he thinks I am beautiful. So he buys me a drink and I say he must buy one, too, and he buys a Dr Pepper, even though it is the same price as a drink of liquor. My drink is supposed to be liquor but it is mostly water, like Saigon tea. They make it the same in New Orleans, the New Orleans tea.

We sip our drinks and he does not have many words to say. He sips and looks at me and sips and I have many words I use on men. You from this town? You in New Orleans for long? You like Bourbon Street? You listen to jazz music? What is your work? But I do not use these words. I tell you I am sometimes very tired. This man's long nose dips down toward his Dr Pepper like he's going to drink through it, but it stops and then he lifts his chin a little and sips at his straw. His face seems very strange-looking and his hair is black but a little greasy and I just let him be quiet if he wants and I am quiet, too. Then he says, "It was nice to see you dance."

"You come often and see me dance and buy me drinks, okay?"

"You look different," he says.

"Miss Noi is a Vietnam girl. You never see that before."

"I seen it," this man says. "I was in Vietnam."

I have many men say they were in my country and they always sound a little funny, like they have a nasty secret or a sickness that you should be careful not to catch. And sometimes they just call it "Nam," saying that word with broken glass in their voice or saying it through their noses and their noses wrinkle up like the word smells when it comes out. But this man says the name of my country quiet and I don't always understand what American voices do, but he sounds sad to me. I say to him, "You didn't like being there? It makes you sad?"

He lifts his face and looks at me and he says, "I was very happy there. Weren't you?"

Well, this is something for me to think about. I could just answer this man, who is only one more man who saw me dance naked. I could just say yes or no and I could talk about reasons why. I am good at bargirl bullshit when I want to talk like that. But this man's eyes look at mine and I look away and sip my drink.

What do I know about men, after all? I can't tell anything anymore. I take men to my bed and I save my money and there have been very many men, I guess. It's like eating too many apples. You take a bite now and you can make yourself remember that apples are sweet, but it is like the apple in your mouth is not even there. You eat too many apples and all you can do is remember them. So this man who comes with his strange face and sounds sad when he talks about Vietnam because he was so happy there—I don't know what to make of him and so I take him to my room and he is very happy about that.

He tells me his name is Fontenot. He lives far away from New Orleans. He owns a little boat and he works fixing car engines. He was in Saigon one year working on car engines and he loved that city very much. I ask him why but he can't really explain. This is all of our talk, every bit of it, except before he makes love to me he says he is sorry he can never get his hands clean. He shows me how the grease from the car engines gets around his fingernails and he can't get them clean. I tell him not to worry and he makes love to me, and when he gets off me and lies down, he turns his head and I think that is because he does not want me to see that he is crying. I want to ask if he is very sad again, but I don't say anything. His face is away from me and he wants it like that and so I say nothing. Those are all the words of that night. In the morning I go into the bathroom and he is in the tub and I kneel beside him and take his hands and I have a cuticle file and I clean the grease away. He kisses my hands when he leaves.

What do I know about men anymore? That is not much to say about Mr. Fontenot. He came to see Miss Noi on a Saturday night and left on Sunday morning. Then the next Saturday night I was naked on the stage and I saw his face at the foot of the runway, looking up with his long nose pointed at my special part, and I felt a strange thing. My face got warm and I turned my back to him and danced away. After I finished my dance, I got dressed and came out to the bar, but he was not there. I asked the guy behind the bar, "Did you see that tall man with the thin neck and the long nose that I had a drink with last week?"

This guy says, "The one who looks like a goddamn goose?"

I don't like this guy behind the bar. I never even learn his name. So I say, "Go to hell, you," and I go outside and there is Mr. Fontenot waiting on the sidewalk. I go to him and I take his arm and we go around the corner and down the block and he says, "I couldn't hang around in there, Miss Noi. It makes me uncomfortable to talk to you in there."

I say, "I know, honey. I know." I see all types of men, though I realize I don't understand any of them deep down. But I know some men feel nervous in a bar. They come there to meet me but then they tell themselves that I really don't belong there, it's not worthy of me. And if I take this type of man to my room, they give me money quiet, folding the bills and putting them under a vase or somewhere, like it's not really happening. I know that kind of man. They can be very sweet sometimes.

We go up to my apartment again. It is a small place, like Saigon. I am comfortable there. Outside my window is a phony balcony. It looks like a balcony but it is only a foot wide, just a grill on the window. But it is nice. It looks like lace, though it is made of iron. I close the shade and turn to Mr. Fontenot and he is sitting on my bed. I go and sit next to him.

"I've been thinking about you," he says.

"You drive all the way back to New Orleans just to see Miss Noi again?"

"Of course," he says. His voice is gentle, but there's also something in it that says I should know this already. This is plenty strange to me, because I know nothing about Mr. Fontenot, really. A few words. He's a quiet man. I know nothing more about him than any man.

Then he says, "Look," and he shows me his hands. I don't understand. "I got one of those things you used on me last week." I look closer and I see that his hands are clean.

This makes me feel one more strange thing, a little sinking inside me. I say, "See? You have no need for Miss Noi anymore."

He takes me serious. He puts his arm around my shoulders and he is right to do this. "Don't say that, Miss Noi."

So then we make love. When we are finished, he turns his face away from me again and I reach over and turn it back. There are no tears, but he is looking very serious. I say, "Tell me one thing you like in Saigon."

Mr. Fontenot wiggles his shoulders and looks away. "Everything," he says.

"Why should I not think you are a crazy man? Everybody knows Americans go to Vietnam and they want to go home quick and forget everything. When they think they like Vietnam while they are there, they come home and they know it was all just a dream."

Mr. Fontenot looks at me one more time. "I'm not crazy. I liked everything there."

" 'Everything' means same as 'nothing.' I do not understand that. One thing. Just think about you on a street in Saigon and you tell me one thing."

"Okay," he says and then he says it again louder, "Okay," like I just push him some more, though I say nothing. It is louder but not angry. He sounds like a little boy. He wrinkles his brow and his little black eyes close. He stays like this for too long.

I ask, "So?"

"I can't think."

"You are on a street. Just one moment for me."

"Okay," he says. "A street. It's hot in Saigon, like Louisiana. I like it hot. I walk around. There's lots of people rushing around, all of them pretty as nutria."

"Pretty as what?"

"It's a little animal that has a pretty coat. It's good."

"Tell me more."

"Okay," he says. "Here's something. It's hot and I'm sweating and I'm walking through your markets in the open air and when I get back to my quarters, my sweat smells like the fruit and the vegetables in your markets."

I look at Mr. Fontenot and his eyes are on me and he's very serious. I do not understand a word he's saying now, but I know he's not saying any bullshit, that's for sure. He sweats and smells like fruit in Saigon. I want to talk to him now, but what am I to say to this? So I just start in about fruit. I tell him the markets have many good fruits, which I like very much. Mangoes, mangosteens, jackfruit, durians, papaya. I ask him and he says he has not eaten any of these. I still want to say words, to keep this going, so I tell him, "One fruit we do not have in South Vietnam is apples. I loved apples in Saigon when GI bring me apples from their mess hall. I never have apples till the GIs give them to me."

As soon as I say this, Mr. Fontenot's brow wrinkles again and I feel like there's a little animal, maybe a nutria, trying to claw his way out from inside Miss Noi. I have made this man think about all the GIs that I sleep with in Saigon. He knows now what kind of girl he is talking to. This time I turn my face away from him to hide tears. Then we stop talking and we sleep and in the morning he goes and I do not come and help him bathe because he learns from Miss Noi already how to clean his hands.

Is this a sad story or a happy story for Miss Noi? The next Saturday

Mr. Fontenot does not come and see me dance naked. I sit at the bar with my clothes on and I am upon a time and I wonder if I'm going to fall off now. Then boom. I go out of that place and Mr. Fontenot is standing on the sidewalk. He is wearing a suit with a tie and his neck reaches up high out of his white shirt and I can bet his hands are clean and he moves to me and one of his hands comes out from behind his back and he gives me an apple and he says he wants to marry Miss Noi.

Once upon a time there was a duck with a long neck and a long beak like all ducks and he lives in a place all alone and he does not know how to build a nest or preen his own feathers. Because of this, the sun shines down and burns him, makes his feathers turn dark and makes him very sad. When he lies down to sleep, you think that he is dead, he is so sad and still. Then one day he flies to another part of the land and he finds a little animal with a nice coat and though that animal is different from him, a nutria, still he lies down beside her. He seems to be all burnt up and dead. But the nutria does not think so and she licks his feathers and makes him well. Then he takes her with him to live in Thibodaux, Louisiana, where he fixes cars and she has a nice little house and she is a housewife with a toaster machine and they go fishing together in his little boat and she never eats an apple unless he thinks to give it to her. Though this may not be very often, they taste very good to her.

CRICKETS

They call me Ted where I work and they've called me that for over a decade now and it still bothers me, though I'm not very happy about my real name being the same as the former President of the former Republic of Vietnam. Thiệu is not an uncommon name in my homeland and my mother had nothing more in mind than a long-dead uncle when she gave it to me. But in Lake Charles, Louisiana, I am Ted. I guess the other Mr. Thiệu has enough of my former country's former gold bullion tucked away so that in London, where he probably wears a bowler and carries a rolled umbrella, nobody's calling him anything but Mr. Thiệu.

I hear myself sometimes and I sound pretty bitter, I guess. But I don't let that out at the refinery, where I'm the best chemical engineer they've got and they even admit it once in a while. They're good-hearted people, really. I've done enough fighting in my life. I was eighteen when Saigon fell and I was only recently mustered into the Army, and when my unit dissolved and everybody ran, I stripped off my uniform and put on my civilian clothes again and I threw rocks at the North's tanks when they rolled through the streets. Very

59

few of my people did likewise. I stayed in the mouths of alleys so I could run and then return and throw more rocks, but because what I did seemed so isolated and so pathetic a gesture, the gunners in the tanks didn't even take notice. But I didn't care about their scorn. At least my right arm had said no to them.

And then there were Thai Pirates in the South China Sea and idiots running the refugee centers and more idiots running the agencies in the U.S. to find a place for me and my new bride, who braved with me the midnight escape by boat and the terrible sea and all the rest. We ended up here in the flat bayou land of Louisiana, where there are rice paddies and where the water and the land are in the most delicate balance with each other, very much like the Mekong Delta, where I grew up. These people who work around me are good people and maybe they call me Ted because they want to think of me as one of them, though sometimes it bothers me that these men are so much bigger than me. I am the size of a woman in this country and these American men are all massive and they speak so slowly, even to one another, even though English is their native language. I've heard New Yorkers on television and I speak as fast as they do.

My son is beginning to speak like the others here in Louisiana. He is ten, the product of the first night my wife and I spent in Lake Charles, in a cheap motel with the sky outside red from the refineries. He is proud to have been born in America, and when he leaves us in the morning to walk to the Catholic school, he says, "Have a good day, y'all." Sometimes I say good-bye to him in Vietnamese and he wrinkles his nose at me and says, "Aw, Pop," like I'd just cracked a corny joke. He doesn't speak Vietnamese at all and my wife says not to worry about that. He's an American.

But I do worry about that, though I understand why I should be content. I even understood ten years ago, so much so that I agreed with my wife and gave my son an American name. Bill. Bill and his father Ted. But this past summer I found my son hanging around the house bored in the middle of vacation and I was suddenly his father Thiệu with a wonderful idea for him. It was an idea that had come to me in the first week of every February we'd been in Lake Charles, because that's when the crickets always begin to crow here. This place is rich in crickets, which always make me think of my own childhood in Vietnam. But I never said anything to my son until last summer.

I came to him after watching him slouch around the yard one Sunday pulling the Spanish moss off the lowest branches of our big oak tree and then throwing rocks against the stop sign on our corner. "Do you want to do something fun?" I said to him.

"Sure, Pop," he said, though there was a certain suspicion in his voice, like he didn't trust me on the subject of fun. He threw all the rocks at once that were left in his hand and the stop sign shivered at their impact.

I said, "If you keep that up, they will arrest me for the destruction of city property and then they will deport us all."

My son laughed at this. I, of course, knew that he would know I was bluffing. I didn't want to be too hard on him for the boyish impulses that I myself had found to be so satisfying when I was young, especially since I was about to share something of my own childhood with him.

"So what've you got, Pop?" my son asked me.

"Fighting crickets," I said.

"What?"

Now, my son was like any of his fellow ten-year-olds, devoted to superheroes and the mighty clash of good and evil in all of its high-tech forms in the Saturday-morning cartoons. Just to make sure he was in the right frame of mind, I explained it to him with one word, "Cricketmen," and I thought this was a pretty good ploy. He cocked his head in interest at this and I took him to the side porch and sat him down and I explained.

I told him how, when I was a boy, my friends and I would prowl the undergrowth and capture crickets and keep them in matchboxes. We would feed them leaves and bits of watermelon and bean sprouts, and we'd train them to fight by keeping them in a constant state of agitation by blowing on them and gently flicking the ends of their antennas with a sliver of wood. So each of us would have a stable of fighting crickets, and there were two kinds.

At this point my son was squirming a little bit and his eyes were shifting away into the yard and I knew that my Cricketman trick had run its course. I fought back the urge to challenge his set of interests. Why should the stiff and foolish fights of his cartoon characters absorb him and the real clash—real life and death—that went on in the natural world bore him? But I realized that I hadn't cut to the chase yet, as they say on the TV. "They fight to the death," I said with as much gravity as I could put into my voice, like I was James Earl Jones.

The announcement won me a glance and a brief lift of his eyebrows. This gave me a little scrabble of panic, because I still hadn't told him about the two types of crickets and I suddenly knew that was a real important part for me. I tried not to despair at his understanding and I put my hands on his shoulders and turned him around to face me. "Listen," I said. "You need to understand this if you are to have fighting crickets. There are two types, and all of us had some of each. One type we called the charcoal crickets. These were very large and strong, but they were slow and they could become confused. The other type was small and brown and we called them fire crickets. They weren't as strong, but they were very smart and quick."

"So who would win?" my son said.

"Sometimes one and sometimes the other. The fights were very long and full of hard struggle. We'd have a little tunnel made of paper and we'd slip a sliver of wood under the cowling of our cricket's head to make him mad and we'd twirl him by his antenna, and then we'd each put our cricket into the tunnel at opposite ends. Inside, they'd approach each other and begin to fight and then we'd lift the paper tunnel and watch."

"Sounds neat," my son said, though his enthusiasm was at best moderate, and I knew I had to act quickly.

So we got a shoe box and we started looking for crickets. It's better at night, but I knew for sure his interest wouldn't last that long. Our house is up on blocks because of the high water table in town and we crawled along the edge, pulling back the bigger tufts of grass and turning over rocks. It was one of the rocks that gave us our first crickets, and my son saw them and cried in my ear, "There, there," but he waited for me to grab them. I cupped first one and then the other and dropped them into the shoe box and I felt a vague disappointment, not so much because it was clear that my boy did not want to touch the insects, but that they were both the big black ones, the charcoal crickets. We crawled on and we found another one in the grass and another sitting in the muddy shadow of the house behind the hose faucet and then we caught two more under an azalea bush.

"Isn't that enough?" my son demanded. "How many do we need?"

I sat with my back against the house and put the shoe box in my lap and my boy sat beside me, his head stretching this way so he could look into the box. There was no more vagueness to my feeling. I was actually weak with disappointment because all six of these were charcoal crickets, big and inert and just looking around like they didn't even know anything was wrong.

"Oh, no," my son said with real force, and for a second I thought he had read my mind and shared my feeling, but I looked at him and he was pointing at the toes of his white sneakers. "My Reeboks are ruined!" he cried, and on the toe of each sneaker was a smudge of grass.

I glanced back into the box and the crickets had not moved and I looked at my son and he was still staring at his sneakers. "Listen," I said, "this was a big mistake. You can go on and do something else."

He jumped up at once. "Do you think Mom can clean these?" he said.

"Sure," I said. "Sure."

He was gone at once and the side door slammed and I put the box on the grass. But I didn't go in. I got back on my hands and knees and I circled the entire house and then I turned over every stone in the yard and dug around all the trees. I found probably two dozen more crickets, but they were all the same. In Louisiana there are rice paddies and some of the bayous look like the Delta, but many of the birds are different, and why shouldn't the insects be different, too? This is another country, after all. It was just funny about the fire crickets. All of us kids rooted for them, even if we were fighting with one of our own charcoal crickets. A fire cricket was a very precious and admirable thing.

The next morning my son stood before me as I finished my breakfast and once he had my attention, he looked down at his feet, drawing my eyes down as well. "See?" he said. "Mom got them clean."

Then he was out the door and I called after him, "See you later, Bill."

LETTERS FROM MY FATHER

I look through the letters my father sent to me in Saigon and I find this: "Dear Fran. How are you? I wish you and your mother were here with me. The weather here is pretty cold this time of year. I bet you would like the cold weather." At the time, I wondered how he would know such a thing. Cold weather sounded very bad. It was freezing, he said, so I touched the tip of my finger to a piece of ice and I held it there for as long as I could. It hurt very bad and that was after only about a minute. I thought, How could you spend hours and days in weather like that?

It makes no difference that I had misunderstood the cold weather. By the time he finally got me and my mother out of Vietnam, he had moved to a place where it almost never got very cold. The point is that in his letters to me he often said this and that about the weather. It is cold today. It is hot today. Today there are clouds in the sky. Today there are no clouds. What did that have to do with me?

He said "Dear Fran" because my name is Fran. That's short for Francine and the sound of Fran is something like a Vietnamese name, but it isn't, really. So I told my friends in Saigon that my name was Trán, which was short for Hôn Trán, which means "a kiss on the forehead." My American father lived in America but my Vietnamese mother and me lived in Saigon, so I was still a Saigon girl. My mother called me Francine, too. She was happy for me to have this name. She said it was not just American, it was also French. But I wanted a name for Saigon and Trán was it.

I was a child of dust. When the American fathers all went home, including my father, and the communists took over, that's what we were called, those of us who had faces like those drawings you see in some of the bookstalls on Nguyễn Huệ Street. You look once and you see a beautiful woman sitting at her mirror, but then you look again and you see the skull of a dead person, no skin on the face, just the wide eyes of the skull and the bared teeth. We were like that, the children of dust in Saigon. At one look we were Vietnamese and at another look we were American and after that you couldn't get your eyes to stay still when they turned to us, they kept seeing first one thing and then another.

Last night I found a package of letters in a footlocker that belongs to my father. It is in the storage shack at the back of our house here in America. I am living now in Lake Charles, Louisiana, and I found this package of letters outside—many packages, hundreds of letters— and I opened one, and these are all copies he kept of letters he sent trying to get us out of Vietnam. I look through these letters my father wrote and I find this: "What is this crap that you're trying to give me now? It has been nine years, seven months, and fifteen days since I last saw my daughter, my own flesh-and-blood daughter."

This is an angry voice, a voice with feeling. I have been in this place now for a year. I am seventeen and it took even longer than nine years, seven months, fifteen days to get me out of Vietnam. I wish I could say something about that, because I know anyone who

listens to my story would expect me right now to say how I felt. My
mother and me were left behind in Saigon. My father went on ahead
to America and he thought he could get some paperwork done and
prepare a place for us, then my mother and me would be leaving for
America very soon. But things happened. A different footlocker was
lost and some important papers with it, like their marriage license
and my birth certificate. Then the country of South Vietnam fell to
the communists, and even those who thought it might happen thought
it happened pretty fast, really. Who knew? My father didn't.

I look at a letter he sent me in Saigon after it fell and the letter
says: "You can imagine how I feel. The whole world is let down by
what happened." But I could not imagine that, if you want to know
the truth, how my father felt. And I knew nothing of the world
except Saigon, and even that wasn't the way the world was, because
when I was very little they gave it a different name, calling it Hồ
Chí Minh City. Now, those words are a man's name, you know, but
the same words have several other meanings, too, and I took the
name like everyone took the face of a child of dust: I looked at it
one way and it meant one thing and then I looked at it a different
way and it meant something else. Hồ Chí Minh also can mean "very
intelligent starch-paste," and that's what we thought of the new name,
me and some friends of mine who also had American fathers. We
would meet at the French cemetery on Phan Thanh Giản Street and
talk about our city—Hồ, for short; starch-paste. We would talk
about our lives in Starch-Paste City and we had this game where
we'd hide in the cemetery, each in a separate place, and then we'd
keep low and move slowly and see how many of our friends we
would find. If you saw the other person first, you would get a
point. And if nobody ever saw you, if it was like you were invisible,
you'd win.

The cemetery made me sad, but it felt very comfortable there somehow. We all thought that, me and my friends. It was a ragged place and many of the names were like Couchet, Picard, Vernet, Believeau, and these graves never had any flowers on them. Everybody who loved these dead people had gone home to France long ago. Then there was a part of the cemetery that had Vietnamese dead. There were some flowers over there, but not very many. The grave markers had photos, little oval frames built into the stone, and these were faces of the dead, mostly old people, men and women, the wealthy Vietnamese, but there were some young people, too, many of them dead in 1968 when there was much killing in Saigon. I would always hide over in this section and there was one boy, very cute, in sunglasses, leaning on a motorcycle, his hand on his hip. He died in February of 1968, and I probably wouldn't have liked him anyway. He looked cute but very conceited. And there was a girl nearby. The marker said she was fifteen. I found her when I was about ten or so and she was very beautiful, with long black hair and dark eyes and a round face. I would always go to her grave and I wanted to be just like her, though I knew my face was different from hers. Then I went one day—I was almost her age at last—and the rain had gotten into the little picture frame and her face was nearly gone. I could see her hair, but the features of her face had faded until you could not see them, there were only dark streaks of water and the picture was curling at the edges, and I cried over that. It was like she had died.

Sometimes my father sent me pictures with his letters. "Dear Fran," he would say. "Here is a picture of me. Please send me a picture of you." A friend of mine, when she was about seven years old, got a pen pal in Russia. They wrote to each other very simple letters in French. Her pen pal said, "Please send me a picture of you and I will send you one of me." My friend put on her white aó dài and went downtown and had her picture taken before the big banyan tree in the park on Lê Thánh Tôn. She sent it off and in return she got a picture of a fat girl who hadn't combed her hair, standing by a cow on a collective farm.

My mother's father was some government man, I think. And the communists said my mother was an agitator or collaborator. Something like that. It was all mostly before I was born or when I was just a little girl, and whenever my mother tried to explain what all this was about, this father across the sea and us not seeming to ever go there, I just didn't like to listen very much and my mother realized that, and after a while she didn't say any more. I put his picture up on my mirror and he was smiling, I guess. He was outside somewhere and there was a lake or something in the background and he had a T-shirt on and I guess he was really more squinting than smiling. There were several of these photographs of him on my mirror. They were always outdoors and he was always squinting in the sun. He said in one of his letters to me: "Dear Fran, I got your photo. You are very pretty, like your mother. I have not forgotten you." And I thought: I am not like my mother. I am a child of dust. Has he forgotten that?

One of the girls I used to hang around with at the cemetery told me a story that she knew was true because it happened to her sister's best friend. The best friend was just a very little girl when it began. Her father was a soldier in the South Vietnam Army and he was away fighting somewhere secret, Cambodia or somewhere. It was very secret, so her mother never heard from him and the little girl was so small when he went away that she didn't even remember him, what he looked like or anything. But she knew she was supposed to have a daddy, so every evening, when the mother would put her daughter to bed, the little girl would ask where her father was. She asked with such a sad heart that one night the mother made something up.

There was a terrible storm and the electricity went out in Saigon.

So the mother went to the table with the little girl clinging in fright to her, and she lit an oil lamp. When she did, her shadow suddenly was thrown upon the wall and it was very big, and she said, "Don't cry, my baby, see there?" She pointed to the shadow. "There's your daddy. He'll protect you." This made the little girl very happy. She stopped shaking from fright immediately and the mother sang the girl to sleep.

The next evening before going to bed, the little girl asked to see her father. When the mother tried to say no, the little girl was so upset that the mother gave in and lit the oil lamp and cast her shadow on the wall. The little girl went to the wall and held her hands before her with the palms together and she bowed low to the shadow. "Good night, Daddy," she said, and she went to sleep. This happened the next evening and the next and it went on for more than a year.

Then one evening, just before bedtime, the father finally came home. The mother, of course, was very happy. She wept and she kissed him and she said to him, "We will prepare a thanksgiving feast to honor our ancestors. You go in to our daughter. She is almost ready for bed. I will go out to the market and get some food for our celebration."

So the father went in to the little girl and he said to her, "My pretty girl, I am home. I am your father and I have not forgotten you."

But the little girl said, "You're not my daddy. I know my daddy. He'll be here soon. He comes every night to say good night to me before I go to bed."

The man was shocked at his wife's faithlessness, but he was very proud, and he did not say anything to her about it when she got home. He did not say anything at all, but prayed briefly before the shrine of their ancestors and picked up his bag and left. The weeks passed and the mother grieved so badly that one day she threw herself into the Saigon River and drowned.

The father heard news of this and thought that she had killed herself from shame. He returned home to be a father to his daughter, but on the first night, there was a storm and the lights went out and the man lit the oil lamp, throwing his shadow on the wall. His little girl laughed in delight and went and bowed low to the shadow and said, "Good night, Daddy." When the man saw this, he took his little girl to his own mother's house, left her, and threw himself into the Saigon River to join his wife in death.

My friend says this story is true. Everyone in the neighborhood of her sister's friend knows about it. But I don't think it's true. I never did say that to my friend, but for me, it doesn't make sense. I can't believe that the little girl would be satisfied with the shadow father. There was this darkness on the wall, just a flatness, and she loved it. I can see how she wouldn't take up with this man who suddenly walks in one night and says, "I'm your father, let me tell you good night." But the other guy, the shadow—he was no father either.

When my father met my mother and me at the airport, there were people with cameras and microphones and my father grabbed my mother with this enormous hug and this sound like a shout and he kissed her hard and all the people with microphones and cameras smiled and nodded. Then he let go of my mother and he looked at me and suddenly he was making this little choking sound, a kind of gacking in the back of his throat like a rabbit makes when you pick him up and he doesn't like it. And my father's hands just fluttered before him and he got stiff-legged coming over to me and the hug he gave me was like I was soaking wet and he had on his Sunday clothes, though he was just wearing some silly T-shirt.

All the letters from my father, the ones I got in Saigon, and the photos, they're in a box in the back of the closet of my room. My closet smells of my perfume, is full of nice clothes so that I can fit in at school. Not everyone can say what they feel in words, especially words on paper. Not everyone can look at a camera and make their face do what it has to do to show a feeling. But years of flat words, grimaces at the sun, these are hard things to forget. So I've been sitting all morning today in the shack behind our house, out here with the tree roaches and the carpenter ants and the smell of mildew and rotting wood and I am sweating so hard that it's dripping off my nose and chin. There are many letters in my lap. In one of them to the U.S. government my father says: "If this was a goddamn white woman, a Russian ballet dancer and her daughter, you people would have them on a plane in twenty-four hours. This is my wife and my daughter. My daughter is so beautiful you can put her face on your dimes and quarters and no one could ever make change again in your goddamn country without stopping and saying, Oh my God, what a beautiful face."

I read this now while I'm hidden in the storage shack, invisible, soaked with sweat like it's that time in Saigon between the dry season and the rainy season, and I know my father will be here soon. The lawn mower is over there in the corner and this morning he got up and said that it was going to be hot today, that there were no clouds in the sky and he was going to have to mow the lawn. When he opens the door, I will let him see me here, and I will ask him to talk to me like in these letters, like when he was so angry with some stranger that he knew what to say.

L O V E

I was once able to bring fire from heaven. My wife knew that and her would-be lovers soon learned that, though sometimes the lesson was a hard one for them. But that was in Vietnam, and when the need arose once more, here in America, I had to find a new way. You see, it has never been easy for a man like me. I know I appear to be what they call here a "wimp." I am not a handsome man, and I am small even for a Vietnamese. I assume the manners of a wimp, too, and I am conscious of doing that. I have done it all my life. I cross my legs at the knee and I step too lightly and I talk too much on subjects that others find boring. But there are two things about me that are exceptional. First, I was for many years a spy. You think that all spies look like the men in the movies. But real spies have a cover identity, even if that cover was in place many years before they began their secret life. The second thing about me is that I have a very beautiful wife. I married her when she was fifteen and I was twenty-five. Her parents were friends of my parents and they liked me very much and they gave me this great blessing and this great curse.

Her name is Bướm, which means in English "butterfly." She is
certainly that. She would fly here and there, landing on this flower
or that, never moving in a straight line. And how do you summon a
butterfly? Only show it a pretty thing. It is not her fault, really. It is
her nature. But it is a terrible thing to be married to a beautiful
woman. We lived in the town of Biên Hòa, very near an air base and
two big American camps, Long Binh and one they called Plantation,
and when my wife walked down the street of Biên Hòa, she was
dressed in black pantaloons and a white blouse like all the other
women but it was so clear how different she was. Her sleeves were
rolled far up and her top two buttons were undone for the heat and
her hair was combed out long and sleek, and the GI jeeps would
slam on their brakes and honk and the Vietnamese men would
straighten up slowly and flare their nostrils and the Vietnamese boys
on their motorbikes would crane their necks going by, even though
more than once I saw them run into some automobile or fruit cart
or a pile of garbage and fly through the air for trying to look twice
at my wife.

Of all these men and boys it was the Vietnamese I worried about.
No American ever tried seriously to go out with my wife. They had
their Vietnamese whores at the camps, and it should be said for my
wife that she never much liked the looks of the Americans anyway.
This is true even today, after we have lived in Gretna, Louisiana, for
more than a dozen years. It was the Vietnamese who I feared. They
loved my wife, all these men, and it was only to be expected that
some of them would try to have her. They would believe that she
could be had. Why else, they reasoned, would she be so beautiful
and swing her hips in that way and unbutton those two extra buttons
on her blouse? How much cooler did she really think that would
make her?

But these men were warned. And some of them never showed

up again after they ignored the warnings. I could bring the fire from heaven to keep them away from my wife. I was a spy, after all. I worked with many Americans at Plantation. They came and they went each year and I would always bring them what they needed. They called me an agent handler, because I had two dozen people working for me. My eyes and ears. The schoolgirls and the woodcutters and the old women and the Regional Forces soldiers and boys from the neighborhoods on their bikes and others like these—they brought me information and I took the information to the Americans, signing onto the post as a day laborer. Most of what I brought them was tactical intelligence. A VC squad with a political cadre coming down from Lái Khê and working the widows' settlement near Biên Hòa. A rocket attack planned on the air base at dawn from a certain place in the woods. Things like that. And when I gave them this information, I was right often enough that the Americans didn't really question me after a while, especially about rocket attacks. If I said there were going to be rockets at dawn from such and such coordinates, then first thing the next morning the United States Air Force would come in and blow those coordinates away.

You can see how this might be a great help to a seemingly wimpy man with a beautiful wife. When my people brought me information about my wife and another man, or I used the evidence of my own eyes, I would send a warning to the man. The fire would come from heaven, I told him in a note delivered by one of my agents. I told him that my wife carries this ancient curse with her. The curse of the little man. I would sometimes go into historical detail. Napoleon Bonaparte, for instance, was very small and conquered 720,000 square miles of Europe. Attila, King of the Huns and ruler of an empire of 1,450,000 square miles, was still smaller, thought even to be a dwarf. History teaches, by the way, that not only is the curse I bring upon the would-be lovers ancient, but the problem of the husband is ancient, too. Napoleon had great troubles with his butterfly of a wife and Attila died in the middle of making love, no doubt due to his being foolish enough to have many wives. But, of course, these are observations that I left out of my warning messages, which were clear and forceful. And if they were not heeded, I would find the coordinates of the place where the man cut wood every morning or where he went to eat his lunch or to fish or some other place where the United States Air Force could find him. We are all creatures of habit.

And how did my wife react when she found some man who was pursuing her suddenly disappear? Perhaps the first time or two she felt that it was something she herself had said or done, or perhaps she thought they did not find her attractive anymore. (This makes me a little sad, to think I made my wife doubt herself. But surely she has always known how beautiful she is and nothing could truly shake that.) Later on she must have known that I was responsible in some dramatic way. But however it was that she felt, I can never say for sure. She would always maintain a face and attitude that revealed nothing. I would speak to her, as I often did, of history or politics or matters of daily life, and she would listen, her face bowed over her sewing, until it was time for us to sleep. Only once did she let on that she knew what had happened to her latest suitor. I believe that this man—a woodcutter with a shack by a stream—never understood what I could do. He was a big man, an arrogant man. One evening soon after this particular reported rocket attack was prevented by the United States Air Force, my wife looked up from her sewing. I had just paused for a few moments in speaking to her due to an itchiness in my throat, so at first I thought she wished me to quickly continue the observations that I had been making on the futility of using our Regional Forces irregulars to guard local government buildings. But instead, she said, "It's sad, the mistakes made in a war."

I knew at once what she was talking about. She had made a terrible mistake in letting this man get too close to her.

"Very sad," I said.

"Do you think someone is actually in control of all these things that happen?" she asked.

"I am sure of it," I said, and a clearer reminder than that was unnecessary. My wife is beautiful, but she is also subtle.

So finally history caught up with my country. I could see it coming for a long time. I stopped enough rockets from hitting the air base at Biên Hòa that in repayment my wife and I, along with our two children, flew from there a week before the place was overrun by the communists. I was not so very sorry to go, for I was coming to a country full of men that my wife would not look at twice. And it's true that in America, things have been much calmer, though this Gretna, Louisiana, is an area with many Vietnamese. But it seems as if somehow the men of Vietnam have lost their nerve in America, even with a beautiful Vietnamese woman. I sometimes receive a respectful compliment about my wife, but these men are beaten down; they are taller than me and even younger than me but wimpier by far.

We live near the Mississippi River and just over the bridge is New Orleans. My wife has seemed happy simply to live in an apartment where she can sit in the living room whenever she wishes and she and her women friends can go out together and shop and get their hair fixed. I work for the telephone company and we have a television set which makes me more interesting to my wife because she does not have to listen in the evenings to the thoughts I have on politics and history and such. I understand her limitations, and a wise man does not try to change the things that can't be changed. It's just that I'd begun to hope that things had changed on their own. For a long time she seemed utterly uninterested in allowing me to be tormented in the ways I was in Vietnam. There was no town street to walk down with the eyes of everyone on the open throat of her blouse or the movement of her hips. The hairdos she liked here seemed intended to impress the other women rather than any man. Things have been very good, very calm. That is, until two months ago.

It was, of course, a Vietnamese. He is a former airborne ranger, a tall man, nearly as tall as an American. And he owns a restaurant in a shopping plaza. The restaurant is called Bún Bò Xào, a name obviously chosen to attract the American diners out for some exotic treat that they can't even distinguish from Chinese. I know this because Bún Bò Xào means Sauteed Beef with Noodles. What if an American restaurant was named Grilled Hamburger with French Fries or Baked Chicken and Mashed Potatoes? Do you see the point? To call a restaurant a name that a whole people will understand as Sauteed Beef with Noodles is an insult to that people. And the bún bò they make there is second-rate anyway, and the nước mắm, the fish sauce, is even worse. This sauce is very special to the tongue of the Vietnamese. I do not expect to taste true Vietnamese nước mắm in America. The nước mắm from Phú Quốc Island was the best of all, clear and with an astonishingly subtle taste for a substance that a fish will give up only after a prolonged process lasting several days. But the sauce in this restaurant is from the Philippines, very bad, not from Thailand, which at least is a pale second-best.

I do not criticize this man's taste and sincerity idly. These were my first clues. My wife and this man forgot that I am a spy. They may have known that I can no longer command the United States Air Force, but they forgot that I know how to read clues. You see, in spite of the bad bún bò and the worse nước mắm, this suddenly became my wife's favorite restaurant. We did not know where to go one Friday night, which is the night we usually go to a restaurant, and she said, oh so lightly, so offhandedly, that she'd heard that this Vietnamese place was quite good. She quoted one of her hairdo companions, a woman who would be plucking chickens and getting high on betel nuts in some Saigon alley if we had won the war. I have tried to avoid Vietnamese restaurants in the United States, but Bướm seemed so set on this, yet in such a casual way, that I indulged her. She is, after all, still a very beautiful woman.

We pulled into the little shopping center and found the place just a few doors down from Ngon Qúa Po-Boys and the Good Luck Bowling Alley. I noticed how my wife's hand casually slipped off my arm as we stepped into the Bún Bò Xào Restaurant and I only had time to make a quick note of the Chinatown lanterns on the ceiling and the lacquer paintings on the wall, mass-produced in Hong Kong, when this tall Vietnamese man in a tuxedo was suddenly bowing before us and shooting little knowing glances at my wife. The owner. Trần Văn Ha. He was so glad to see us and I felt a chill going up and down me from my scalp to my toes.

So we ate this second-rate food and the owner visited our table twice to make sure everything was all right. I explained carefully to him how it was not, how the food was falling short of this or that standard of excellence. He listened to me with his temples throbbing and I could hear my wife peeping in repressed contradiction to me. It was all so clear that I almost laughed at them then and there and said, Do you take me for a fool? Have you forgotten how severely I deal with matters such as this?

But the fact was that I no longer had access to the fire. I did not even have my eyes and ears who could go out and gather more information for me and deliver the necessary warnings. So I held my tongue about all but the food. Nor did I speak of these things on the way home nor that evening nor even, a week later, when my little butterfly said she had a craving for Vietnamese food and suggested the Bún Bò Xào Restaurant. I simply said no to the restaurant and with my spy experience kept a cool exterior, a calm and placid exterior. Inside, however, I was a whirlwind of feelings and plans. At no time in the past dozen years had I such a strong sense that I was in a foreign country, behind enemy lines, as it were, without any resources but my own. But soon my head cleared enough to understand that no matter where you are in the world, the forces of history and culture have been at work, and these forces create solutions to problems for the man who knows how to find them.

Take New Orleans, Louisiana, for instance. Napoleon snatched the city from the Spanish, who he defeated in Europe, and then two years later he sold it to the United States. This city was the casual possession of a small man who commanded fire of his own. But the city had a long history even before Napoleon held it. For a hundred years it had been a city with French and Spanish people but with many from the Caribbean, too, the West Indies and elsewhere, black people with fire of a different kind. You can't live around New Orleans without hearing about voodoo. And one night soon after I learned about Trần Văn Ha, I saw a program on our television where a very thin little black man taught hard lessons to his enemies with voodoo. My wife was sitting there with me and I kept my face very calm, never letting her know that I was listening to the voice of history right there in her presence, and even when the thin little black man made some mistakes that let the lumbering Americans catch him, I knew that I had to grow and learn and command the fire once more.

So on the very next day I called in sick to the phone company and I went across the bridge and past the great mandarin hat of the Superdome and down into the French Quarter, where the television and the movies all suggested voodoo was practiced. I walked the main streets of this area and there were boutiques and T-shirt shops and pizza parlors and jazz places and places where women danced whose husbands, if they had the power I once had, would have long ago bombed New Orleans into rubble. But the shop I found among all of this was run by white people, large Americans with neat shelves full of books and jars and dolls that I clearly sensed had nothing to do with the real voodoo.

So I went out of that shop and looked up and down Bourbon Street and I realized that this was all like Trần Văn Ha's Vietnamese restaurant, a phony thing. I went up to the next corner and turned down a side street, then took another turn and another until I was in a cobbled street of narrow little houses with spindlework porches and I walked along and I smiled at the black people on their stoops and I stopped at several of the stoops and asked if there was a voodoo man in the neighborhood. I have learned the lessons of history and I felt a kinship with these people and I was comfortable asking them for help, even though most of them looked at me very strangely. Finally an old man with a gray film in his eyes and a walking stick leaning on the post next to him said to me, "What you want him for?"

I said, "I have a beautiful wife who has a wandering eye."

The old man nodded and said, "I know that trouble," and he told me how to find the house of a voodoo man, a Doctor Joseph. He said, "You ax Doctor Joseph what you want. He be a powerful low-down papa." (I learned later that a papa is what many people call a male voodoo witch. And a "low-down" papa is willing to perform black magic and do evil deeds.)

I thanked the old man and made my way to another street much like the one I'd just left. I found the house, but I was expecting something different. This was like all the other houses, no strange symbols hung over the door or animal bones dangling on string or anything at all, except I did see a tiny sign by the doorbell. I went up onto the porch and the sign was a three-by-five card, laminated

and nailed there, and it said, DOCTOR JOSEPH. HARD PROBLEMS SOLVED.
If he had a great power like the old man said, then I liked Doctor
Joseph already. This was my own style, of course. Low-key. I rang
the bell and waited and then Doctor Joseph himself answered the
door. I know this because he said so. As if he already knew me and
knew what I wanted, he opened the door and instantly said, "I am
Doctor Joseph. Come in."

I stepped into a foyer that smelled of mildew and incense and
my eyes were slow, straining to open to the darkness, and I couldn't
see a thing, but I followed in Doctor Joseph's wake and we entered
a front sitting room. He waved his hand and I sat in an enormous
soft old chair and I could feel the springs of the cushion beneath me.
Doctor Joseph sat opposite me in a cane-backed chair and he had
seemed from the moment he opened the door like a very large man,
bigger even than any American, but now that he was sitting before
me, I could see that I was mistaken. It may have been a little spell
he'd cast over me. I hoped so. But now he let me see that he was
not big. He was as thin as any Vietnamese and he was a younger
man than I'd expected, though this, too, may have been a spell. His
eyes were very clear, very large, and the tight black curls of his hair
had not the slightest touch of gray. His lower lip pushed up into an
inverted smile and he was obviously ready for business, so I began.

I told Doctor Joseph everything about my wife, about the burden
I've had to bear. I did not tell him that I once used the U.S. Air
Force to correct my problems. I am still, at heart, a spy, even in the
presence of a low-down papa, though being the papa that he was,
he probably knew all of this anyway. After hearing me out, he tented
his fingers before him and looked past me to the window where the
filmy curtains let in the morning light that illuminated the room. He
kept his eyes outside for a long while and I finally looked away from
him, too. The room was very small, and except for the two chairs

and a wooden pedestal table beside Doctor Joseph, there were no objects at all in the room. The empty walls were very dark in spite of the light from the window, and when I looked closer, they seemed to be actually painted black. There was a heavy curtain at a doorway which must have led to the rest of the house, and perhaps back there were all the potions and mysterious objects of the voodoo doctor. I don't know. All that was in this room was the smell of incense and the low-down papa's gaze, which was traveling beyond me.

Finally Doctor Joseph's eyes came back to my face and when they did, I felt a burning in my sinuses and a weakness in my arms and legs. Then he said, "How much is this woman worth to you?"

I figured he was talking about his fee. I shrugged and he knew what I was thinking because he kind of snorted and said, "You and I will deal with that later. I'm speaking of a different realm. Three times you will have an opportunity to deny her. If you are going to call on the High Heavens, then you best know exactly what you want and exactly how bad you want it."

I was losing track of his words, but I could sense he wanted some kind of declaration from me before he would proceed. So I gave him the only answer I could possibly give. I did not even think about it. I said, "She is worth bringing fire from heaven."

Doctor Joseph nodded his head at this and his eyes bored deeper into me. I felt like I was about to sneeze. He said, "I could give you some good gris-gris for the doorstep of this man, but I think something stronger is called for."

I nodded and I found that I could not raise either of my hands and I twitched my nose at the threatened sneeze, hoping Doctor Joseph would not take this as disrespect. Then he rose from his chair and he did not need to tell me to stay seated because I knew for certain that I had no command of my body at that moment. He disappeared through the curtain and I waited and it struck me that

I was not even breathing, but then Doctor Joseph reappeared in the room, a sea wave of incense smells following him. He passed his chair and was looming before me and I sank down, the springs sproinging beneath me, and Doctor Joseph bent over me and I closed my eyes tight. "Here," he said and something dropped lightly into my lap.

I opened my eyes and he had pulled back. In my lap was a small brown paper parcel and Doctor Joseph said, "Inside is a hog bladder. You will also find a vial of blood. You must fill the bladder with the shit of a he-goat and then pour in the blood, tie up the bladder with a lock of your wife's hair, and then at the stroke of noon throw the bladder over your rival's house."

I nodded dumbly.

Then Doctor Joseph's inverted smile poked up again from his chin and he waved his hand and I don't remember getting up and crossing the room and going out the door, though I must have. But I just found myself standing in the street before his house and under my arm in a brown paper parcel was a hog bladder and a vial of the blood of who-knows-what and I was faced with a quest for goat shit. And I thought to myself, What am I doing? I thought of Bướm's face and I could see in my mind that it was very beautiful, but history taught that a beautiful woman would always bring torture to her husband. Simply ask the American actor Mickey Rooney. I should drop this paper parcel in the nearest trash can and leave that woman, I thought. It might strike you as strange, but this was not a common thought for me, to just remove myself from the field and let my butterfly fly away. It was a very uncommon thought. In fact, this may well have been the first time I had it. I later realized that this was also my first opportunity to deny my wife. But the thought vanished as quickly as it came. I pulled the parcel from under my arm and looked at it and I wondered where in New Orleans I would find goat shit.

I am a small man but very clever, and soon I found myself
approaching the gate to the petting zoo in Audubon Park. I was in
luck, I thought, because it was a weekday morning and there was no
one in sight. Just me and a pen full of sheep and goats who were as
fidgety as unwilling whores, waiting for the petting that would come
at them every day. Before going in, I sat down on a bench to figure
out how to handle this. My hands began to work at the string on
the parcel, but then I realized that the goat shit didn't have to go
straight into the bladder. I could gather the droppings in something
more easily handled and then put them in the bladder later. I was
very pleased with myself at this thought. I knew how to plan effec-
tively.

So I got up and went back to the concession stand and ordered
a box of popcorn, thinking to dump the corn and use the box. I
glanced away for a moment, hearing the crunch of popcorn being
scooped into the box, but thank Buddha I glanced over to the girl
just as she stuck my box under a silver metal spout and reached up
to the pump. "No butter!" I cried, and the girl recoiled as if she'd
been hit. This could not be helped. I was concerned about inadvert-
ently altering Doctor Joseph's formula. Who knows what butter might
have done?

With the box in hand, however, I grew calm. So much so that
I returned to the bench near the petting zoo and sat and ate the
popcorn and enjoyed it very much. And this turned out to be a big
mistake. I did think to wipe the salt out of the box with my handkerchief, but taking the time on the bench to eat the popcorn set up
the arrival of a class of schoolchildren just as I stepped into the pen.
I heard them laughing and talking and then saw them approaching
along a path and I had to decide whether to back out of the pen and
sit on the bench and wait for everyone to clear out or head quickly
for the goats. The sun was getting high and I figured that it could

be one class after another for the rest of the day, so I looked around the pen. There was a scattering of pellets here and there, but I didn't know exactly what a sheep's shit might look like and I didn't want to make a mistake. I spotted a white goat rubbing itself against a wooden post and I went over to it and lingered at its tail.

The goat continued to rub and the children were at the gate and I started to pat the animal on the hindquarters, both to look less conspicuous and perhaps to coax something out. But the goat looked up and twitched its ears at the gabble of the children and the voice of the teacher riding over the others and saying to calm down and be nice to the animals. The goat pulled away from the post and I could feel it tense up and I knew that there were little hands heading this way.

"Come on," I said, low, and I watched the goat's tail flick once, twice, and then there was a cascade of black pellets. I have particularly good reflexes and not more than half a dozen of them fell before my popcorn box was in place and clattering full of what I needed.

Then a child's voice rose from behind me, right at my elbow, howling in amazement, "Miss Gibbs, this man is putting goat doodies in his popcorn!"

It was now that I once again thought about my wife's face. I considered it in my mind and asked if it was worth what I was going through. I knew that many eyes were turning to watch what I was doing and part of me was saying, Let her fly away. And this was the second chance I had to deny my wife. But something was happening quite apart from my free will at that moment. I have heard the one or two rare brave soldiers that I knew in my home country speak of a time under fire when your mind knows you are in serious danger, but your body will not budge; it holds its position in spite of the terrible force moving toward you. It was this that I felt as the child ranted on about this strange thing that I was doing. I kept my face down, my eyes focused on the flow of goat shit into the box in my hand, and I did not move. I held my ground until the tail twitched again and the flow stopped and the goat wisely galloped away from the little demon behind me.

I, too, moved away, never looking back at my tormentor or Miss Gibbs or any of the others. I followed the white goat; we escaped together along the perimeter of the pen, and it struck me that I must appear to the children and their teacher to be pursuing the goat for still more seasoning in my popcorn. But I veered away at last and waded through the children, heading for the gate and escape. To keep me from seeing the wondering glances of these little faces, I went over in my mind all that I'd just accomplished. I was very conscious of the weight of the popcorn box and the press of the paper parcel tucked tightly under my arm. I could get a lock of my wife's hair tonight. The tough part was done. I had the shit of a he-goat. And this stopped me cold as I touched the gate latch.

A he-goat. I had not checked the sex of the goat. I spun around and there were children all around me, drawn close, no doubt, to see this strange man and his strange snack depart. But when I turned, they drew back squealing. The white goat had stopped by the far fence. I knew it was *my* white goat because it was standing where I had last seen it and because it was looking at me almost in sympathy, as if it understood what I was going through with the attentions of these other little creatures.

It was a very hard thing for me to do, but I moved back into the pen, amidst the children. I would not look at them, but in my peripheral vision I could tell they were all turning to watch me, some of them even following me. I approached the goat and it looked very nervous. I spoke to it. "It's all right," I said. And then the toughest thing of all. I went to the goat's tail and I crouched down, and I heard two dozen little voices gasp. Thanks to Buddha I saw what I needed to see underneath the white goat, and I rushed out of the pen and the park as if the darkest voodoo demon was pursuing me for my very soul.

That night, as my wife slept, I bent near her with her own best sewing scissors and she was very beautiful in the dim light, her face as smooth and unlined as the face of the fifteen-year-old girl that I married. How was it that fate had brought such a woman as this to a man like me? Even if my surface hides quite a different sort of man. She sighed softly in her sleep and though it was a lovely sound, it only made me restless. I could not bear to look very long at my wife's beauty until this whole thing was resolved, so I went to the back of her head and gently raised some of her hair so the lock I took would not be missed, and the silkiness of her hair made my hand tremble. Badly. I feared even that I might slip and cut her ear or her throat. But I took a deep breath and my blade made a crisp little snip and I was ready to work my voodoo magic.

The next morning Buờm said she was shopping at the malls with her friends. I said, "You know those women would be plucking chickens and getting high on betel nuts in the alleys of Saigon if we had won the war."

Buờm huffed faintly at this and she even whispered to the toaster, "Try saying something new."

It's true I'd made this observation before and I said, sincerely, "I'm sorry, my pretty butterfly. You have a nice time with your friends."

Buờm turned to me and there was something in her face that I could not place. Part of me wanted to believe that it was a wistful look, almost tender, appreciative that I am the kind of Vietnamese husband who might even apologize to his wife. But another part of me thought that the look was simply repressed exasperation, a Vietnamese wife's delicate loathing. Either way, we said no more and when I left the house, I did not head for the telephone company.

I drove to a local library and read the newspapers and the news magazines for a few hours. The world was full of struggle and you had to be clever to survive, that much was clear, and in the backseat of my car in a gym bag was a hog bladder full of blood and the shit of a he-goat and it was tied up (this was not an easy thing to do, as it turned out) with a lock of my wife's hair. I had Trần Văn Ha's address and I knew the neighborhood he lived in. At a quarter to twelve, I carefully folded the newspaper I was reading and replaced it on the shelf and I walked past the librarians with the softest tread, the calmest face (I was still a splendid spy, after all), and I drove up Manhattan Boulevard and under the West Bank Expressway and a few more turns brought me to Ha's street and I found his house on the corner.

I still had five minutes, so I parked across the street and slumped lower behind the wheel and observed the place. His was a shotgun house in a neighborhood of shotgun houses. They get their name from the fact that you could stand on the front porch and shoot a shotgun straight through to the back porch and the buckshot would pass through every room in the house. It occurred to me that this was the perfect design for a man in my situation. These houses were probably invented by an architect with a butterfly wife. He wanted to make it easy to draw a bead on his rivals. Just as I was about to answer this with the observation that a shotgun was not my style, something struck me about a shotgun house.

Doctor Joseph said I was to throw the bladder over the house. I had a ranch house or Cape Cod or such in my mind, a place where I would stand near the front porch and throw the bladder over the peak of the roof and it would roll down the other side and the task would be done. But the shotgun house is very long, stretched out deep into the lot. I could not throw the bladder that far. I was not a good thrower to start with, and this was just too far. Would the magic work if I threw the bladder over the house from one side to the other? Ha's place sat very near to the house next door and there was a fence in between.

It was a high, solid fence, I noticed, so that the neighbors could not see into his bedroom window where he met his lovers. This thought made me very angry and I looked at my watch and I had only two minutes to figure this out. I grabbed the gym bag from the backseat and stepped out of the car. Over the house, I thought. Over the house. If it goes over from side to side, it is still over the house. Surely that's all right, I thought. And I was lucky that Ha's house was on a corner lot. I could not deal with the narrow passage and high fence, but the other side of the house was open to the street and I walked briskly around the corner.

On this side there were three large trees, side by side. They seemed to block the house, but looking closer, I could see that there was a space of a few feet between each one. I looked at my watch and I had no time to waste now, only a matter of a few seconds. I set the gym bag down at my feet and drew out the bladder, long and dark gray and with a bandanna of Bướm's silky hair. I placed myself between two of the trees and the alarm began to beep on my watch and I did not know how to hold the bladder, how to move my arm. Overhand or underhand? The alarm beeped on and I felt panic like a frightened goat running around in my chest and I chose to use an underhand throw. My arm went down, I kept my eye on the peak of the roof, and I flung the hog bladder as hard as I could, just as the alarm stopped beeping.

The bladder flew almost straight up, hooking just enough to crash through the leaves of the tree to my left and drape itself on a branch. I won't tell you exactly what it looked like to me, this bulbous skin doubled now and dangling from the limb of the tree. Yes I will tell you. It looked like a monstrous set of testicles, and it made me crazy with anger at Trân Văn Ha and I knew it could not remain there. Hanging there like that, it would probably work magic that was the exact opposite of what I'd intended. I decided that the bladder had been flung at noon and in a real sense it was still in the process of going over the house. The trip had no time limit on its completion, I reasoned, so I went to the tree, which was an oak with some large lower branches, and I began to climb.

As with many small men, I am very agile. I have not had much experience climbing trees, but the sight of the bladder above me and the thought of Ha and his desire for my wife drove me up the tree in a trance of rage. The bark scraped, the leaves grabbed at me, the gulf beneath me grew larger and larger, but I went up and up without a look down or a single thought of my own safety until I was nearly as high as the top of the roof and I'd drawn opposite the bladder. At this point I reached for a limb to steady me but it was dead and cracked off and clattered down onto the roof and my head snapped back with a little shock of understanding. I was in a tree and high off the ground.

But the bladder was hanging just beyond arm's length now and the peak of the roof was only an easy toss away from me and by the High Heavens I was going to complete this curse on Trân Văn Ha. I wrapped my arms and legs around the limb before me and began to inch my way out to the bladder. The little twigs along the limb clutched at me and I made the mistake of letting my eyes wander from my goal and I saw the distant earth and felt my breath fly away, leaving my lungs empty and my heart pounding. But I closed my eyes for a moment and when I opened them again, they were fixed on the hog bladder filled with the hard-earned goat pellets and I inched farther along, just a little more, a little more, and finally I reached out my hand and grasped the bladder.

And just as I did, I heard a voice from below. "What the hell is this?" the voice said. I looked down and it was Trần Văn Ha with his shirt unbuttoned and in his bare feet, like he had thrown his clothes on hastily. His face was turned upward to me and when I looked down, he must have recognized me, because his mouth gaped open and he staggered back a step. "You," he said.

"Yes, me," I said and the bladder was firmly in hand. I wondered what would happen if I threw it over the roof now. Would the earth crack open and swallow him up? Would he disappear in a puff of smoke? For a moment, I actually felt personally powerful up in that tree, like I was a B-52 opening its bomb-bay doors. I was ready to make one more defense of my wife, my honor, my manhood. But then I heard a woman's voice, and Trần Văn Ha lowered his face and looked toward the sound.

"Don't," he said to the voice. But already there was a figure gliding across the lawn, a woman, her hair long and black and silky, and the face lifted to me and it was Bướm. It was my beautiful butterfly of a wife and she, too, gaped, not expecting to see me. And I didn't feel powerful anymore. I was a small man up a tree holding a hog bladder full of goat pellets while my unfaithful wife stood beside her lover and watched me. This is what I'd come to. The man who once could bring fire from heaven now could only bring shit from the trees. I glanced at the peak of the roof and then I looked down at the two upturned faces and I knew I had to work my own magic here. But just as Doctor Joseph had prophesied, I was visited by my third opportunity to deny my wife. As beautiful as my wife's face was, it had only brought me pain, I thought. The hand with the bladder moved out away from the limb, hovered over this face, and I thought of how this woman had tormented me. But am I truly the right man for a woman this beautiful? Could I truly blame her? I looked at Trần Văn Ha and there was nothing redeeming at all in his face and I raised my arm not just to drop the bladder but to propel it. This I did, squarely at the amazed forehead of this man who had tempted my wife. I am glad to say that the bomb found its target. Unfortunately, this accuracy was obtained at some cost, for I followed the bladder out of the tree and I now lie in a hospital bed with both legs in traction and my left arm encased in plaster and folded over my chest.

But I am still more than I may seem to be on the surface. Every day I have been in this hospital, my wife has come and sat with me and held my right hand with her face bowed. Then this evening she brought her sewing and pulled her chair close to me, and before she began to sew, she asked what thoughts I had about the ways the Vietnamese in America were becoming part of American society. What did history have to say about all of that? she asked. I have many thoughts on that subject and I spoke to her for a long time. I spoke to her, in fact, until I dozed off, and I woke only briefly to feel her adjust the pillow behind my head and gently cover my good arm with the sheet.

MID-AUTUMN

We are lucky, you and I, to be Vietnamese so that I can speak to you even before you are born. This is why I use the Vietnamese language. It is our custom for the mother to begin this conversation with the child in the womb, to begin counseling you in matters of the world that you will soon enter. It is not a custom among the Americans, so perhaps you would not even understand English if I spoke it. Nor could I speak in English nearly so well, to tell you some of the things of my heart. Above all you must listen to my heart. The language is not important. I don't know if you can hear all the other words, the ones in English that float about us like the pollen that in the spring makes me sneeze and that lets the flowers bear their own children. I think I remember from our country that this is a private conversation, that it is only my voice that you can hear, but I do not know for sure. My mother is dead now and cannot answer this question. She spoke to me when I was in her womb and sometimes, when I dream and wake and cannot remember, I have the feeling that the dream was of her voice plunging like a naked swimmer into that sea and swimming strongly to me, who waited deep beneath the waves.

And when you move inside me, my little one, when you try to swim higher, coming up to meet me, I look at the two oaken barrels I have filled with red blooms, the hibiscus. They have no smell to speak of, but they are very pretty, and sometimes the hummingbirds come with their invisible wings and with their little bodies as slick as if they had just flown up from the sea. I look also at the white picket fence, very white without any stain of mildew, though the air is warm here in Louisiana all the time, and very wet. And sometimes, like at this moment, I look beyond this yard, lifting my eyes above the ragged line of trees to the sky. It is a sky that looks like the skies in Vietnam. Sometimes full of tiny blooms of clouds as still as flowers floating on a bowl in the center of a New Year's table. Sometimes full of great dark bodies, Chinese warriors rolling their shoulders, huffing up with a summer storm that we know will pass. One day you will run out into the storm, laughing, like all the children of Vietnam.

I saw you for the first time last week. The doctor spread a jelly on my stomach and it was the coldest thing I have ever felt, even more cold than the snow I once held melting in my hands. He ran a microphone up and down my stomach and I saw you on a screen, the shape of you. I could see inside you. I could see your spine and I could see your heart beating and this is what reminded me of my duty to you. And my joy. To speak. And he told me you were a girl.

Please understand that I love you, that you are a girl. My own mother never knew my sex as she spoke to me. And I know that she was a Vietnamese mother and so she must have been disappointed when she came to find out that I was a girl, when she held me for the first time and she shared the cast-down look of my father that I was not a son for them. This is the way in Vietnam. I know that the words she spoke to me in the womb were as a boy; she was hoping that I was a boy and not ever bringing the bad luck on themselves by acting as if I was anything else but a son. But, little one, I am glad you are a girl. You will understand me even better.

A marriage in Vietnam is a strange and wonderful thing. There is a genie of marriage. We call him the Rose Silk Thread God, though he is not quite a god. I can say this because I am already married, but if I was single and living once more in the village where I grew up in Vietnam, I would call him a god and do all the right things to make him smile on me. A special altar is made and we light candles and incense in honor of this genie. There is a ceremony on the day of marriage led by the male head of the groom's family, and everyone bows before the altar and prays, and a plea to the genie for his protection and help is written on a piece of rose-colored silk paper and then read aloud. A cup is filled with wine and the head of the groom's family sips from it and gives it to the groom, who sips from it and gives it to his bride. She drinks, and I am told that this is the most delicious thing that she will ever taste. I do not know who told me this. Perhaps my mother. Perhaps I learned it when I was in her womb. Then after the bride has drunk the wine that has touched the lips of the men, the sheet of silk paper is burned. The flame is pale rose, and the threads of silk rise in the heat before they vanish.

My little one, I was once very young. I was sixteen and I was very beautiful and I met Bạo when he was seventeen. It was at the most wonderful time of year for lovers to meet, at the Mid-Autumn Festival. I saw him in the morning as I was coming up the footpath from the cistern. My hands and my face and my arms up nearly to my shoulders were slick and cool from my plunging them into the water of the cistern. The cistern held the drinking water for my hamlet, but no one had been looking and I knew I was clean because I had bathed that morning in the river and the water had looked so still and fine that I could not resist plunging my arms in and my face. When I came up out of the water, the sun that had been harsh with me all morning was suddenly my friend, tugging gently at my skin and making me feel very calm.

I filled my family's jug and started up the path, and when I encountered this tall boy coming down the path with a strong step, my first thought was that he was coming to catch me and punish me for touching the water that the hamlet must drink. I looked at his face and his eyes were so very black and they seized on my face with such a fervor that I almost dropped the jug. I thought it was fear that I felt, but later I knew it had not been fear.

He lunged forward and caught the jug of water and it splashed him on the face and the chest and he laughed. When he laughed I grew weaker still and he had to take the jug onto his own shoulder and turn and walk with me up the path to my house. We did not say many words. We laughed several times in silent recollection of the falling jug and the splashing water. And we looked at each other with side glances as we walked. Sometimes I would look and he would not be looking; sometimes I knew he was looking and I did not look; but other times one of us would look and the other would be looking at just the same time and we would laugh again. At last my legs grew heavy, though, as we neared my house. I told him we now had to part, and as he slowly took the jug of water from his shoulder and gave it to me, he said that his name was Bạo and he was from a different hamlet but he was staying here for a time with a cousin and he asked if I would be out celebrating the moon tonight and I said yes.

The Mid-Autumn Festival is all about the moon, my little one. It is held on the fifteenth day of the eighth lunar month, when there is the brightest moon of the year. The Chinese gave us the celebration because one of their early emperors loved poetry and he wrote many poems himself. Since all poets are full of silver threads that rise inside them as the moon grows large, the emperor yearned to go to the moon. On the fifteenth day of the eighth lunar month this yearning grew unbearable, and he called his wizard to him and told him he must find a way. So the wizard worked hard, chanting spells and burning special incense, and finally in a blinding flash of light the wizard fell to the ground, and there in the palace courtyard was the root of a great rainbow which arched up into the night sky and went all the way to the moon.

The emperor saddled his best horse and armed himself with a sheaf of his own poems and he spurred the horse onto the rainbow and he galloped off to the moon. When he got there, he found a beautiful island in the middle of a great, dark sea. On the island he dismounted his horse and he was surrounded by fairies who lifted him up and danced and sang their poems and he sang his and it was the most wonderful time of his life, borne on the shoulders of these lovely creatures and feeling as if he belonged there, his deepest self belonged in this place, so full of wonder it was. But he could not stay. His people needed him. There was another world to deal with. So with great reluctance he got onto his horse and rode back down to his palace.

The next morning the rainbow was gone. The emperor did all the things he needed to do for his people and one night he thought that he had earned a rest, that he could return to the moon at least until morning. But the wizard came at his call and sadly explained that there was no return to the moon. Once you came down the rainbow, there was no way back. The emperor was very sad, so he proclaimed that every year on the fifteenth night of the eighth lunar month, the anniversary of his trip, there would be a celebration throughout the kingdom to remember the beautiful land that was left behind.

My little one, you would love all the paper lanterns that we light on this night. They are in the shapes of dragons and unicorns and stars and boats and horses and hares and toads. We light candles inside them and we swing them on sticks in the dark and the village is full of these wonderful pinwheels of light, the rushing of these bright shapes. I saw Bạo again in such a light, with the swirling of lanterns and the moon just coming over the horizon, fat as an elephant and the color of the sun in fog. I saw him in the center of the hamlet where we had all gathered to celebrate and the lights were whirling and when our eyes met, he suddenly staggered under the weight of an invisible water jug, he carried it around and around in circles on his shoulder, a wonderful pantomime, and then he lost his footing and I could almost see the jug there on his shoulder tipping, tipping, and it fell and crashed and he jumped back from all the splashing water and we laughed.

At the festival of the moon, it is not forbidden for an unbetrothed boy and girl to speak together. We moved toward each other and I could feel the heat of the swinging lanterns on my face as the children ran near me and cut in before me, but Bạo and I kept moving and we came together in the center of the village square and we spoke. He asked if my family was well and I asked about his family and I was happy to find that the father of his cousin was a good friend of my father. Bạo asked if my water jug was safe and I asked if his shoulder was in pain from carrying the jug and we slowly edged our way to the darkness beyond the celebrating and then we walked down the path to the cistern and beyond, to the edge of the river.

This was perhaps more than our hamlet's customs would allow us, but we did not think of that. I was a strongheaded girl, my little one, and Bạo was a good boy. I sensed that of him and I was right. He was very respectful to me. I felt very safe. We stood by the river and a sampan slipped silently past and it was hung with orange lanterns, the color of the moon from earlier this night, when it was near the horizon and Bạo did his pantomime for me.

Now the moon was higher and it had grown slimmer and it had turned so white that it nearly hurt my eyes to look at it. Nearly hurt them but not quite, and so it was the most beautiful of all. It was as bright as it could be and still be a good thing. And Bạo slipped his arm around my waist and I let him keep it there and the joy of it was as strong as it could be and still be a good thing. We stood looking up at the moon and trying to see the fairies there in the middle of the dark sea and we tried to hear them singing their poems.

My little one, Bạo was my love and both our families loved us, too, so much so that they agreed to let us marry. In Vietnam this was a very rare thing, that the marriage agreement should be the same as the agreement of hearts between the bride and the groom. You will be lucky, too. This is a good thing about being in America. A very good thing, and I wonder if you can tell that there are tears in my eyes now, if you can sense this little fall of water, surrounded as you are by your own sea. But do not worry. These tears are happy ones, tears for you and the life you will have, which will be very beautiful.

I look at the gate in our white picket fence and soon your father will come through. I want to tell you that you are a lucky girl. Even as my tears change. Bạo and I were betrothed to be married. And then he was called into the Army and he went away before the ceremony could be arranged and he died in a battle somewhere in the mountains. The gate is opening now and your father, my husband, is coming through and he is a good man. He keeps this fence and our house free from the mildew. He scrubs it with bleach and hoses it every six months and he stops at my hibiscus, not seeing me here at the window. I must soon stop speaking. He is a good man, an American soldier who loved his Vietnamese woman for true and for always. He will find me by the window and touch my cheek gently with the back of his fine, strong hand and he will touch my belly, trying to think he is touching you.

You will love him, my little one, and since I know you understand my heart, I do not want you to be sad for me. I had my night on the moon and when I came back down the rainbow, the world I found was also good. It is sad that there is no return, but we can still light a lantern and look into the night sky and remember.

IN THE
CLEARING

Though I have never seen you, my son, do not think that I am unable to love you. You were in your mother's womb when the North of our country took over the South and some of those who fought the war found themselves running away. I did not choose to run, not with you ready to enter this world. I did not choose to leave my homeland and become an American. I have chosen so few of the things of my life, really. I was eighteen when Saigon was falling and you were dreaming on in your little sea inside your mother in a thatched house in An Khê. Your mother loved me then and I loved her and I would not have left except I had no choice. This has always been a strange thing to me, though I have met several others here where I live in New Orleans, Louisiana, who are in the same condition. It is strange because I know how desperately many others wanted to get out, even hiding in the landing gears of the departing airplanes. I myself had not thought of running away, did not choose to, but it happened to me anyway.

I am sorry. And I write you now not to distract you from your duty to your new father, as I am sure your mother would fear. I write with a full heart for you because I must tell you a few things about being a person who is somewhere between a boy and a man. I was just such a person when I held a rifle in my hands. It was a black thing, the M16 rifle, black like a charcoal cricket, and surprisingly light, with a terrible voice, a terrible quick voice like the river demons my own father told stories about when it was dark and nighttime in our village and I wanted to be frightened.

That is one thing I must tell you. As a boy you wish to be frightened. You like the night; you like the quickness inside you as you and your friends speak of mysterious things, ghosts and spirits, and you wish to go out into the dark and go as far down the forest path as you can without turning back. You and your friends go down the path together and no one dares to say that you have gone too far even though you hear every tiny sound from the darkness around you and these sounds make you quake inside. Am I right about this? I dream of you often and I can see you in this way with your friends and it is the same as it was with me and my friends.

This is all right, to embrace the things you fear. It is natural and it will help build the courage you must have as a man. But when you are a man, don't become confused. Do not seek out the darkness, the things you fear, as you have done as a boy. This is not a part of you that you should hold on to. I myself did not hold on to it for more than a few minutes once the rifle in my hand heard the cries of other rifles calling it. I no longer dream of those few minutes. I dream only of you.

I cannot remember clearly now any of the specific moments of my real fear, of my man's fear with no delight in it at all, no happiness, no sense of power or of my really deep down controlling it, of being able to turn back with my friends and walk out of the forest. I can only remember a wide rice paddy and the air leaning against me like a drunken man who says he knows me and I remember my boots full of water and always my thought to check to see if I was wrong, if there was really blood in my boots, if I had somehow stepped on a mine and been too scared to even realize it and I was walking with my boots filled with blood. But this memory is the sum of many moments like these. All the particular rice paddies and tarmac highways and hacked jungle paths—the exact, specific ones—are gone from me.

Only this remains. A clearing in a triple-canopy mahogany forest in the highlands. The trees were almost a perfect circle around us and in the center of the clearing was a large tree that had been down for a long time. We were a patrol and we were sitting in a row against the dead trunk, our legs stuck out flat or tucked up to our chests. We were all young and none of us knew what he was doing. Maybe we were stupid for stopping where we did. I don't know about that.

But our lieutenant let us do it. He was sitting on the tree trunk, his elbows on his knees, leaning forward smoking a cigarette. He was right next to me and I knew he wanted to be somewhere else. He was pretty new, but he seemed to know what he was doing. His name was Binh and he was maybe twenty-one, but I was eighteen and he seemed like a man and I was a private and he was our officer, our platoon leader. I wanted to speak to him because I was feeling the fear pretty bad, like it was a river catfish with the sharp gills and it was just now pulled out of the water and into the boat, thrashing, with the hook still in its mouth, and my chest was the bottom of the boat.

I sat trying to think what to say to Lieutenant Binh, but there was only a little nattering in my head, no real words at all. Then another private sitting next to me spoke. I do not remember his name. I can't shape his face in my mind anymore. Not even a single feature. But I remember his words. He lifted off his helmet and placed it on the ground beside him and he said, "I bet no man has ever set his foot in this place before."

I heard Lieutenant Binh make a little snorting sound at this, but I didn't pick up on the contempt of it or the bitterness. I probably would've kept silent if I had. But instead, I said to the other private, "Not since the dragon came south."

Lieutenant Binh snorted again. This time it was clear to both the other soldier and me that the lieutenant was responding to us. We looked at him and he said to the other, "You're dead meat if you keep thinking like that. It's probably too late for you already. There've been men in this place before, and you better hope it was a couple of days ago instead of a couple of hours."

We both turned our faces away from the rebuke and my cheeks were hotter than the sun could ever make them, even though the lieutenant had spoken to the other private. But I was not to be spared. The lieutenant tapped me on the shoulder with iron fingertips. I looked back to him and he bent near with his face hard, like what I'd said was far worse than the other.

He said, "And what was that about the dragon?"

I was too frightened now to make my mind work. I could only repeat, "The dragon?"

"The dragon," he said, his face coming nearer still. "The thing about the dragon going south."

For a moment I felt relieved. I don't know how the lieutenant sensed this about me, but somehow he knew that when I spoke of the dragon going south, it was not just a familiar phrase meant to refer to a long time ago. He knew that I actually believed. But at that moment I did not understand how foolish this made me seem to him. I said, "The dragon. You know, the gentle dragon who was the father of Vietnam."

The story my father told of the gentle dragon and the fairy princess had always been different from the ones about ghosts that I sought in the candlelight to chill me, though my father did believe in ghosts, as do many Vietnamese people and even some Americans. But the story of how our country began was always told in the daylight and with many of our family members gathered together, and no one ever said to me that this was just a made-up story, that this was just a lovely little lie. When I studied American history to become a citizen here, there was a story of a man named George Washington and he cut down a little tree and then told the truth. And the teacher immediately explained that this was just a made-up story. He made this very clear for even something like that. Just cutting down a tree and telling the truth about it. We had to keep that story separate from the stories that were actual true history.

This makes me sad about this country that was chosen for me. It makes me sad for a whole world of adults. It makes me sad even for Lieutenant Binh as I remember his questions that followed, all with a clenched face and a voice as quick and furious as the rifles at our sides. "Is this the dragon who slept with the fairy?" he demanded, though the actual words he used at that moment of my own true history were much harsher.

"He married a fairy princess," I said.

"Who married them?" the lieutenant said.

I couldn't answer the question. It was a simple question and it was, I see now, an unimportant question, but sitting in that clearing in the middle of a forest full of men who would kill me, having already fired my rifle at their shapes on several occasions and felt the rush of their bullets past my face and seen already two men die, though I turned my face from that, but having seen two men splashed with their own blood and me sitting now in a forest with the fear clawing at my chest, I faced that simple little question and I realized how foolish I was, how much a child.

The lieutenant cried, "Is this the fairy princess who's going to *lay eggs?*"

And in a moment as terrible as when I first felt the fear of my adult self, I now turned my face from the lieutenant and I looked across the clearing at the tree line and I knew that someone out there was coming near and I knew that dragons and fairies do not have children and the lieutenant's voice was very close to me and it said, "Save your life."

I don't know if some time passed with me sitting there feeling as crumbly and dry as the tree trunk I leaned against. Maybe only a few seconds, maybe no seconds at all. But very soon, from the tree line before me, there was a flash of light and another and I could only barely shift my eyes to the private sitting next to me and his head was a blur of red and gray and I was as quick as my rifle and over the trunk and beside my lieutenant and we were very quiet together, firing, and all of the rest is very distant from me now. Half of our platoon was dead in those first few seconds, I think. When air support arrived, there was only the lieutenant and me and another private who would soon die from the wounds he received in those few minutes in the clearing.

Not many months later the lieutenant came to me where we were trying to dig in on the rim of Saigon and he said, "It's time." And all the troops of the Army of the Republic of Vietnam were streaming past us into the city, without leaders now, without hope, and so I followed Lieutenant Binh, I and a couple of other soldiers in his platoon that he knew were good fighters, and I did not understand exactly what he meant about its being time until we were in the motorboat of a friend of his and we were racing down the Saigon River. This was the last little bit of my childhood. I was holding my rifle across my chest, ready to fight wherever the lieutenant was leading me. But the lieutenant said, "You won't need that now."

He was taking me and the others into the South China Sea and when I realized I was leaving my country and my wife and my unborn son, I was only able to turn my face to him, for I knew there was no going back. He looked at me with a quick little smile, a warm smile, one man to another, and a nod of the head like he thought I was a good fighter, a good man, a man he respected, and all of that was true, and he thought he was helping me save my life, and maybe that was true, but maybe it wasn't true at all. You must understand, though, that I did not choose to leave.

My son, I love you. Your mother does not love me now and you have a new father. Has she told you about me? Are you reading this? I pray you are; with all the little shiny pebbles of my childhood faith that I can find in the dust, I pray it. And I am writing to tell you this. Thousands of years ago a gentle and kindly dragon grew lonely in the harsh wide plains of China and he wandered south. He found a land full of beautiful mountains and green valleys and fresh, clear rivers that ran so fast in their banks that they made a singing sound.

But even though the land was beautiful, he was still lonely. He traveled through this new country of his and at last he met a beautiful fairy princess. She, too, was lonely and the two of them fell in love and they decided to live together as man and wife and to love each other forever. And so they did live together in the beautiful land and one day the princess found that she had laid a hundred eggs in a beautiful silk pouch and these eggs hatched and they were the children of the dragon and the princess.

These children were very wonderful, inheriting bravery and gentleness from their father and beauty and charm and a delicacy of feeling from their mother. They grew and grew and they were fine, loving children, but finally the dragon had to make a very difficult decision. He realized that the family was too large for them all to live together in one place. So he called his family to him and told them that even though he loved them all very much, he would have to divide the family into two parts. His wife would take fifty of the children and travel to the east. He would take the other fifty children and travel to the south. Everyone was very sad about having to do this, but they all understood that there was no other way.

So the princess took fifty of the children and went far away to the east, where she became the Queen of the Ocean. And the dragon took fifty children far away to the south, where he became the King of the Land. The dragon and the princess remained with the children until they were adults, wise and strong and able to take care of themselves. Then the dragon and the princess vanished and were reunited in the spirit world, where they lived happily together for the rest of eternity. The children married and prospered and they created Vietnam from the far north to the southern tip and they are the ancestors of all of us. Of you, my son, and of me.

For a time in my life, the part of me that could believe in this story was dead. I often think, here in my new home, that it is dead still. But now, at least, I do not wish it to be dead and it does not make me feel foolish, so perhaps my belief is still part of me. I love you, my son, and all I wish for you is that you save your life. Tell this story that I have told you. Try to think of it as true.

A GHOST
STORY

Let's say I got onto a bus, a Greyhound bus, and you saw me coming down the aisle, an Oriental man. Your eye wouldn't be practiced enough to know by looking at me that I'm Vietnamese—I'm just Oriental at first glance—and you certainly wouldn't know that I have a special story to tell, a story about ghosts. All you see is a late-middle-aged sort of shabby Oriental man, a little frayed at the collar and cuffs, his hair a little shaggy over the ears, and he's heading your way and there is a seat next to you. As he approaches, would you raise your newspaper to cover your face or maybe turn to look outside even though we are sitting in the New Orleans bus station and there's nothing to see out there but a sidewalk and a driver throwing some suitcases into the baggage compartment? This way he would know he wasn't welcome in that seat, and being an Oriental gentleman, he would know how to take the hint and walk on past and sit someplace else. Or would you keep your eyes on him as he approaches and maybe even give him a little smile so he knows he's welcome to sit in that empty seat? It's just far enough to Biloxi that it's good to sit next to someone for the trip. Biloxi is where I go to see my daughter about once a month, and if you would keep your eyes on me to let me know it's okay for me to sit next to you, I would tell you a true story about Vietnam.

This happened in the central highlands, not far from the city of An Khê in the year 1971. One day in late spring a Vietnamese Army major named Trung visited his mistress in the city and they spent the afternoon in a garden and the early evening in her bed, where they made love with the pollen of the flowers still clinging to their faces and arms. Afterward, the room was full of a pale light and they fell asleep. But when the major awoke, it was very dark. He had slept much too long and he leaped from the bed cursing and sweating and he threw on his clothes. He was stationed in a base camp on the other side of the mountains and he had a meeting with the base commander first thing in the morning. The major had to return to the camp now, in the middle of the night. His lover was very frightened for him. In the daylight the road through the mountain belonged to the Republic. But at night the communists could come out of the forests whenever they wished, making this trip very dangerous. Nevertheless, the major had no choice. He kissed his lover good-bye and went out to his car.

He was frightened, but he was a serious officer in the Army of the Republic of Vietnam, a very brave man, and before he opened the door to his car, he held his hands out in front of him and he vowed to master the tiny tremor in them. He would not leave until both his hands were absolutely still. The moon was very bright, but there were many clouds and they passed over the moon and the major could not see his hands. But he waited patiently until the clouds parted and he could clearly observe that his hands had become motionless before him. Then he got into the car and drove away, not even looking back to the window of his lover's house, where her face could be seen weeping.

The major drove very fast and he was soon on the road that wound up into the tops of the mountains, and whenever the moon was free of the clouds, the major, in fear of the communists, turned off his headlights and leaned forward to follow the twisting road by the silver light. This light of the moon that would have been very bright to show the bodies of two lovers entwined was only barely bright enough to guide him through the mountains. But the major knew what danger he was in, and when the moon disappeared and the road could not be distinguished from the deep chasms just beyond, it was only with great reluctance that he turned on his headlights.

He drove on like this, turning and twisting up and up and at each turn his hands tightened on the steering wheel for fear of a roadblock, a hundred rifles pointed at him, beginning to fire, shattering glass, the end of his life. But he finally reached what he knew was the highest point of the mountains. He saw a white road marker in the beam of his headlights, a jagged stone sitting at the turning of the road, and then he was in a pass with the road leveling off for a time, the trees mounting darkly on both sides of him, and the only chasm for the moment being the darkness before him, beyond the reach of his lights. The road began to descend, though gently for now, and he followed a turn to the right and something flashed before him in the light, his heart seized up, but it was a rabbit dashing across the road. He could see the final high kick of the long hind legs as the animal leaped into the darkness of the trees, and the major even laughed aloud, in relief but also in scorn at his own moment of fear.

The road turned sharply to the left and the moon appeared in a break in the clouds, but its light was snagged and slivered by the surrounding trees. The major knew that in a mile or so he would be through the pass and the road would cling once again to the side of the mountain and wind its way down, with a chasm on one side. He glanced at the tree-striped face of the moon, and when he brought

his eyes back before him, a woman appeared in his lights, standing
in his lane of the road and he was rushing toward her and he could
hardly believe she was there, a slim young woman in a beautiful white
aó dài, and she raised her hand to him, a clear gesture telling him
to stop, and all of this happened in a few seconds, but as this lovely
woman held her ground, her hand raised, and the major rushed toward
her, he thought of the Viet Cong and their tricks and he would not
stop his car in this mountain at night for anyone and he swerved
sharply, his tires crying out on the pavement, and he went around
her, the wheel heavy in his hands, and he yanked at it and he was
back in his lane and there was nothing in his lights but the road.

A trick, he thought, a trick, using a local girl to lure me into a
trap. And then she was before him again, or another girl, perhaps a
sister—how could it be the same girl? he was hurtling along the
road, leaving her behind—but a beautiful young woman in a white
aó dài was before him and she raised her hand and this time he could
see her face, for some reason her face was very clear—round, smooth
skinned, a thin nose as if she had French blood, and her mouth was
wide. Pleasing at first glance but the mouth grew wider, the mouth
widened even as he watched it in his headlights and his hands prepared
to swerve around the girl—it was the same girl as before, he was
sure of it—but the mouth was growing wider and wider, a great
crack in this beautiful round face, and the mouth opened, gaping
wide, like the chasm of the mountainside, and a tongue came out,
huge, bloating as it came, swelling as wide as her face, as wide as
her shoulders, undulating forward from her mouth, red and soft and
as wide as the road now, and the monstrous tongue licked at the car
and the car lifted up, and the major's eyes and his head were filled
with a vision of the tongue and then all was darkness.

He drifted into consciousness and he felt himself lying on the
ground. He opened his eyes and gasped, for the young woman's face

was before him, bending over him, and there was moonlight on the face and he stared at her mouth, a wide mouth but a human mouth, and it opened and no great tongue came out, only words. "Major Trung," she said, and her voice was very soft, softer than his lover's kiss, even when his lover touched his tongue with hers. The young woman said, "You must sleep for a time now. There is an ambush ahead. I am Nguyễn thị Linh of the street called Lotus in An Khê. You will see me again. I wish for you to be alive." The major tried to answer, but he could not speak. The darkness rushed back upon him and he fell unconscious.

When the major woke for the second time, the road was still dark, though there was a faint silver glow in the air. He raised himself onto his elbows and looked around. He was lying beside the road, and his car, which he expected to find crashed into the trees, was sitting just off the road, as if it had been carefully parked there. The major stood up and he was surprised to find not a single pain in his body, no bruises, no scratches, nothing whatever to show that he had crashed his car and had been thrown out. He looked at his watch and found that he'd been unconscious for two hours. He decided that he'd had a hallucination. The strain of the drive through the mountains, the pleasures of the afternoon, the flower pollen—perhaps one of the flowers was a rare thing, producing a drug that worked on him so that he had parked his car and had gotten out and slept and dreamt all of the rest about the girl in the white aó dài, this girl Nguyễn thị Linh of the street called Lotus. That was it. A kind of lotus had affected him and had named itself in the very dream it provoked.

So the major got into his car and drove on. He still had time to make it back to the base by dawn, and he smiled at this strange narcotic fantasy that he'd experienced. But he did not go a mile before he found a terrible sight. Along the road were the bodies of many men, dead soldiers strewn from the forest and down the slope and across the highway. He pulled his car over and stepped out into the stench of blood and cordite. He needed to take only a few steps until he recognized a man's face twisted upward from the ground in the agony of a death two hours old. This was the wreckage of one of the major's own night patrols, clearly ambushed and destroyed in this spot, just as the young woman had warned in the major's dream. But now he was not so sure it was a dream. Just in case, he bowed low and spoke aloud his thanks to the woman in his vision. Then he got back into his car and returned safely to the base.

This is a simple enough ghost story, and if you have turned your face to the bus window while I spoke and if it is clear to me that I have been boring you, as I can do to people—my daughter's American husband, for instance—then I will stop right there and let that be the story for you. But there is more. If you've looked at me while I've spoken and there is a light in your eyes and no condescension, then I will tell you more, for I know this story to be true.

The next week, when the major returned to An Khê, he did not go directly to his lover's house. First of all he went to the street called Lotus. It was a narrow street at the edge of the city on a little rise so that it looked out over the tops of banana trees, across a plain, to the mountains. The street was very quiet, though the sun was not yet high. The major heard the sound of the wind and the muttering of chickens and that was all. He faced a stretch of modest wooden houses with slate roofs and he thought he would knock on the nearest door and ask about the girl.

But then a young man came around the side of a house on a bicycle and drove past and the major hailed him. The young man stopped and the major said, "Do you know a girl named Nguyễn thị Linh?"

The boy's reaction was surprising to the major. He gave a short little sneering laugh. "I know the girl, to my regret. But I will not speak ill of the dead."

The major's breath stopped and he felt a chill, like a winter wind, at the news that Linh was dead. Somehow, though, he was not surprised. He knew that no living person could project her spirit in such a way as he had encountered. The chill soon passed, but his breath was just as hard to draw as he grew furious with the boy for his disrespectful words about this beautiful girl who had saved his life. The major very nearly stepped forward to strike the young man, but suddenly a calmness came over him. This was merely a jealous boy, one who had seen Miss Linh's beauty and desired it and who was rejected by her. The major knew this as surely as if Miss Linh had suddenly bent near him and whispered the facts of the case into his ear.

The major said, "And do her parents live in this street?"

"The red house at the end," the boy said and he did not wait for any further words but turned away and rode off on his bicycle.

The major walked down the block and at the end found a small wooden house perhaps once painted red but faded now into a mellower shade, a pink from some sunset. He went to the door and knocked, and after a time, a woman appeared. She was old and bent but slim and with a thin nose and she looked up into the major's face with searching eyes.

"I am Major Trung," he said. "May I come in?" These words sounded strange to the major as he said them; they were as if he needed to give no explanation here. But without asking anything of him, the woman nodded and opened the door and stepped aside, and when the major was in the room, his eyes went at once to a shrine set against a wall. The shrine held flowers and candles and incense curling its smoke into the air and in the center was a large photograph of the girl from the mountain road. Miss Linh was unmistakable in this photo——the round face, the wide mouth, the thin nose, like her mother's.

He turned to the woman and said, "Is this your daughter?"

The old woman nodded and touched her eyes lightly with a handkerchief. "Yes, she passed into the spirit world four years ago."

"I'm sorry," the major said.

"We are all sorry," the woman said. "The whole world should be sorry. This war took the sweetest daughter a mother could have."

The major said, "Yes, madame, and she saved the life of this soldier just last week." And with that, the major sat the old woman down and told her his story.

After he was done, the old woman simply nodded and turned her face toward the window. "I am glad to know that my daughter's spirit has not forgotten this world," she said.

Then the old woman lowered her face and such a stillness and sadness seemed to come over her that the major knew he could say no more. He rose and bowed to the woman and turned and bowed to the shrine of Miss Linh, saying a silent prayer of thanks, and he left the house on the street called Lotus and he wandered into the grove of trees nearby and sat down, because a great weariness had come over him. He spoke her name once more——"Linh"——and a pale light filled the grove of trees and he fell into a deep sleep.

When the major woke, it was very dark. He leaped to his feet with the fright of waking from a bad dream, but he could remember no dream and he realized where he was and what had happened. He had slept all day and into the night in the grove of trees near Miss Linh's house and once again he felt a calmness come over him. He had to drive back to the base camp, but he knew that Linh's spirit would be there in the mountains to protect him. So he walked back to his car, bowing to her house, which was dark with sleep now as he passed. In his car, his hands were steady and his heart was light, and he drove off without even thinking of his earthly lover, who no doubt was weeping now in another part of the city.

The night sky had no stars and no moon. All was black and the whole world for the major was the column of light his car pushed before him. But he drove across the plain and up into the mountains and the road rose and cut back and rose and the mountain on the one side and the chasm on the other were the same, deep black, and the major was calm. There was nothing in his head but a light rustling, like a summer wind moving banyan leaves or the panels of an aó dài rising behind a beautiful girl. He kept his eyes on the turns of the pavement in his headlights and at every turn he half-expected Miss Linh to appear before him. And he would stop on his own. He would go to her.

And the road went up and up until he passed the white road marker and the road leveled and he felt a change in the darkness, he could sense the difference in the dark of the chasm and the dark of the mountain, which rose on both sides of him now. This was near the place of Linh's last appearance and his heart began to race. He felt like a boy carrying a flower across a schoolyard to a girl he'd been watching all year and now his courage was strong enough to move his legs but not strong enough to give him a voice or enough breath. The road descended gently and turned to the right, the place where he'd seen the rabbit kicking up its heels and disappearing, and then the sharp left and it was now, he thought, now, but the lights showed only the road, there was no young woman in an aó dài, and he slowed his car as he passed the place where she'd first appeared but there was nothing. The major felt a hot flush in his cheeks, the bloom of disappointment, and he thought, Perhaps it's because I am not in danger this night. Then for a moment he even wished that the VC were doing their job, waiting to kill him, so that Miss Linh would have to come.

Even as this thought shaped itself, the road dipped and before him Miss Linh appeared in the far reach of his lights. The major cried out, wordless, a sound of pleasure like the yip of a dog about to be fed. And he slowed the car, pressed at the brake, and as he neared her, he could see her face, lovely, round, and the wide mouth was smiling, a smile he returned, broadly, and he pulled off the road and came to a stop.

The major leaped out of the car and stood where he was because she was coming toward him and he wanted to watch her move. She floated, this highland girl from An Khê, floated like the most beautiful of the Saigon girls, and the panels of her white aó dài lifted delicately, and she was smiling. Her thin nose seemed like the very best of the faces of Western women and the rest of Miss Linh's face was the best of the Orient. The major trembled as she drew near and she stopped just before the car, in the brightest beam of the headlights, and she seemed so substantial to the major, a spirit that had all the delicious tangibleness of an earthly body. "Miss Linh," he said, with a great sigh, as if he had been destined all his life to be on this mountaintop with her.

"Major Trung," she said, and her voice was as soft as a summer wind moving through banyan leaves, and he knew it had been her voice rustling in his head all through his journey to this place.

"I'm so glad you're here," he said.

"And I'm glad you are here," she said. "This was our appointed time." And she smiled at him. Her lovely, wide mouth widened farther as the smile grew and the smile did not stop when it reached the edge of her mouth but pushed the mouth farther, quickly now, and the major's hands clenched as the smile opened and the great tongue came out, red and soft, and it grew and filled his sight and licked forward and touched him, a lover's tongue, wet and insistent and clinging, and the major's feet left the ground, the tongue lifted him up and he was yanked forward and he had time for one glance at Miss Linh's eyes gleaming in the light, enormous eyes, as big as twin moons, and then there was darkness all around him and the pain crushed along the back of him, from his head to his feet, though he died quite quickly, long before he was chewed into pulp and swallowed.

Now, if you've been listening to me and even took note of my claim that I know this story to be true, you may be surprised at this turn of events. You thought perhaps that I myself was the major, and things would have turned out differently. But that is a foolish, romantic notion. I have no hesitation in telling you that. The major died horribly in the jaws of this enticing woman. And if you care about what I'm saying and you do not despise me for calling you foolish, even if I have no guile anymore and I call you this seriously, without charm, then you are a very rare American indeed, and I will tell you how I know this story to be true.

When Saigon was falling to the communists in April of 1975, I was working for your embassy and I kept waiting for my boss, an American foreign service officer, to come and get me out. He had left the week before and he told me to wait. But things happened—I do not blame him—and it was getting very late—the communists were already in the outskirts of the city—and I knew I had to go from my apartment on Nguyễn Huệ Street to the American embassy because the last helicopters would soon be taking off.

So I went out and got in my car, an American car from the embassy. It was only a few blocks, but I thought that my having the embassy car would help validate my claim with the Marines at the front gate, for I knew there were many of my countrymen trying to leave at the last minute. I went only a couple of blocks, had barely gotten beyond the Continental Palace Hotel, when I sensed the craziness in the streets. People were running everywhere now, frantic, carrying whatever possessions they could on their backs and running, many of them in the direction of the embassy. So I turned into Gia Long and up at the far corner there was a great commotion. I slowed down, and even as I did, I saw her.

It was Miss Linh. I know it was her. The man who told me Major Trung's story—his brother—actually showed me Miss Linh's photograph, the one that had sat on the mother's shrine. I knew her round face, the thin nose, and of course that wide mouth that I watched now with special attention. She stepped into the street before me and held up her hand. I stopped the car and I got out quickly and walked away at a right angle to her, peeking over my shoulder to see what she would do. She did nothing. She watched me walking away and she smiled. But just a faint smile.

I cut through some yards and made it into the next street and I headed for the embassy on foot, fighting my way through very heavy crowds now. When I came to the next corner, I could see back down to the intersection Miss Linh had prevented me from entering. Two vehicles were already on fire there and I could see people in the crowd waving clubs. Miss Linh had saved me. But you can understand how this gave me no peace of mind.

A helicopter pounded overhead and I had no time to think of ghosts. The evacuation would soon be over, I knew, and I ran hard until I was in the street of the embassy, and there my heart sank. The embassy gates were besieged by a vast throng of my people and I could tell the gates were barred and no one was going in. There were figures trying to go up the wall and I heard automatic rifle fire and these figures leaped back down. I turned my eyes to the roof of the embassy and a chopper was sitting there with its rotors still moving as a single-file stream of people was climbing into its belly. I could tell even from this distance that almost all of the people going into the helicopter were Americans.

And then the voice came softly into my ear, whispering my name. I spun around and it was Miss Linh, her round face hovering before me like a bloated summer moon. I reared back and gasped and she smiled and I didn't want that mouth to widen any further. My voice spoke and I heard it as if from a great distance. "Is this our appointed time?" I asked.

Miss Linh nodded yes, the smile steady on her lips, and she took a step toward me and I squeezed my eyes shut, I could not bear to see her monstrous tongue. But I felt nothing for a moment and then another moment, and I opened my eyes and I did not see her. I turned around and Miss Linh was standing near me in the street, and as I looked at her, she raised her hand to an approaching car. The car was large and black, a limousine with American flags on the fenders licking at the rush of air. But Miss Linh held her ground and the car stopped and then she stepped to the back door and opened it. Inside was a very important American, the boss of my boss. He recognized me and he said to get in. I looked at Miss Linh. She smiled at me, a lovely wide smile that ended in a nod toward the gaping door. So I stepped into the car and I was taken away to America.

Are you confused again, my round-eyed friend? Look at me, look where I am, listen to how I speak compulsively to strangers, even strangers from this alien land, listen to the kind of treatment I expect even now, even from you who have pretended to listen to me this long with interest. How do I know the major's story is true? Because as I sat in the darkness of the limousine and it drove away, I looked out the window and saw Miss Linh's tongue slip from her mouth and lick her lips, as if she had just eaten me up. And indeed she has.

SNOW

I wonder how long he watched me sleeping. I still wonder that. He sat and he did not wake me to ask about his carry-out order. Did he watch my eyes move as I dreamed? When I finally knew he was there and I turned to look at him, I could not make out his whole face at once. His head was turned a little to the side. His beard was neatly trimmed, but the jaw it covered was long and its curve was like a sampan sail and it held my eyes the way a sail always did when I saw one on the sea. Then I raised my eyes and looked at his nose. I am Vietnamese, you know, and we have a different sense of these proportions. Our noses are small and his was long and it also curved, gently, a reminder of his jaw, which I looked at again. His beard was dark gray, like he'd crawled out of a charcoal kiln. I make these comparisons to things from my country and village, but it is only to clearly say what this face was like. It is not that he reminded me of home. That was the farthest thing from my mind when I first saw Mr. Cohen. And I must have stared at him in those first moments with a strange look because when his face turned full to me and I could finally lift my gaze to his eyes, his eyebrows made a little jump like he was asking me, What is it? What's wrong?

I was at this same table before the big window at the front of the restaurant. The Plantation Hunan does not look like a restaurant, though. No one would give it a name like that unless it really was an old plantation house. It's very large and full of antiques. It's quiet right now. Not even five, and I can hear the big clock—I had never seen one till I came here. No one in Vietnam has a clock as tall as a man. Time isn't as important as that in Vietnam. But the clock here is very tall and they call it Grandfather, which I like, and Grandfather is ticking very slowly right now, and he wants me to fall asleep again. But I won't.

This plantation house must feel like a refugee. It is full of foreign smells, ginger and Chinese pepper and fried shells for wonton, and there's a motel on one side and a gas station on the other, not like the life the house once knew, though there are very large oak trees surrounding it, trees that must have been here when this was still a plantation. The house sits on a busy street and the Chinese family who owns it changed it from Plantation Seafood into a place that could hire a Vietnamese woman like me to be a waitress. They are very kind, this family, though we know we are different from each other. They are Chinese and I am Vietnamese and they are very kind, but we are both here in Louisiana and they go somewhere with the other Chinese in town—there are four restaurants and two laundries and some people, I think, who work as engineers at the oil refinery. They go off to themselves and they don't seem to even notice where they are.

I was sleeping that day he came in here. It was late afternoon of the day before Christmas. Almost Christmas Eve. I am not a Christian. My mother and I are Buddhist. I live with my mother and she is very sad for me because I am thirty-four years old and I am not married. There are other Vietnamese here in Lake Charles, Louisiana, but we are not a community. We are all too sad, perhaps, or too tired. But maybe not. Maybe that's just me saying that. Maybe the others are real Americans already. My mother has two Vietnamese friends, old women like her, and her two friends look at me with the same sadness in their faces because of what they see as my life. They know that once I might have been married, but the fiancé I had in my town in Vietnam went away in the Army and though he is still alive in Vietnam, the last I heard, he is driving a cab in Hô Chí Minh City and he is married to someone else. I never really knew him, and I don't feel any loss. It's just that he's the only boy my mother ever speaks of when she gets frightened for me.

I get frightened for me, too, sometimes, but it's not because I have no husband. That Christmas Eve afternoon I woke slowly. The front tables are for cocktails and for waiting for carry-out, so the chairs are large and stuffed so that they are soft. My head was very comfortable against one of the high wings of the chair and I opened my eyes without moving. The rest of me was still sleeping, but my eyes opened and the sky was still blue, though the shreds of cloud were turning pink. It looked like a warm sky. And it was. I felt sweat on my throat and I let my eyes move just a little and the live oak in front of the restaurant was quivering—all its leaves were shaking and you might think that it would look cold doing that, but it was a warm wind, I knew. The air was thick and wet, and cutting through the ginger and pepper smell was the fuzzy smell of mildew.

Perhaps it was from my dream but I remembered my first Christmas Eve in America. I slept and woke just like this, in a Chinese restaurant. I was working there. But it was in a distant place, in St. Louis. And I woke to snow. The first snow I had ever seen. It scared me. Many Vietnamese love to see their first snow, but it frightened me in some very deep way that I could not explain, and even remembering that moment—especially as I woke from sleep at the front of another restaurant—frightened me. So I turned my face sharply from the window in the Plantation Hunan and that's when I saw Mr. Cohen.

I stared at those parts of his face, like I said, and maybe this was a way for me to hide from the snow, maybe the strangeness that he saw in my face had to do with the snow. But when his eyebrows jumped and I did not say anything to explain what was going on inside me, I could see him wondering what to do. I could feel him thinking: Should I ask her what is wrong or should I just ask her for my carry-out? I am not an especially shy person, but I hoped he would choose to ask for the carry-out. I came to myself with a little jolt and I stood up and faced him——he was sitting in one of the stuffed chairs at the next table. "I'm sorry," I said, trying to turn us both from my dreaming. "Do you have an order?"

He hesitated, his eyes holding fast on my face. These were very dark eyes, as dark as the eyes of any Vietnamese, but turned up to me like this, his face seemed so large that I had trouble taking it in. Then he said, "Yes. For Cohen." His voice was deep, like a movie actor who is playing a grandfather, the kind of voice that if he asked what it was that I had been dreaming, I would tell him at once.

But he did not ask anything more. I went off to the kitchen and the order was not ready. I wanted to complain to them. There was no one else in the restaurant, and everyone in the kitchen seemed like they were just hanging around. But I don't make any trouble for anybody. So I just went back out to Mr. Cohen. He rose when he saw me, even though he surely also saw that I had no carry-out with me.

"It's not ready yet," I said. "I'm sorry."

"That's okay," he said, and he smiled at me, his gray beard opening and showing teeth that were very white.

"I wanted to scold them," I said. "You should not have to wait for a long time on Christmas Eve."

"It's okay," he said. "This is not my holiday."

I tilted my head, not understanding. He tilted his own head just like mine, like he wanted to keep looking straight into my eyes. Then he said, "I am Jewish."

I straightened my head again, and I felt a little pleasure at knowing that his straightening his own head was caused by me. I still didn't understand, exactly, and he clearly read that in my face. He said, "A Jew doesn't celebrate Christmas."

"I thought all Americans celebrated Christmas," I said.

"Not all. Not exactly." He did a little shrug with his shoulders, and his eyebrows rose like the shrug, as he tilted his head to the side once more, for just a second. It all seemed to say, What is there to do, it's the way the world is and I know it and it all makes me just a little bit weary. He said, "We all stay home, but we don't all celebrate."

He said no more, but he looked at me and I was surprised to find that I had no words either on my tongue or in my head. It felt a little strange to see this very American man who was not celebrating the holiday. In Vietnam we never miss a holiday and it did not make a difference if we were Buddhist or Cao Ðài or Catholic. I thought of this Mr. Cohen sitting in his room tonight alone while all the other Americans celebrated Christmas Eve. But I had nothing to say and he didn't either and he kept looking at me and I glanced down at my hands twisting at my order book and I didn't even remember taking the book out. So I said, "I'll check on your order again," and I turned and went off to the kitchen and I waited there till the order was done, though I stood over next to the door away from the chatter of the cook and the head waiter and the mother of the owner.

Carrying the white paper bag out to the front, I could not help but look inside to see how much food there was. There was enough for two people. So I did not look into Mr. Cohen's eyes as I gave him the food and rang up the order and took his money. I was counting his change into his palm—his hand, too, was very large—and he said, "You're not Chinese, are you?"

I said, "No. I am Vietnamese," but I did not raise my face to him, and he went away.

Two days later, it was even earlier in the day when Mr. Cohen came in. About four-thirty. The grandfather had just chimed the half hour like a man who is really crazy about one subject and talks of it at any chance he gets. I was sitting in my chair at the front once again and my first thought when I saw Mr. Cohen coming through the door was that he would think I am a lazy girl. I started to jump up, but he saw me and he motioned with his hand for me to stay where I was, a single heavy pat in the air, like he'd just laid this large hand of his on the shoulder of an invisible child before him. He said, "I'm early again."

"I am not a lazy girl," I said.

"I know you're not," he said and he sat down in the chair across from me.

"How do you know I'm not?" This question just jumped out of me. I can be a cheeky girl sometimes. My mother says that this was one reason I am not married, that this is why she always talks about the boy I was once going to marry in Vietnam, because he was a shy boy, a weak boy, who would take whatever his wife said and not complain. I myself think this is why he is driving a taxi in Hồ Chí Minh City. But as soon as this cheeky thing came out of my mouth to Mr. Cohen, I found that I was afraid. I did not want Mr. Cohen to hate me.

But he was smiling. I could even see his white teeth in this smile. He said, "You're right. I have no proof."

"I am always sitting here when you come in," I said, even as I asked myself, Why are you rubbing on this subject?

I saw still more teeth in his smile, then he said, "And the last time you were even sleeping."

I think at this I must have looked upset, because his smile went away fast. He did not have to help me seem a fool before him. "It's all right," he said. "This is a slow time of day. I have trouble staying awake myself. Even in court."

I looked at him more closely, leaving his face. He seemed very prosperous. He was wearing a suit as gray as his beard and it had thin blue stripes, almost invisible, running through it. "You are a judge?"

"A lawyer," he said.

"You will defend me when the owner fires me for sleeping."

This made Mr. Cohen laugh, but when he stopped, his face was very solemn. He seemed to lean nearer to me, though I was sure he did not move. "You had a bad dream the last time," he said.

How did I know he would finally come to ask about my dream? I had known it from the first time I'd heard his voice. "Yes," I said. "I think I was dreaming about the first Christmas Eve I spent in America. I fell asleep before a window in a restaurant in St. Louis, Missouri. When I woke, there was snow on the ground. It was the first snow I'd ever seen. I went to sleep and there was still only a gray afternoon, a thin little rain, like a mist. I had no idea things could change like that. I woke and everything was covered and I was terrified."

I suddenly sounded to myself like a crazy person. Mr. Cohen would think I was lazy and crazy both. I stopped speaking and I looked out the window. A jogger went by in the street, a man in shorts and a T-shirt, and his body glistened with sweat. I felt beads of sweat on my own forehead like little insects crouching there and I kept my eyes outside, wishing now that Mr. Cohen would go away.

"Why did it terrify you?" he said.

"I don't know," I said, though this wasn't really true. I'd thought about it now and then, and though I'd never spoken them, I could imagine reasons.

Mr. Cohen said, "Snow frightened me, too, when I was a child. I'd seen it all my life, but it still frightened me."

I turned to him and now he was looking out the window.

"Why did it frighten you?" I asked, expecting no answer.

But he turned from the window and looked at me and smiled just a little bit, like he was saying that since he had asked this question of me, I could ask him, too. He answered, "It's rather a long story. Are you sure you want to hear it?"

"Yes," I said. Of course I did.

"It was far away from here," he said. "My first home and my second one. Poland and then England. My father was a professor in Warsaw. It was early in 1939. I was eight years old and my father knew something was going wrong. All the talk about the corridor to the sea was just the beginning. He had ears. He knew. So he sent me and my mother to England. He had good friends there. I left that February and there was snow everywhere and I had my own instincts, even at eight. I cried in the courtyard of our apartment building. I threw myself into the snow there and I would not move. I cried like he was sending us away from him forever. He and my mother said it was only for some months, but I didn't believe it. And I was right. They had to lift me bodily and carry me to the taxi. But the snow was in my clothes and as we pulled away and I scrambled up to look out the back window at my father, the snow was melting against my skin and I began to shake. It was as much from my fear as from the cold. The snow was telling me he would die. And he did. He waved at me in the street and he grew smaller and we turned a corner and that was the last I saw of him."

Maybe it was foolish of me, but I thought not so much of Mr.

Cohen losing his father. I had lost a father, too, and I knew that it was something that a child lives through. In Vietnam we believe that our ancestors are always close to us, and I could tell that about Mr. Cohen, that his father was still close to him. But what I thought about was Mr. Cohen going to another place, another country, and living with his mother. I live with my mother, just like that. Even still.

He said, "So the snow was something I was afraid of. Every time it snowed in England I knew that my father was dead. It took a few years for us to learn this from others, but I knew it whenever it snowed."

"You lived with your mother?" I said.

"Yes. In England until after the war and then we came to America. The others from Poland and Hungary and Russia that we traveled with all came in through New York City and stayed there. My mother loved trains and she'd read a book once about New Orleans, and so we stayed on the train and we came to the South. I was glad to be in a place where it almost never snowed."

I was thinking how he was a foreigner, too. Not an American, really. But all the talk about the snow made this little chill behind my thoughts. Maybe I was ready to talk about that. Mr. Cohen had spoken many words to me about his childhood and I didn't want him to think I was a girl who takes things without giving something back. He was looking out the window again, and his lips pinched together so that his mouth disappeared in his beard. He seemed sad to me. So I said, "You know why the snow scared me in St. Louis?"

He turned at once with a little humph sound and a crease on his forehead between his eyes and then a very strong voice saying, "Tell me," and it felt like he was scolding himself inside for not paying attention to me. I am not a vain girl, always thinking that men pay such serious attention to me that they get mad at themselves for ignoring me even for a few moments. This is what it really felt like and it surprised me. If I was a vain girl, it wouldn't have surprised me. He said it again: "Tell me why it scared you."

I said, "I think it's because the snow came so quietly and everything was underneath it, like this white surface was the real earth and everything had died—all the trees and the grass and the streets and the houses—everything had died and was buried. It was all lost. I knew there was snow above me, on the roof, and I was dead, too."

"Your own country was very different," Mr. Cohen said.

It pleased me that he thought just the way I once did. You could tell that he wished there was an easy way to make me feel better, make the dream go away. But I said to him, "This is what I also thought. If I could just go to a warm climate, more like home. So I came down to New Orleans, with my mother, just like you, and then we came over to Lake Charles. And it is something like Vietnam here. The rice fields and the heat and the way the storms come in. But it makes no difference. There's no snow to scare me here, but I still sit alone in this chair in the middle of the afternoon and I sleep and I listen to the grandfather over there ticking."

I stopped talking and I felt like I w. making no sense at all, so I said, "I should check on your order."

Mr. Cohen's hand came out over the table. "May I ask your name?"

"I'm Miss Giàu," I said.

"Miss Giau?" he asked, and when he did that, he made a different word, since Vietnamese words change with the way your voice sings them.

I laughed. "My name is Giàu, with the voice falling. It means 'wealthy' in Vietnamese. When you say the word like a question, you say something very different. You say I am Miss Pout."

Mr. Cohen laughed and there was something in the laugh that made me shiver just a little, like a nice little thing, like maybe stepping into the shower when you are covered with dust and feeling the water expose you. But in the back of my mind was his carry-out and there was a bad little feeling there, something I wasn't thinking about, but it made me go off now with heavy feet to the kitchen. I got the bag and it was feeling different as I carried it back to the front of the restaurant. I went behind the counter and I put it down and I wished I'd done this a few moments before, but even with his eyes on me, I looked into the bag. There was one main dish and one portion of soup.

Then Mr. Cohen said, "Is this a giau I see on your face?" And he pronounced the word exactly right, with the curling tone that made it "pout."

I looked up at him and I wanted to smile at how good he said the word, but even wanting to do that made the pout worse. I said, "I was just thinking that your wife must be sick. She is not eating tonight."

He could have laughed at this. But he did not. He laid his hand for a moment on his beard, he smoothed it down. He said, "The second dinner on Christmas Eve was for my son passing through town. My wife died some years ago and I am not remarried."

I am not a hard-hearted girl because I knew that a child gets over the loss of a father and because I also knew that a man gets over the loss of a wife. I am a good girl, but I did not feel sad for Mr. Cohen. I felt very happy. Because he laid his hand on mine and he asked if he could call me. I said yes, and as it turns out, New Year's Eve seems to be a Jewish holiday. The Vietnamese New Year comes at a different time, but people in Vietnam know to celebrate whatever holiday comes along. So tonight Mr. Cohen and I will go to some restaurant that is not Chinese, and all I have to do now is sit here and listen very carefully to Grandfather as he talks to me about time.

RELIC

You may be surprised to learn that a man from Vietnam owns one of John Lennon's shoes. Not only one of John Lennon's shoes. One shoe that he was wearing when he was shot to death in front of the Dakota apartment building. That man is me, and I have money, of course, to buy this thing. I was a very wealthy man in my former country, before the spineless poor threw down their guns and let the communists take over. Something comes into your head as I speak: This is a hard man, a man of no caring; how can he speak of the "spineless poor"? I do not mean to say that these people are poor because they are cowards. I am saying that being poor can take away a man's courage. For those who are poor, being beaten down, robbed of rights, repressed under the worst possible form of tyranny is not enough worse than just being poor. Why should they risk the pain and the maiming and the death for so little benefit? If I was a poor man, I, too, would be spineless.

But I had wealth in Vietnam and that gave me courage enough even to sail away on the South China Sea, sail away from all those things I owned and come to a foreign country and start again with nothing. That is what I did. I came at last to New Orleans, Louisiana, and because I was once from North Vietnam and was Catholic, I ended up among my own people far east in Orleans Parish, in a community called Versailles, named after an apartment complex they put us in as refugees. I lived in such a place for a time. The ceilings were hardly eight feet high and there was no veranda, nowhere even to hang a wind chime. The emptiness of the rooms threatened to cast me down, take my courage. In Saigon, I owned many wonderful things: furniture of teak, inlaid with scenes made of tiles of ivory and pearl, showing how the Trưng sisters threw out the Chinese from our country in the year 40 A.D.; a part of an oracle bone from the earliest times of my country, the bone of some animal killed by ritual and carved with the future in Chinese characters; a dagger with a stag's antler handle in bronze. You might think that things like this should have protected me from what happened. There is much power in objects. My church teaches that clearly. A fragment of bone from a saint's body, a bit of skin, a lock of hair—all of these things have great power to do miracles, to cure, to heal.

But you see, though the Trưng sisters threw the Chinese out, just one year later the Chinese returned and the Trưng sisters had to retreat, and finally, in the year 43, they threw themselves into a river and drowned. And the oracle bone, though I did not know exactly what it said, probably dealt with events long past or maybe even foresaw this very world where I have ended up. And the dagger looked ceremonial and I'm sure was never drawn in anger. It would have been better if I had owned the tiniest fragment of some saint's body, but the church does not sell such things.

And here I sit, at the desk in the study in my house. I am growing rich once more and in the center of my desk sits this shoe. It is more like a little boot, coming up to the ankle and having no laces but a loop of leather at the back where John Lennon's forefinger went through to pull the shoe onto his foot, even that morning which was his last morning on this earth. Something comes into your head when I tell you this. It is my talent in making wealth to know what others are thinking. You wonder how I should come to have this shoe, how I know it is really what I say it is. I cannot give away the names of those who I dealt with, but I can tell you this much. I am a special collector of things. A man in New York who sells to me asked if I was interested in something unusual. When he told me about this shoe, I had the same response—how can I know for sure? Well, I met the man who provided the shoe, and I have photographs and even a newspaper article that identifies him as a very close associate of John Lennon. He says that certain items were very painful for the family, so they were disposed of and he was in possession of them and he knew that some people would appreciate them very much. He, too, is a Catholic. The other shoe was already gone, which is unfortunate, but this shoe was still available, and I paid much money for it.

Of course, I have made much money in my new country. It is a gift I have, and America is the land of opportunity. I started in paper lanterns and firecrackers and cay nêu, the New Year poles. I sold these at the time of Têt, our Vietnam New Year celebration, when the refugees wanted to think about home. I also sold them sandwiches and drinks and later I opened a restaurant and then a parlor with many video games. Versailles already has a pool hall, run by another good businessman, but I have video games in my place and the young men love these games, fighting alien spaceships and wizards and kung-fu villains with much greater skill than their fathers fought the communists. And I am now doing other things, bigger things, mostly in the shrimp industry. In ten years people from Vietnam will be the only shrimp fishermen in the Gulf of Mexico. I do not need an oracle bone to tell you this for sure. And when this is so, I will be making even more money.

I may even be able to break free of Versailles. I sit at my desk and I look beyond John Lennon's shoe, through the window, and

what do I see? My house, unlike the others on this street, has two
stories. I am on the second story at the back and outside is my
carefully trimmed yard, the lush St. Augustine grass faintly tinted
with blue, and there is my brick barbecue pit and my setting of
cypress lawn furniture. But beyond is the bayou that runs through
Versailles and my house is built at an angle on an acre and a half and
I can see all the other backyards set side by side for the quarter mile
to the place where the lagoon opens up and the Versailles apartments
stand. All the backyards of these houses—all of them—are plowed
and planted as if this was some provincial village in Vietnam. Such
things are not done in America. In America a vegetable garden is a
hobby. Here in Versailles the people of Vietnam are cultivating their
backyards as a way of life. And behind the yards is a path and beyond
the path is the border of city land along the bayou and on this land
the people of Vietnam have planted a community garden stretching
down to the lagoon and even now I can see a scattering of conical
straw hats there, the women crouched flat-footed and working the
garden, and I expect any moment to see a boy riding a water buffalo
down the path or perhaps a sampan gliding along the bayou, heading
for the South China Sea. Do you understand me? I am living in the
past.

I have enough money to leave Versailles and become the American
that I must be. But I have found that it isn't so simple. Something
is missing. I know I am wrong when I say that still more money,
from shrimp or from whatever else, will finally free me from the past.
Perhaps the problem is that my businesses are all connected to the
Vietnam community here. There was no way around that when I
started. And perhaps it's true that I should find some American
business to invest in. But there is nothing to keep me in this place
even if my money is made here. I do not work the cash registers in
my businesses.

Perhaps it is the absence of my family. But this is something they chose for themselves. My wife was a simple woman and she would not leave her parents and she feared America greatly. The children came from her body. They belong with her, and she felt she belonged in Vietnam. My only regret is that I have nothing of hers to touch, not a lock of hair or a ring or even a scarf—she had so many beautiful scarves, some of which she wore around her waist. But if my family had come with me, would they not in fact be a further difficulty in my becoming American? As it is, I have only myself to consider in this problem and that should make things simpler.

But there are certain matters in life that a man is not able to control on his own. My religion teaches this clearly. For a rich man, for a man with the gift to become rich even a second time, this is a truth that is sometimes difficult to see. But he should realize that he is human and dependent on forces beyond himself and he should look to the opportunity that his wealth can give him.

I do not even know John Lennon's music very well. I have heard it and it is very nice, but in Vietnam I always preferred the popular singers in my own language, and in America I like the music they call "easy listening," though sometimes a favorite tune I will hear from the Living Strings or Percy Faith turns out to be a song of John Lennon. It is of no matter to a man like John Lennon that I did not know his music well before I possessed his shoe. The significance of this object is the same. He is a very important figure. This is common knowledge. He wrote many songs that affected the lives of people in America and he sang about love and peace and then he died on the streets of New York as a martyr.

I touch his shoe. The leather is smooth and is the color of teakwood and my forefinger glides along the instep to the toe, where there is a jagged scrape. I lift my finger and put it on the spot where the scrape begins, at the point of the toe, and I trace the gash, follow the fuzzy track of the exposed underside of the leather. All along it I feel a faint grinding inside me, as if this is a wound in flesh that I

touch. John Lennon's wound. I understand this scrape on the shoe.
John Lennon fell and his leg pushed out on the pavement as he died.
This is the stigmata of the shoe, the sign of his martyrdom.

With one hand I cup the shoe at its back and slide my other
hand under the toe and I lift and the shoe always surprises me at its
lightness, just as one who has moments before died a martyr's death
might be surprised at the lightness of his own soul. I angle the shoe
toward the light from my window and I look inside. I see the words
SAVILE ROW on the lining, but that is all. There is no size recorded
here and I imagine that this shoe was made special for John Lennon,
that they carefully measured his foot and this is its purest image in
the softest leather. I am very quiet inside but there is this great
pressure in my chest, coming from something I cannot identify as
myself. This is because of what I will now do.

I wait until I can draw an adequate breath. Then I turn in my
chair and gently lower the shoe to the floor and I place it before my
bare right foot. I make the sign of the cross and slip my foot into
John Lennon's shoe, sliding my forefinger into the loop at the back
and pulling gently, just as John Lennon did on the day he joined the
angels. The lining is made of something as soft as silk and there is a
chill from it. I stand up before my desk and the shoe is large for me,
but that's as it should be. I take one step and then another and I am
in the center of my room and I stand there and my heart is very full
and I wait for what I pray will one day be mine, a feeling about what
has happened to me that I cannot even imagine until I actually feel
it. I have asked the man in New York to look for another of John
Lennon's shoes, a left shoe. Even if it is from some other pair, I want
to own just one more shoe. Then I will put both of John Lennon's
shoes on my feet and I will go out into the street and I will walk as
far as I need to go to find the place where I belong.

PREPARATION

Though Thūy's dead body was naked under the sheet, I had not seen it since we were girls together and our families took us to the beaches at Nha Trang. This was so even though she and I were best friends for all our lives and she became the wife of Lê Văn Lý, the man I once loved. Thūy had a beautiful figure and breasts that were so tempting in the tight bodices of our aó dàis that Lý could not resist her. But the last time I saw Thūy's naked body, she had no breasts yet at all, just the little brown nubs that I also had at seven years old, and we ran in the white foam of the breakers and we watched the sampans out beyond the coral reefs.

We were not common girls, the ones who worked the fields and seemed so casual about their bodies. And more than that, we were Catholics, and Mother Mary was very modest, covered from her throat to her ankles, and we made up our toes beautifully, like the statue of Mary in the church, and we were very modest about all the rest. Except Thūy could seem naked when she was clothed. We both ran in the same surf, but somehow her flesh learned something there that mine did not. She could move like the sea, her body filled her clothes like the living sea, fluid and beckoning. Her mother was always worried about her because the boys grew quiet at her approach and noisy at her departure, and no one was worried about me. I was an expert pair of hands, to bring together the herbs for the lemon grass chicken or to serve the tea with the delicacy of a wind chime or to scratch the eucalyptus oil into the back of a sick child.

And this won for me a good husband, though he was not Lê Văn Lý, nor could ever have been. But he was a good man and a surprised man to learn that my hands could also make him very happy even if my breasts did not seem so delightful in the tight bodice of my aó dài. That man died in the war which came to our country, a war we were about to lose, and I took my sons to America and I settled in this place in New Orleans called Versailles that has only Vietnamese. Soon my best friend Thūy also came to this place, with her husband Lê Văn Lý and her children. They left shortly for California, but after three years they returned, and we all lived another decade together and we expected much longer than that, for Thūy and I would have become fifty years old within a week of each other next month.

Except that Thūy was dead now and lying before me in this place that Mr. Hoa, the mortician for our community, called the "preparation room," and she was waiting for me to put the makeup on her face and comb her hair for the last time. She died very quickly, but she knew enough to ask for the work of my hands to make her beautiful in the casket. She let on to no one—probably not even herself—when the signs of the cancer growing in her ovaries caused no pain. She was a fearful person over foolish little things, and such a one as that will sometimes ignore the big things until it is too late. But thank God that when the pain did come and the truth was known, the end came quickly afterward.

She clutched my hand in the hospital room, the curtain drawn around us, and my own grip is very strong, but on that morning she hurt me with the power of her hand. This was a great surprise to me. I looked at our locked hands, and her lovely, slender fingers were white with the strength in them and yet the nails were still perfect, each one a meticulously curved echo of the others, each one carefully stroked with the red paint the color of her favorite Winesap apples. This was a very sad moment for me. It made me sadder even than the sounds of her pain, this hand with its sudden fearful strength and yet the signs of her lovely vanity still there.

But I could not see her hands as I stood beside her in the preparation room. They were somewhere under the sheet and I had work to do, so I looked at her face. Her closed eyes showed the mostly Western lids, passed down by more than one Frenchman among her ancestors. This was a very attractive thing about her, I always knew, though Lý never mentioned her eyes, even though they were something he might well have complimented in public. He could have said to people, "My wife has such beautiful eyes," but he did not. And his certain regard for her breasts, of course, was kept very private. Except with his glance.

We three were young, only sixteen, and Thūy and I were at the Cirque Sportif in Saigon. This was where we met Lý for the first time. We were told that if Mother Mary had known the game of tennis, she would have allowed her spiritual children to wear the costume for the game, even if our legs did show. We loved showing our legs. I have very nice legs, really. Not as nice as Thūy's but I was happy to have my legs bare when I met Lê Văn Lý for the first time. He was a ball boy at the tennis court, and when Thūy and I played, he would run before us and pick up the balls and return them to us. I was a more skillful player than Thūy and it wasn't until too late that I realized how much better it was to hit the ball into the net and have Lý dart before me on this side and then pick up my tennis ball and return it to me. Thūy, of course, knew this right away and

her game was never worse than when we played with Lê Văn Lý
poised at the end of the net waiting for us to make a mistake.

And it was even on that first meeting that I saw his eyes move
to Thủy's breasts. It was the slightest of glances but full of meaning.
I knew this because I was very attuned to his eyes from the start.
They were more like mine, with nothing of the West but everything
of our ancestors back to the Kindly Dragon, whose hundred children
began Vietnam. But I had let myself forget that the Kindly Dragon
married a fairy princess, not a solid homemaker, so my hopes were
still real at age sixteen. He glanced at Thủy's breasts, but he smiled
at me when I did miss a shot and he said, very low so only I could
hear it, "You're a very good player." It sounded to me at sixteen
that this was something he would begin to build his love on. I was
a foolish girl.

But now she lay before me on a stainless-steel table, her head
cranked up on a chrome support, her hair scattered behind her and
her face almost plain. The room had a faint smell, a little itch in the
nose of something strong, like the smell when my sons killed insects
for their science classes in school. But over this was a faint aroma of
flowers, though not real flowers, I knew. I did not like this place and
I tried to think about what I'd come for. I was standing before Thủy
and I had not moved since Mr. Hoa left me. He tied the smock I
was wearing at the back and he told me how he had washed Thủy's
hair already. He turned up the air conditioner in the window, which
had its glass panes painted a chalky white, and he bowed himself out
of the room and closed the door tight.

I opened the bag I'd placed on the high metal chair and I took
out Thủy's pearl-handled brush and I bent near her. We had combed
each other's hair all our lives. She had always worn her hair down,
even as she got older. Even to the day of her death, with her hair
laid carefully out on her pillow, something she must have done herself,

very near the end, for when Lý and their oldest son and I came into the room that evening and found her, she was dead and her hair was beautiful.

So now I reached out to Thủy and I stroked her hair for the first time since her death and her hair resisted the brush and the resistance sent a chill through me. Her hair was still alive. The body was fixed and cold and absolutely passive, but the hair defied the brush, and though Thủy did not cry out at this first brush stroke as she always did, the hair insisted that she was still alive and I felt something very surprising at that. From the quick fisting of my mind at the image of Thủy, I knew I was angry. From the image of her hair worn long even after she was middle aged instead of worn in a bun at the nape of the neck like all the Vietnamese women our age. I was angry and then I realized that I was angry because she was not completely dead, and this immediately filled me with a shame so hot that it seemed as if I would break into a sweat.

The shame did not last very long. I straightened and turned my face to the flow of cool air from the air conditioner and I looked at all the instruments hanging behind the glass doors of the cabinet in the far wall, all the glinting clamps and tubes and scissors and knives. This was not the place of the living. I looked at Thủy's face and her pale lips were tugged down into a faint frown and I lifted the brush and stroked her hair again and once again, and though it felt just the way it always had felt when I combed it, I continued to brush.

And I spoke a few words to Thủy. Perhaps her spirit was in the room and could hear me. "It's all right, Thủy. The things I never blamed you for in life I won't blame you for now." She had been a good friend. She had always appreciated me. When we brushed each other's hair, she would always say how beautiful mine was and she would invite me also to leave it long, even though I am nearly fifty and I am no beauty at all. And she would tell me how wonderful my talents were. She would urge me to date some man or other in Versailles. I would make such and such a man a wonderful wife, she said. These men were successful men that she recommended, very well off. But they were always older men, in their sixties or seventies. One man was eighty-one, and this one she did not suggest to me directly but by saying casually how she had seen him last week and he was such a vigorous man, such a fine and vigorous man.

And her own husband, Lê Văn Lý, was of course more successful than any of them. And he is still the finest-looking man in Versailles. How fine he is. The face of a warrior. I have seen the high cheeks and full lips of Lê Văn Lý in the statues of warriors in the Saigon Museum, the men who threw the Chinese out of our country many centuries ago. And I lifted Thūy's hair and brushed it out in narrow columns and laid the hair carefully on the bright silver surface behind the support, letting the ends dangle off the table. The hair was very soft and it was yielding to my hands now and I could see this hair hanging perfectly against the back of her pale blue aó dài as she and Lý strolled away across the square near the Continental Palace Hotel.

I wish there had been some clear moment, a little scene; I would even have been prepared not to seem so solid and level-headed; I would have been prepared to weep and even to speak in a loud voice. But they were very disarming in the way they let me know how things were. We had lemonades on the veranda of the Continental Palace Hotel, and I thought it would be like all the other times, the three of us together in the city, strolling along the river or through the flower markets at Nguyễn Huệ or the bookstalls on Lê Lợi. We had been three friends together for nearly two years, ever since we'd met at the club. There had been no clear choosing, in my mind. Lý was a very traditional boy, a courteous boy, and he never forced the issue of romance, and so I still had some hopes.

Except that I had unconsciously noticed things, so when Thūy spoke to me and then, soon after, the two of them walked away from the hotel together on the eve of Lý's induction into the Army, I realized something with a shock that I actually had come to understand slowly all along. Like suddenly noticing that you are old. The little things gather for a long time, but one morning you look in the mirror and you understand them in a flash. At the flower market on Nguyễn Huệ I would talk with great spirit of how to arrange the flowers, which ones to put together, how a home would be filled with this or that sort of flower on this or that occasion. But Thūy would be bending into the flowers, her hair falling through the petals, and she would breathe very deeply and rise up and she would be inflated with the smell of flowers and of course her breasts would seem to have grown even larger and more beautiful and Lý would look at them and then he would close his eyes softly in appreciation. And at the bookstalls—I would be the one who asked for the bookstalls—I would be lost in what I thought was the miracle of all these little worlds inviting me in, and I was unaware of the little world near my elbow, Thūy looking at the postcards and talking to Lý about trips to faraway places.

I suppose my two friends were as nice to me as possible at the Continental Palace Hotel, considering what they had to do. Thūy asked me to go to the rest room with her and we were laughing together at something Lý had said. We went to the big double mirror and our two faces were side by side, two girls eighteen years old, and yet beside her I looked much older. Already old. I could see that. And she said, "I am so happy."

We were certainly having fun on this day, but I couldn't quite understand her attitude. After all, Lý was going off to fight our long war. But I replied, "I am, too."

Then she leaned near me and put her hand on my shoulder and

she said, "I have a wonderful secret for you. I couldn't wait to tell it to my dear friend."

She meant these words without sarcasm. I'm sure of it. And I still did not understand what was coming.

She said, "I am in love."

I almost asked who it was that she loved. But this was only the briefest final pulse of naïveté. I knew who she loved. And after laying her head on the point of my shoulder and smiling at me in the mirror with such tenderness for her dear friend, she said, "And Lý loves me, too."

How had this subject not come up before? The answer is that the two of us had always spoken together of what a wonderful boy Lý was. But my own declarations were as vivid and enthusiastic as Thūy's—rather more vivid, in fact. So if I was to assume that she loved Lý from all that she'd said, then my own declaration of love should have been just as clear. But obviously it wasn't, and that was just as I should have expected it. Thūy never for a moment had considered me a rival for Lý. In fact, it was unthinkable to her that I should even love him in vain.

She lifted her head from my shoulder and smiled at me as if she expected me to be happy. When I kept silent, she prompted me. "Isn't it wonderful?"

I had never spoken of my love for Lý and I knew that this was the last chance I would have. But what was there to say? I could look back at all the little signs now and read them clearly. And Thūy was who she was and I was different from that and the feeling between Lý and her was already decided upon. So I said the only reasonable thing that I could. "It is very wonderful."

This made Thūy even happier. She hugged me. And then she asked me to comb her hair. We had been outside for an hour before coming to the hotel and her long, straight hair was slightly ruffled and she handed me the pearl-handled brush that her mother had given her and she turned her back to me. And I began to brush. The first stroke caught a tangle and Thūy cried out in a pretty, piping voice. I paused briefly and almost threw the brush against the wall and walked out of this place. But then I brushed once again and again, and she was turned away from the mirror so she could not see the terrible pinch of my face when I suggested that she and Lý spend their last hours now alone together. She nearly wept in joy and appreciation at this gesture from her dear friend, and I kept on brushing until her hair was perfect.

And her hair was perfect now beneath my hands in the preparation room. And I had a strange thought. She was doing this once more to me. She was having me make her hair beautiful so she could go off to the spirit world and seduce the one man there who could love me. This would be Thūy's final triumph over me. My hands trembled at this thought and it persisted. I saw this clearly: Thūy arriving in heaven and her hair lying long and soft down her back and her breasts are clearly beautiful even in the white robe of the angels, and the spirit of some great warrior who fought at the side of the Trưng sisters comes to her, and though he has waited nineteen centuries for me, he sees Thūy and decides to wait no more. It has been only the work of my hands that he has awaited and he lifts Thūy's hair and kisses it.

I drew back from Thūy and I stared at her face. I saw it in the mirror at the Continental Palace Hotel and it was very beautiful, but this face before me now was rubbery in death, the beauty was hidden, waiting for my hands. Thūy waited for me to make her beautiful. I had always made her more beautiful. Just by being near her. I was tempted once more to turn away. But that would only let her have her condescending smile at me. Someone else would do this job if I did not, and Thūy would fly off to heaven with her beautiful face and I would be alone in my own shame.

I turned to the sheet now, and the body I had never looked upon in its womanly nakedness was hiding there and this was what Lý had given his love for. The hair and the face had invited him, but it was this hidden body, her secret flesh, that he had longed for. I had seen him less than half an hour ago. He was in Mr. Hoa's office when I arrived. He got up and shook my hand with both of his, holding my hand for a long moment as he said how glad he was that I was here. His eyes were full of tears and I felt very sorry for Lê Văn Lý. A warrior should never cry, even for the death of a beautiful woman. He handed me the bag with Thūy's brush and makeup and he said, "You always know what to do."

What did he mean by this? Simply that I knew how to brush Thūy's hair and paint her face? Or was this something he had seen about me in all things, just as he had once seen that I was a very good tennis player? Did it mean he understood that he had never been with a woman like that, a woman who would always know what to do for him as a wife? When he stood before me in Mr. Hoa's office, I felt like a foolish teenage girl again, with that rush of hope. But perhaps it wasn't foolish; Thūy's breasts were no longer there for his eyes to slide away to.

Her breasts. What were these things that had always defined my place in the world of women? They were beneath the sheet and my hand went out and grasped it at the edge, but I stopped. I told myself it was of no matter now. She was dead. I let go of the sheet and turned to her face of rubber and I took out her eye shadow and her lipstick and her mascara and I bent near and painted the life back into this dead thing.

And as I painted, I thought of where she would lie, in the cemetery behind the Catholic church, in a stone tomb above the ground. It was often necessary in New Orleans, the placing of the dead above the ground, because the water table was so high. If we laid Thūy in the earth, one day she would float to the surface and I could see that day clearly, her rising from the earth and awaking and finding her way back to the main street of Versailles in the heat of the day, and I would be talking with Lý, he would be bending near me and listening as I said all the things of my heart, and suddenly his eyes would slide away and there she would be, her face made up and her hair brushed and her breasts would be as beautiful as ever. But the thought of her lying above the ground made me anxious, as well. As if she wasn't quite gone. And she never would be. Lý would sense her out there behind the church, suspended in the air, and he would never forget her and would take all the consolation he needed from his children and grandchildren.

My hand trembled now as I touched her eyes with the brush, and when I held the lipstick, I pressed it hard against her mouth and I cast aside the shame at my anger and I watched this mouth in my mind, the quick smile of it that never changed in all the years, that never sensed any mood in me but loyal, subordinate friendship. Then the paint was all in place and I pulled back and I angled my face once more into the flow of cool air and I tried to just listen to the grinding of the air conditioner and forget all of these feelings, these terrible feelings about the dead woman who had always been my friend, who I had never once challenged in life over any of these things. I thought, What a coward I am.

But instead of hearing this righteous charge against me, I looked at Thúy and I took her hair in my hands and I smoothed it all together and wound it into a bun and I pinned it at the nape of her neck. She was a fifty-year-old woman, after all. She was as much a fifty-year-old woman as I was. Surely she was. And at this I looked to the sheet.

It lay lower across the chest than I thought it might. But her breasts were also fifty years old, and they were spread flat as she lay on her back. She had never let her dear friend see them, these two secrets that had enchanted the man I loved. I could bear to look at them now, vulnerable and weary as they were. I stepped down and I grasped the edge of the sheet at her throat, and with the whisper of the cloth I pulled it back.

And one of her breasts was gone. The right breast was lovely even now, even in death, the nipple large and the color of cinnamon, but the left breast was gone and a large crescent scar began there in its place and curved out of sight under her arm. I could not draw a breath at this, as if the scar was in my own chest where my lungs had been yanked out, and I could see that her scar was old, years old, and I thought of her three years in California and how she had never spoken at all about this, how her smile had hidden all that she must have suffered.

I could not move for a long moment, and then at last my hands acted as if on their own. They pulled the sheet up and gently spread it at her throat. I suppose this should have brought back my shame at the anger I'd had at my friend Thủy, but it did not. That seemed a childish feeling now, much too simple. It was not necessary to explain any of this. I simply leaned forward and kissed Thủy on her brow and I undid the bun at the back of her neck, happy to make her beautiful once more, happy to send her off to a whole body in heaven where she would catch the eye of the finest warrior. And I knew she would understand if I did all I could to make Lê Văn Lý happy.

THE
AMERICAN
COUPLE

My sister and I dressed up like ducks and our sign said DON'T DUCK A DEAL and so I ended up in Puerto Vallarta, Mexico, with my husband. This was the deal my sister and I made after the show. She would take the money that went along with the special vacation package that turned out to be behind curtain number two, and I would take my husband to Puerto Vallarta. If we'd had a chance to make the deal just before ours, I would have won a car. I could see a very slight bulge just to the left of center in curtain number three, and sure enough, when they opened it to show the couple dressed like killer bees what they'd passed over, there was a Ford Escort, which was pulled up just a little bit too far. They do that sometimes. I noticed it. The killer bees did not notice it and they won the goat behind curtain number one, a goat that nibbled the hem of the electric-blue dress on the beautiful blond model holding the goat's leash. Everyone laughed except the couple dressed like bees, and my sister and I laughed, too, though when I leaned over to my sister and told her that I had known where the car was, she slapped her forehead in distress and stopped laughing. I am very observant. This is a good thing, I think, though in Vietnam, where I was born and raised, it is not thought to be a good trait in a woman, unless she keeps it to herself.

My husband is of two minds on this matter. Sometimes I will notice something that will help him in his business. He is a very fine businessman. He is a very big success in America, just as he was when he was in Vietnam, even though he had to start over again from the beginning in this country. In Vietnam he made much money in the export of duck feathers. This is what inspired my costume on "Let's Make a Deal." Duck feathers were the fourth largest export business in the Republic of South Vietnam and they make very soft pillows and very warm blankets. Once, a man who my husband trusted came to the office and said that he was dealing only with my husband, but I observed a duck feather in the cuff of his trouser and that duck was not one of ours. My husband was very proud of my observations on that day, but I know I make him nervous because he thinks there is a great deal that I can see and know about him at all times.

It's true that I know quite a few things from what my eyes tell me. It's true that I was happy to have a chance to bring him to Puerto Vallarta and that I myself struck the deal with my sister that made this possible. We flew in over the mountains and he was sleeping beside me and I watched out the window. The mountains were covered in a lush green that looked like velour and it was very much like Vietnam. There was a river running over the mountain, a brown river, as brown as a Mexican child, and our plane followed it until I could see the city out ahead of us strung along the sea. It was very beautiful coming in and I nudged my husband, hoping he would wake and bring his face near to mine and watch with me. But he became instantly concerned with finding his shoes, which he always slips off when he sleeps, and by the time he felt like nothing was lost and he was not being caught off guard by anything, we were too low for romance and all I could see outside were ragged fields and a neighborhood of poor houses, tin and wood, also like Vietnam, like the places all around Saigon, which is the city I am from.

The airport was pretty ragged, too. All the strips of land in between the runways were overgrown and the airport building was long and low and it looked mostly like cinder block, which they tried to hide by giving big sections of the outside walls a different texture, a certain roughness, but it reminded me of crepe paper and they painted these parts in bright colors, red and yellow and lime green. It just all seemed pretty cheap, and I could see my husband's eye for business picking up on that right away, along with all the weeds. He'd been to the slick American places—Las Vegas and Miami Beach and Lake Tahoe—and he knew what the customer expected. In the taxicab he was snorting at the potholes in the road—the cab had to slow almost to a stop several times—and at the occasional piles of stony rubble and at all the weedy fields. This whole corridor to the fancy hotels should be done up right, he was thinking. And he wasn't all that happy about doing this trip anyway, I knew. He was sorry to be away from his work, even for a week, and he didn't like my sister being his benefactor. Especially not since she and I had dressed up like ducks.

I didn't like that either, really. I must admit I love the game shows. I love American television in general. The soap operas. You'd think I would've had enough of daily disaster, but the soaps remind me that somewhere somebody knows what life can really be. It makes me enjoy even more all of this wonderful lightness before my eyes in America. And I particularly like one of the soap operas with an older woman character. This actress has been around for years, and even though the shows are taped, she always seems to me on the edge of disaster. The actress personally. She is saying her lines and I can sense some light go out in her brain and you can see her eyes slide just ever so briefly off camera. She's looking for the prompt cards, you see. She's forgotten her lines. And this must be happening to her all the time, for these moments to be left on the tape, even if they are subtle, and maybe I'm the only viewer in the country, other than perhaps another professional actor, to notice. There's always this real-life drama going on. I like her very much. This woman has guts, continuing to act without a memory. Sometimes she gets the other actor in the scene positioned just right and her gaze lifts over the actor's shoulder and you can see the faint scanning of her eyes as she reads. It is very subtle, this movement, but I can see it, and at those moments I feel very good for her. She can see what there is to say. But I also feel good for her, a little thrilled even, like watching an ice skater doing a leap, when her character suddenly becomes chatty and slightly unfocused and it's because she is cut off from the prompt cards and she's improvising around until she can find her way back to the script. This is what's good about America. There is always some improvisation, something new, and when things get strained, you don't fall back on tradition but you make up something new.

Still, if I could have been part of all that without dressing up like a duck, that would have been better. I wish I could have won Mexico by answering questions or solving puzzles or guessing prices. Something like that. I'm very good at all those things. Just last week I did several things that no one else could do—I identified Jeremy Brett as playing both Sherlock Holmes on public television and Freddy in the movie "My Fair Lady" and I read the phrase "Desperation Tactics" even without any vowels and I knew that a KitchenAid dishwasher and a year's supply of Toast 'Ems cost between six hundred fifty and seven hundred dollars. But you have to try out for these shows and they stay away from people who have an accent. I put the words of

English together as well as most Americans, but you can hear my foreignness in my pronunciation.

And only once did I get as far as the tryout anyway. I finally had sense enough to turn my name around and leave out the middle two. I turned Trần Nam Thanh Gabrielle into Gabrielle Tran. My parents had given me a French name because they had always admired the French, for their food and for their riding club in Saigon, mostly. But arranging my name like Gabrielle Tran won me a tryout—I guess the producers thought I might be like Nancy Kwan, the actress who I enjoy on the old movies and who can speak English very clearly when she wants to.

I was very good at doing what they asked when exciting things happened in the game. You'd think that they'd have long ago gotten used to asking for this. But the man with the headphones and a clipboard seemed almost shy when he got around to it. Like we were on a date and he was asking for something sexual and a little strange. There were three of us trying out at once, three women, and he said, "When something very good happens, could you . . ." And he stammered around for a bit and then said, "Could you show it physically. That is, could you kind of, you know, bounce up and down? Jiggle around." So we all laughed at this, but then we did it and I did it very well. He even stopped us and put his hand on my shoulder and said to the others, "Yes. Like this. Watch Mrs. Tran."

I was very good, you see. And it was natural to me. I was having fun. But then when they started talking to us, asking our names and where we lived and such, I could see the little squinting that went on when I spoke. They asked questions and I got them right and I bounced up and down, but I knew I wasn't going to make it. And I think I probably talked a little too much, as well. I even kidded the host—I won't mention his name—about the kiss he gave his hostess during a break. They had both disappeared while the director walked around setting cameras, and when they returned, they did it without looking at each other at all and the host's TV makeup was smudged around his lips. It's not as if I said this on the air, but instantly I could tell that it wasn't the thing to do.

My husband told me that it was all I should have expected. In America he is in the food-service business. Not restaurants. He thinks that's like being a trained elephant in a circus, running a Vietnamese restaurant in America with paper lanterns and China soup bowls and all of that. He thinks it's just putting on your foreignness and playing a part. Instead, he makes food for institutions that need meals—like hospitals, schools, airplanes, banquet facilities. He is a very good businessman. He appreciates America very much for being the sort of place where a man like him can succeed. But he has no use for the things I like about America. He said that I should have known the game shows would never take a woman who has my face or my voice.

But in a way I proved him wrong. The proof was that he and I were going up in the elevator at the five-star Fiesta Vallarta Hotel in beautiful Puerto Vallarta, where we would spend an exciting four days and three nights. The crowd at "Let's Make a Deal" knew the value of this. They let out a long sigh of envy. I know they'd been asked to make this sound, just like the winners had been asked to jump up and down. And it's true that I'd seen shows when the crowds made long sighs over an electric coffee maker or a lava lamp and they didn't even laugh at themselves afterward. They were playing this wonderful game in this wonderful world where these things can make people happy. When your coffee drips through a filter in the morning and it tastes so good, you sigh. Or you turn off the lights, all but your lava lamp, and these wondrous shapes rise beside your bed and you turn to your husband and say, Look how beautiful. And you say, I won that. We got that for free. Well, the trip was really worth a sigh, and I won that.

So my husband and I went up to the tenth floor and we entered our room and the glass doors in the far wall were open and the filmy white curtains were fluttering and we stepped through them, out onto the balcony, and there was a wonderful view, the sharp ocean horizon, Banderas Bay a jade green out far, and to the left was the curve of the shore, the hotels all nestled there and also the distant city with its red-tiled roofs and palms and the mountains rising behind, thick with trees. It was very nice. I had seen but I did not look at the band of brown water, maybe seventy-five meters wide, stretching along the beach. I supposed it was the tide-drifted water from the mountain river I'd seen coming in, water full of mud and leaves from the jungle. Sort of romantic, if you think about it, jungle water hugging our shore. But of course my husband's eyes went straight for this stain on the bay and he didn't see any romance in it. He just shook his head.

"Look," I said and I pointed to half a dozen pelicans flying past at our tenth-floor level, very close, their necks curled back and their wonderful flappy lower jaws somehow tucked in. We could see their eyes and I said, "Look, Vinh," and they wheeled around for me and passed by again.

We live in Louisiana, in New Orleans. Pelicans are the state bird, but we never see pelicans in Louisiana. Here were six of them almost at arm's length. But Vinh only nodded and he leaned on the rail of the balcony, his arms stiff, and I wanted to put my hand on his shoulder. I see many things, and I knew that somewhere inside, part of him was unhappy that the businessman could not stop running his mind. How do I know this? Because this sigh he made was not just in exasperation that these businessmen had not done better in Puerto Vallarta. A neater airport, better roads, a nicer corridor of elegance to get us to the hotels, a beach with perfect white sand and green water. What were those things to my husband that they should make him sigh? Even though I knew that these were the thoughts on the surface of his mind. He even said, as his elbows stayed locked, "They should do better with this place."

I nearly reminded him that this was free. But I did not want to give him more reason to diminish what I had done. I said nothing, and I almost raised my hand to put it on his shoulder, but my husband is old-fashioned, really. He would rather touch me first. So I simply nodded at his words. They were true. And we both looked down at the pool, shimmering with sunlight, and the sun was hot on our faces and we were soon floating there on red, white and green Fiesta Vallarta inner tubes, and all about the pool were hibiscus with their yellow flowers and elephant-ear plants and philodendron and bougainvillea and my husband paddled near to me and said, "The pool is very good. They take care of it very good. The water is clean and not too much chlorine." He paddled away and I felt like he had just embraced me. He is a good man. He was telling me that I had done all right, that he was going to try to enjoy this vacation, even that he was a little bit sorry he had been brooding so far. This is his way. It is a good thing that he is married to an observant woman.

I looked around the pool and three other couples caught my eye. All of them were American. I could see that from their faces and the way they held themselves, loose but every once in a while like somebody told them to stand up straight. And more than that. Somehow I knew that they were all game-show winners. They didn't know this about one another yet, but I did. And it didn't surprise me, really. For a long time, an exciting four days and three nights at the five-star Fiesta Vallarta Hotel in beautiful Puerto Vallarta was a prize on just about all of the game shows. I had already imagined a hotel constantly full of game-show winners, and so when I saw these three couples around the pool, I knew at once what they were. Not to mention the fact that each couple had at least one person, usually the wife, with a very animated face, and one woman who actually jiggled up and down in excitement when her husband unexpectedly brought her a drink from the pool bar.

They didn't yet know about one another what I already knew about them. They were scattered about and I floated near them in turn and I played a little game for myself, trying to figure out which type of show each had been on. One woman was wearing a black two-piece suit and she still had on jewelry, a pair of hammered silver and turquoise earrings and a heavy matching necklace, and even the bra of her suit was held together by a metal brooch. She was maybe fifty and hoping to look in her thirties and her hair was bleached a blond so shiny and light that in the glint of the sun it seemed almost the color of her hammered silver. She seemed easy for me to place on one of the puzzle-solving shows, not just because she was working a crossword puzzle in a tightly folded newspaper but because of the smugness of her smile as she did it and the fact that she was doing it in ink.

The next was a young couple, and this was the woman who jiggled up and down about the drink and she flashed blinding smiles all over the pool. But when she lay back on her lounge chair and I floated past the wrinkled bottoms of her feet, I knew they'd logged many hundreds of miles in shopping malls and I figured she was from one of the price-guessing shows.

I paddled around to the other side of the pool, which was quite big, and I passed an American man playing with great patience with a little Mexican girl wearing water wings. The child's father was standing a few meters away in the water and the little girl would swim from her father to the American and back again with great glee. The American was very loud and very gentle in his encouraging the girl and the father was pleased but a little nervous, as well. The American was bald with a big laugh and a big blond mustache and he was wearing dog tags. His hair was too shaggy for a current military man and he was perhaps in his early forties, and I knew from his age and the dog tags that he was a Vietnam veteran, one of those who was either unable or reluctant to forget where he had been. But it was his wife who I realized was the game-show woman. She was sitting on her lounge chair and she was reading a book and I know she was the veteran's wife because of the looks she gave him now and then as he grew particularly loud. His voice bellowed, "Swim, little darling, swim over there to your daddy now," and the wife lowered her book and her head angled slightly to the side and there was something around her eyes and her mouth that was very hard to read. Like she loved this man and was distressed by him in such equal parts that there was only something very small and placid that she could ever show about him. Or maybe even feel.

I looked toward Vinh and he was still floating on his inner tube, though his stomach was not visible, like he was slowly sinking through the hole. I wondered if this was comfortable for him, if I should go over and try to help him adjust himself on the tube. If I just let him float and slowly sink, he might finally decide to slip into the water and feel refreshed and then comfortably readjust himself and he would like this place even more. But he might sink farther until he felt stuck and it would irritate him and make his business mind reawaken and criticize these people for offering inner tubes instead of inflatable mattresses and this would be the final little irritation that prevented him from having a moment's real enjoyment for the rest of the trip. It could go either way. So I watched his tube slowly turning and he was very still and I looked back to the wife with the book and I decided she'd appeared on a question-answering show.

As it turned out, however, I was wrong about two of the three. The one with the jewelry turned out to be from the pricing game and the young one who jiggled was a puzzle expert. I know this because after a while the three women, each in her own time, ended up in the hot tub at the side of the pool. As each arrived, there were little hello-to-a-stranger nods and I didn't want to miss any of their talk, so I pulled myself from the pool and plucked the bodice of my one-piece up into place——I am happy to be very slim but I am small-chested—and I approached the hot tub. A beautiful dark-skinned Mexican woman was ahead of me going up the steps of the hot tub. She was wearing a skimpy two-piece suit and was in the process of making it skimpier, twirling and tucking the cloth of the panties of it into the separation of her own very lovely bottom so that it was now like a string bikini, and the eyes of the three American women rose and then whirled like the steam from the water. The Mexican settled into the water and the three others moved just a little bit closer to one another in the shared put-down they'd felt from the flamboyant sexiness of this woman.

They hardly gave me a glance as I eased into the hot water in the space between them and the Mexican, who had thrown her head back and closed her eyes as if the most handsome lover in the world had asked her if he could kiss her throat. The Americans could hardly say what they had on their minds, for fear that this woman spoke English, but at least her presence broke the ice between them.

The bouncy one that I had pegged as a shopper spoke first. She looked at the other two and said, "Well, y'all look like you're from the same side of the border as this little old girl."

I looked at the Mexican woman and she did not move; she kept receiving the kisses of Valentino's ghost or whoever and I myself felt downright invisible. This wasn't a bad feeling, but I did glance out into the pool, and at moments like these a sense of Vinh's no-nonsense business eye was something of a comfort to me. He could always see through anything, it seemed to me, and I could imagine myself stand-ing beside him on a hill above it all.

This all happened in a brief moment and when I looked back to the others, they were chuckling at the remark, though the woman with the veteran for a husband was covering up the laugh with her hand, like she was a little guilty about it. The woman wearing the jewelry said, "You don't sound like you're too far over the border. Texas?"

"Louisiana," the bouncy one said, and I sank lower into the hot tub, some sort of reflex. Then she said, "Not New Orleans either. I'm from up north, where the real Southerners are."

The one with the jewelry said, "So you don't do Mardi Gras?"

"No way, honey. That's for the people with no shame whatsoever." And her eyes moved to the Mexican woman and the eyes of the other two followed, though the woman from the question-answering show was the last one over and the first one to look away again. When she did, she saw me and it seemed to be with a little shock, like she hadn't noticed me before. Maybe she hadn't. Or since I was submerged now to my chin, maybe it looked like I was just this disembodied head floating on the surface of the hot tub. I smiled at her like she was the red light on the camera.

"I bet you're from California," Northern Louisiana said to the woman with the jewelry.

"Minnesota," said the other. "Not Minneapolis either. I'm from up north, where the real Northerners are."

Everybody laughed and I wanted to sink a little deeper, but I'd run out of submergible parts. I thought about getting out of the tub, but I still wanted to hear them discover the game-show connection, and fortunately that happened very quickly. Northern Louisiana asked Minnesota what it was that brought her to Mexico, no doubt eager to let these women know that she was a winner on a show. But Minnesota got the first chance. She declared that she'd won on "The Price Is Right" and Northern Louisiana jiggled up and down in excitement and proclaimed her own triumph on "Wheel of Fortune."

I pouted briefly at getting these two wrong, and the third woman finally spoke and said she'd won on "Tic, Tac, Dough" and then I nearly drowned in the hot tub because they all three began to jump up and down in the excitement of this revelation and the waves of hot water rushed over my face, splashing up my nose and into my mouth and eyes.

I was happy that no one noticed. I rose up and gasped quietly to myself while the others talked all at once. The Mexican woman was looking at me, but I nodded to her that I was all right, and after a slow, contemptuous look at the three Americans, she closed her eyes and put her head back once more, though this time she turned slightly to one side as if to ask her lover to kiss a new spot, just under her ear. I was ready to get out of the tub, away from all the excitement, but I lingered for a time watching this woman, so comfortable in her body, so relaxed with matters that touched on sex.

A little later Vinh and I were walking along the beach. It was the Mexican woman who stayed in my mind, not the game-show winners. I knew I was seeing them too flatly. They were complicated human beings, like all of us, in spite of how hard they worked at making their surfaces simple. But they bored me right now. I thought about the Mexican woman and I wished I could take Vinh's hand. Perhaps this was foolish of me, to have this hesitation. I am a smart woman, a modern woman. Vinh has never said a word to me that would discourage me from doing something like taking his hand as we walked on the beach. But there are forces in me that are very strong. Just as strong as the forces that make the two women from Northern Louisiana and Minnesota speak and dress and act the way they do. They have no control of those things. I doubt if they could change any of those things even if they were conscious of them and wanted to. I spent the first twenty years of my life living in a country and a culture that expected certain attitudes from women and men and you can't just put all that aside because your mind says, Why not? Nobody's mind is that strong. You have to wait. Things have to change from the inside.

Like Vinh. He walked beside me on the beach and the waves rustled near us, running up now and then and licking our feet, and there was bright sun and a blue sky overhead while across the bay, the mountains had disappeared into a dark gray sky and there were leaps of lightning over there and the contrast between this sunny beach and that storm-dark mountain was very romantic. But Vinh could not see these things. He was brooding again, thinking about Delta Airlines or the Superdome or the Hilton hotels, thinking about five hundred chicken dinners or a thousand Swedish meatballs. A man strapped into a harness beneath a parachute was rising from the beach just ahead of us, a cable running out to a speedboat in the bay going taut and dragging him into the air, and I stopped to watch it rise and Vinh realized what I did and he, too, stopped, following my eyes into the air but not really seeing anything, because he said, "Can you remind me to call Nicholson when we get back? They've got some big engineering conference coming in."

"Okay," I said, still watching the man on the parachute getting smaller and smaller in the blue sky, and I thought that this was something I might like to do. To get up there above all of this and just float around.

"You'll remember?" Vinh asked because I had answered without looking at him. It wasn't in irritation that he said this. It was just that I was important to him in this way. He depended on me. I have a very good memory.

I lowered my eyes and he was looking at me with a face that seemed eager, almost like a child. Sometimes he seemed to really enjoy the work he did. I was glad for that. I said, "I'll remember. You know I'm like an elephant."

My Vinh smiled at this. I have said this same thing to him many times and it always makes him smile. And that always makes me smile, that this should amuse him so. I smiled and then a young Mexican girl appeared at Vinh's side and she had lizards on both shoulders and on the top of her head, large lizards.

"You take picture of you and iguana?" she asked. "Very cheap."

Vinh looked at her and stepped back, startled, I think, at these large green creatures crouching on the girl. "No, gracias," he said.

"Like in the movies," the girl said.

"Where's your camera?" Vinh said, and the girl shrugged and looked toward me. I was carrying a bag large enough, I suppose, to hold a camera. Vinh said to her, "You should have a camera. If you want to make money, you get a camera and shoot the picture yourself. Comprende?"

I don't think the girl comprended. But even if she did, making an investment in a camera to improve her business probably was worthless advice. I said to Vinh, "She never has that much money at one time, to be able to buy a camera."

Vinh nodded and sighed. "She'll never get anywhere."

By now I'm sure the girl thought we were both a little cracked, so she drifted away. I came to Vinh's side and we walked on. "Iguanas," he muttered.

I said, "Do you know why iguanas?"

He shook his head no.

I said, "Because Puerto Vallarta is a very romantic place, and it has to do with iguanas."

Sometimes I will surprise my husband with a piece of information, and though it usually has something to do with the parts of American culture he has little patience for, his natural curiosity gets the better of him. This was one of those times. He looked at me sideways, not exactly turning his head to me; he was trying to say that he wasn't really interested in this but I'd better tell anyway. In these situations I don't say anything immediately. I choose to ignore this look of his. I make him ask for it. The culture I grew up in does give a woman certain subtle ways of maintaining her dignity.

"There's a reason?" he finally asked.

"A reason?" I said, as if I'd already forgotten about it.

"Yes," he said firmly. "A reason for the iguanas on the beach."

"Oh, yes," I said, and I waited.

Vinh stopped walking abruptly. I took a few more steps, as if I didn't notice. "Gabrielle," he called after me, and I stopped and turned and looked surprised not to find him beside me. I returned at once, being the good wife that I am. When I got to him, he settled himself so as not to seem too eager to hear whatever this was that I knew. He even used the casual form of my name, though he said it with the French pronunciation and I don't think he has ever learned that in English he could have a little joke on me with it. "Gaby, why is it that they think tourists want to have their pictures taken with iguanas?"

"It's nothing really. It's just a foolish thing."

"Gabrielle," he said in the voice I was waiting for. My husband is very attractive at this sort of moment. Someone else might get angry or imperious or dismissive or whiney. But Vinh turns gently urgent, like he is a child with a little pain that his momma has to make better. "Please tell me," he said.

So I told him about Liz and Dick. Elizabeth Taylor in "National Velvet" is a wonderfully beautiful girl. Even later, in "Cleopatra," she is very beautiful. You might think that a Vietnamese would not appreciate that kind of full-bosomed beauty. But people often admire qualities that are quite different from their own. And Richard Burton of that same time is equally attractive, say in "Look Back in Anger" or "The Bramble Bush." His voice, particularly, can thrill a woman. He, too, was in "Cleopatra" and that, of course, is when the story I told Vinh really began. Liz and Dick—Cleopatra and Antony—fell in love, and since they were both married to other people and that was in 1962, there was a big uproar. Then the next year Richard Burton came to Puerto Vallarta to make a film. (I didn't tell Vinh the name of the film at this point so that I could hold back the big answer to his question and keep his attention. He was still wondering about the iguanas.) Elizabeth Taylor followed him to this place and they rented two houses with a bridge between them, over a cobbled street, and the world was watching that bridge very closely for months. By now Vinh was getting a little impatient, I knew. Just impatient enough—I always could sense when I was about to lose his attention. So I told him that the name of the movie was "The Night of the Iguana" and there were Puerto Vallarta iguanas featured in it and that's why the little girl had her business.

Vinh was disappointed at the payoff of this story. I knew he would be. He almost always was. His brow wrinkled up and he pursed his lips and I wasn't upset at his reaction. I liked it very much that he continued to insist that I finish these little stories even though his deeply practical self almost always ended up finding them trivial or foolish or simply incomprehensible. He still always asked me to go on. He insisted. And I don't exactly understand it, but I took it as a kind of faithfulness to me.

"Iguanas," he muttered and I heard the word again late that afternoon, across the lobby lounge in the Fiesta Vallarta Hotel. Vinh and I had a handful of drink coupons, an unexpected extra benefit from curtain number two, and we'd come down to the lounge in the open-air end of the lobby facing the sea. The three American game-show couples were already there, and I could feel Vinh tense up because they were loud and they were having a frivolous good time and I knew that what pleasure Vinh hoped might be squeezed out of this trip had to do with being quiet and peaceful.

Northern Louisiana and her husband were at the bar and they

were both facing into the lounge, their elbows thrown back behind them onto the counter. The husband was young and so blond his hair and mustache seemed almost white, made even more pale by the deep tan of his skin. I was thinking his work kept him out in the Louisiana sun, but Minnesota and her husband were sitting in overstuffed chairs at a little table nearby and he was at least thirty years older than Mr. Northern Louisiana and his hair, though thinned out quite a bit, was just about the same bleached white color and his skin, though more leathery, was just as tan. I couldn't see him sweating under a Minnesota sun, so I figured maybe they both went to the same franchise of tanning salons that turned all their clients out like this.

The Tic-Tac-Dough woman was at an adjoining table and she was smiling and speaking to the others and it was from her that I heard the word "iguana." She was probably telling them the same story I'd told Vinh, since her specialty (I'd been right about her) was question answering and this was a set of those countless facts that clung to her mind. I have a similar static-cling mind, and as I watched her, her husband crossed my sight carrying two drinks from the bar. He handed one down to her and turned to sit and his T-shirt had a map of Vietnam and the words I'VE BEEN AND I'M PROUD. This didn't surprise me because I'd felt certain I'd read the sign of the dog tags correctly. The veteran sank into the overstuffed chair, and as he was trying to arrange himself, he glanced our way. Vinh was tugging at my elbow. He wanted to leave, I'm sure, but I kept my attention on the veteran, whose eyes widened slightly at us and then slid away as Minnesota laughed loud and said to his wife, "Eileen, honey, nobody today would even give them a second thought. What's a little adultery anymore?"

Vinh had my elbow in a strong grip now, but I leaned near to him and said, "We've got free drinks coming and I need one right now."

Vinh whispered, "I'd rather pay in a quieter place."

I answered, "There is no such place." This was a little gamble. I didn't want to turn him more strongly against the vacation, but I did want to sit and watch these people. It was like television, like the games and the soaps were mixed together.

Vinh sighed and nodded to me that it was all right, that as long as he was stuck in this whole thing, he really couldn't do anything but go along with me. So I took him to a table not next to the three couples but not far from them either. Vinh turned his chair at a right angle to all the other people and he faced the line of bougainvillea at the end of the lounge and the sea beyond. I listened carefully for a while.

Minnesota went on about how acceptable adultery had become and I watched her husband and he seemed to be trying to figure something out about the ice in his drink and I suppose he was used to this kind of talk and she finally grabbed his arm and said that present company was of course excluded. And then Northern Louisiana told a story about how one of the game shows she'd tried out for turned her down because she wouldn't let the host kiss her on the lips and this had come out in a discussion with the director of the show, who was prepping the contestants, and he said that the host always kissed the women contestants on the lips. Not her, she'd told him, and that's for damn sure, honey, they didn't do that where she came from. And then the question-and-answer woman, whose name apparently was Eileen, said that she wished she'd gotten on "Jeopardy"; that was the show she really wanted to get on, and it didn't have anything to do with not wanting to kiss somebody. If something like that had prevented her, it wouldn't have been so disappointing.

And somewhere along the way, as I was sipping the drink that the waiter brought and feeling invisible, I realized that the veteran was glancing now and then in my direction. I wondered if he'd learned enough about us over there to recognize a Vietnamese when he saw one. I knew he was thinking about it, wondering if Vinh and I were from Vietnam. And after a time I began to worry just a little bit what his attitude might be. The very visible veterans I'd encountered were unpredictable. They seemed to be one extreme or the other about us. We were fascinating and long-suffering and unreal or we were sly and dangerous and unreal. I kept my own eyes on his wife, who was certainly pitched to a lower key than the other two women and whose sense of disappointment about the show she had appeared on intrigued me. I would have expected her to feel only proud of winning at whatever she did. Though maybe this expectation is my own little prejudice showing through. Why shouldn't this American woman have the same sort of disappointment of dignity that I myself felt? She interested me. She felt disappointed and she hadn't even had to dress up as a duck.

To overcome a slight lull in the conversation, Northern Louisiana declared how wonderful a coincidence it was that they should all meet, all Americans and all game-show winners. At this, the veteran turned to me and said, "Are you from America, too?"

This took me by surprise. When I first saw the movie "The Invisible Man" with Claude Rains, it got me to thinking about what it would be like to be invisible. And the scary part was always getting yourself into a place where you shouldn't be and then suddenly becoming visible again. Well, that's how I felt at that moment. The man had a loud voice and the attention of all these people suddenly swung around to me. And to Vinh, as well. Before I answered, I looked at him, to see if he wished to speak for us. He glanced over to the veteran, but his gaze returned to the sea and I faced the group and I tried very hard to make my pronunciation just right and I said, "Yes, we're from America. I won this trip on 'Let's Make a Deal.' "

Everyone laughed very loud and I was certain that it was friendly laughter, all of it, laughter at this sudden extension of the coincidence, no laughter at me, no one imagining me dressed up like a duck, no one thinking how absurd for this Asian woman to be a game-show winner. Minnesota cried over the laughter, "Four winners. What a hoot."

The Vietnam vet seemed particularly pleased. I could tell, though, that there was still a question in his mind about our home country, but his hunch about us was getting stronger. All of this was in his face, the way he finished laughing before the others and began to squint at us with a little smile. At least I could read him enough to know he wasn't a Vietnamese-as-the-enemy type of veteran. I looked at the faces of the others as the laughter faded and they were all friendly, and I mean no disrespect or arrogance when I say this, but I felt a little bit proud of them, like they were children who behaved really well when you didn't expect it.

The veteran said, "May I ask where you're from?"

I understood what he meant, but I chose not to show it all at once. "New Orleans," I said. Perhaps not to betray my little game with the veteran, I did not look at him directly when I answered. I glanced across all the other faces and the young woman from Northern Louisiana could not hide a little jolt of distaste over this. Even that pleased me somehow. These were human beings and they had to have their own narrowness, their own prejudices. This woman showed it to me not because I was an Asian claiming game-show equality with her but because I was from New Orleans.

"I mean originally," the veteran said, and he added, "You don't mind me asking?"

I was turning back to the man and ready to smile at him and say I didn't mind at all and let him wait a few more moments before I confirmed his hunch, but before I could say a word, I was surprised to hear Vinh's voice, not hostile or angry but still very firm, say, "We are from the Republic of Vietnam originally. Now we are American citizens and so are our children and so will be our children's children."

For him to take over and answer the question would not surprise me. But the elaboration of it, talking about our children and our children's children (though in Vietnamese culture the unborn and even the unconceived children are already thought to be part of the family), this is what surprised me. He was looking directly at the veteran and the veteran was looking directly at him, and maybe Vinh thought he was drawing a line, like the man does, the male animals do, here's the line of my territory—look at it and don't get too close. But maybe not. Because when the veteran suddenly smiled broadly and jumped up and strode the few steps over to us and bent and insisted on a handshake from my husband, Vinh gave his hand without hesitation and he was very intently looking into the face of this American, as if he was a man who needed a thousand baked chicken dinners and hadn't decided who to buy them from.

The veteran said, "I'm Frank Davies and this is my wife, Eileen." He checked back over his shoulder and his wife was looking a little confused, not knowing whether to continue to talk with the other Americans or to come over to us, as her husband was motioning for her to do. Then the pinch of confusion was gone and the face I saw at the pool returned, the placid face exactly in between exasperation and affection. "Come on, honey," Frank Davies said, and the couple at the bar turned to get the bartender's attention and the woman from Minnesota said something to her husband and Eileen Davies rose and came over and shook our hands and she and her husband sat down with us.

I saw no discomfort on Vinh's face at all of this. I could tell if he was really wishing to make a quick escape, and he wasn't. This interested me greatly. He turned slightly toward these two people but not all the way. He was still angled more toward the balcony and the bougainvillea and the sea than he was toward the veteran and his wife, but he clearly accepted their being with us. He did not look away from them, and there was not a single little glance to me as if to say, Look what you've led me into now. He was apparently content.

Frank Davies said, "I was in Vietnam, as you can see," and he thumped himself on his chest. Vinh and I both dutifully read his T-shirt once more.

Eileen's hand came out now and fell lightly on her husband's as it returned from his chest and landed on the arm of the chair. The gesture seemed to be a reminder not to say certain things that he had said many times before. When he felt her hand, Frank looked at his wife and he began, "My wife . . ." But he paused, again measuring his words. I expected him to tell us that his wife didn't like him talking too much about all of that, but apparently even this was something he'd agreed not to say, for he finished the sentence: ". . . she's the winner in the family."

This was a reference to her game-show victory, but when Frank heard himself say this, you could see his face flinch as he unexpectedly interpreted his own words in another way. He could not resist: "I wish I'd been part of a winner for you folks."

Eileen smiled faintly and I looked at Vinh and he thought for a moment and then he squared around in his chair, leaving the sea. "What are you drinking?" he asked.

"Coca-Cola," Frank proclaimed. "I've given up the hard stuff."

"And you?" Vinh smiled over to Eileen, and she looked at me before she answered. Her eyes searched my face for a moment and it seemed like she was trying to see if it was okay with me for her to answer him, if there was some sort of hidden protocol from our culture that she needed to observe in requesting a drink from my husband.

I felt so sure that this was what was going on that I was about to remind her that we were from New Orleans, but before I could speak, she looked back to Vinh and said, "White wine."

Vinh called over the waiter and ordered the drinks and Frank caught the waiter by the sleeve before he went to get them and said, "Coca-Cola from a bottle. Not a can, por favor."

The waiter nodded at him as if he understood this request and Vinh said, "You've given up cans, too?" When Vinh was in his sharpest business mood, he could probe people like this, and it was not always with a friendly intent. But Frank laughed loud and he said that he sure as hell was. Vinh smiled and nodded, and this may be surprising, but I was having trouble now reading his mood. I make so many presumptions about people from the things I observe, and I'm usually right. But I've been around Vinh long enough to observe when he has made his feelings invisible to me, and this was one of those times.

So the drinks came and we talked, Vinh and me and this proud-to-be Vietnam veteran and his wife, Eileen. We asked where Frank had served and it turned out that he'd been a helicopter mechanic in Qui Nhon. He told us a story about how he'd had trouble with a "butter bar" because Frank was going up on his own time as a door gunner and he was supposed to be just a mechanic. When I got a chance, I asked what a butter bar was and he said a second looey and that was not much help. It had to be some kind of Army man, perhaps a rank. But as his words flowed on, I was sitting there thinking about Frank Davies going into the place where the Army men eat their meals and there was an incident at one of the tables, Frank was arguing with a bar of butter and they came to blows and Frank squeezed the bar and it was oozing through his fingers and all the men were sighing like a game-show audience, but Frank was in big trouble.

Then Eileen was at my elbow. She'd moved her chair closer to mine and she leaned near and she said in a low voice, "The men do go on about the war, don't they?"

This snapped me out of my little fantasy and I looked over to Frank and he had turned his attentions strictly on my husband, and Vinh was listening to him, leaning slightly forward and listening as if with great interest. He spoke to Frank and I didn't catch the words, but Frank nodded vigorously and said more and I turned to Eileen and replied, "My husband doesn't often talk about all of that."

"Was he a soldier?" Eileen asked.

"Yes," I said, "a very good one. He was a major in the airborne. But later, about a year before the end of the war, he was reassigned to Saigon City Hall, where he worked in a special program to develop business in the city. They were trying until the very end to make the economy work, to make people want to defend their way of life. Everyone respected my husband."

Eileen looked over to her husband and pursed her lips. "Frank was a good soldier, too. He wanted to do so much. He really felt like he was responsible for everyone."

I looked at Frank and his hands were before him, gesturing, shaping some point. He was talking about helicopter engines. I said, "He has so much energy."

Eileen sighed softly, in both appreciation and exasperation, it seemed. "I just wish I could get him to focus it where it's needed."

I wondered where that might be, but I did not ask. Perhaps I should have. Perhaps Eileen had something she needed to talk about and she was waiting for me to ask. But I did not. I have no trouble intruding on people's lives by reading the things that they show. But I have trouble asking my way in. So I sipped my own glass of white wine and Eileen and I watched the men talking for a while longer and then she leaned forward and touched her husband on the arm and said it was time to go.

Frank turned to her and looked at his watch and said she was right. He rose and shook our hands—his hand taking mine was large and hard but surprisingly gentle—and Eileen thanked each of us and said she hoped we could speak again soon and they moved off. I watched them carefully. Frank led the way with an air almost of determination, like weaving between these tables and overstuffed chairs took the skills of an experienced tracker. Eileen followed two paces behind. Passing by, Frank bumped one of the chairs and kept on moving and Eileen paused to straighten it.

When he was clear of the lounge area, Frank stopped and turned and waited for his wife, but when she drew near him, he was looking out over our heads, back out to the sea, and she spoke a word to turn him and they walked off. They were side by side now, but they did not hold hands, though American couples often do.

Vinh and I remained in the bar for only a brief time. In the elevator, we were alone, but as the doors were closing, a young couple got into the car with us. She had one of those hairdos that looked like she'd slept standing on her head, full of wild waves and wrinkles. The man had a very thick neck and they were both wearing bathrobes. But their hair was not wet and they did not smell of suntan lotion, so I knew they'd spent the day in bed. Newlyweds. And I knew at once that they, too, were from a game. When they entered, the wife's robe fell open at the top and showed a lot of bare cleavage, and the husband clamped it shut and looked at me and said, "She's like that." "So are you," she said, slapping at his hand. "My little show-off," he said and he tried to kiss her on the cheek. She turned her face in mock anger and then kissed him and I looked to the front of the car. "The Newlywed Game." Unquestionably.

And I thought about Frank and Eileen, leaving the lounge. How they had moved away with a space between them and he had not taken her hand and she did not take his, for whatever reason. As Vinh and I lay beside each other that night in the dark, well before Vinh's breathing was due to turn soft and regular with sleep, I said, "What do you think of them?"

From the few moments of silence that followed, I knew that he understood who I was talking about, even though he finally said, "Who's that?" If he really didn't know, then he would have asked that question immediately. Instead, he'd been trying to think what to say, or perhaps trying to understand for himself why he'd been as receptive as he had to the couple. So now he either knew the reason and didn't want to tell me or he was as puzzled as me; I didn't know which.

"Frank and Eileen Davies," I said.

"Oh, them," he said, and then there was silence again.

I waited for a while and decided not to let him off the hook. "Well?"

"What's that?" He forced a slur into his voice. But I knew he wasn't really sleeping.

"You seemed to be very friendly with Frank."

"Was I friendly exactly?"

"You ordered him a drink."

"I couldn't avoid that. There they were."

"When the two of you were speaking, you leaned forward for his words. You don't do that to just anyone."

Vinh thrashed about with his covers. "I hate it when you do that," he said.

Two could play his little game. I let a few moments pass and then said, "What's that?"

"You know what I'm talking about. When you start telling me what my little gestures and looks mean. *I* don't even know."

I could hear music from somewhere. Very faint. I couldn't control the sigh that billowed up from my chest. It was very clear, the sound of my sigh in the dark room, but I wasn't sure that Vinh had noticed. I wished that he had. I wished that he had my own little gifts so he could tell me why it was that I made that sound right then.

Then he said, softly enough that I could hear the music behind his words, "I'm not being critical."

I didn't answer. I turned my face toward the sliding doors. I'd left one of them open and the curtain moved a little in a breeze and the music was out there, out in the bay. There was a horn and there were guitars and a violin. "I don't know," Vinh said.

"You don't know what?" I asked, and I truly didn't.

"I don't know what it is about that man."

I found I didn't care, for the moment. I rose and moved to the windows and listened to the music. It was a looping kind of melody, a mariachi waltz. I brushed the curtain aside and stepped out onto the balcony and far out in the dark bay was a triangle of colored lights, red and blue, and it was moving slowly and I looked harder and could see the boat, its decks flashing faintly, color wheels whirling there, and I could imagine the couples waltzing, the sweat still on them from the fast songs, and now they were holding each other close and gliding across the deck, their skin flushed with colored light.

"What is it?" Vinh's voice came to me faintly, as if it was he who was far across the bay. I could even hear the rasp of the maracas now. And then the maracas faded, and then the strings, and the horn, and I watched until the boat disappeared down the shore. When I slipped back into bed, Vinh was asleep.

The next morning I left Vinh snoring faintly in the bed. It was pretty early. I wanted him to have at least the pleasure of sleeping late on this vacation that I'd given him, so I put on my bathing suit and eased the room door shut behind me and I went down to the pool. The lounge chairs were all upended and the Mexican boys with their white trousers rolled almost to their knees were mopping up, and one of them was skimming the surface of the water with a thin screen at the end of a pole. I stood there not wanting to go back upstairs. The morning sun felt very nice—a soft kiss on my forehead that wouldn't stop—and finally one of the boys saw me and he bowed and put one of the chairs on its legs and motioned me over. I thanked him and stretched out there and I looked back up the facade of the hotel and tried to figure out which was our balcony. But I caught myself at this. Did I hope to see Vinh's face looking down at me? This hope made me angry at myself for some reason. So I closed my eyes and thought of the cruise boat on the bay last night and the anger just sharpened. This surprised me and I wished I could step outside of myself and look back. Maybe I could see something that would give me a clue about what I was feeling. But all I could see was the fall of dim light-shapes in my closed eyes and then a woman said, "Can I sit beside you?"

I opened my eyes and found Eileen Davies. "Of course," I said and I got up and helped her put a lounge chair beside mine. I sat back down and watched her take off her robe and she had a one-piece suit on, a little frumpy, though her figure was pretty good in the way that Americans like their women. That was my first impression, but as she folded her robe very carefully and put it inside the large canvas bag at her feet, I could see that her bottom was probably a little too large and the pocks that the TV ads call "unsightly cellulite" were beginning to appear on the backs of her thighs. All of this was, no doubt, a development in the last few years. When her man was in Vietnam, I was sure that her figure had been very fine indeed.

She was beside me now and she smiled over at me and said, "We're the early ones."

"Yes," I said. "It's a habit I can't break."

"I like the mornings," she said. "You can feel sometimes that you're all alone in the world." After a moment Eileen seemed to hear how that sounded and her hand fluttered out toward me as if to grab back any inference I might have made. "Just for a little while," she said. "I wouldn't want to feel like that for more than maybe an hour or so."

"An hour's about right," I said.

"I love my husband." Eileen did not need to declare this to further explain the alone-in-the-world remark. I figured it must've come from the same place that made her give him that look I'd seen a couple of times.

For myself, I could have replied in a number of ways. I could have just stayed silent or I could have made some little nod or uh-huh or something. But instead I said, "I love my husband, too."

My saying this didn't seem to strike Eileen as odd, though it certainly struck me that way. She just nodded and laid her head back and pulled her sunglasses down from her forehead. I lay back, too, but if we were going to grow quiet and sleepy side by side here in the sun, I didn't want to leave off speaking on such a strange note. So I tried to make small talk. "Have you ever been down here before?"

"No. Have you?"

"No." This still wasn't enough and I tried to figure out how to say more about never being here.

But for some reason I'd lost control of all my social skills and the silence persisted and before I could think of some new track of small talk, Eileen said, "The Love Boat stopped here."

I should have known what she was talking about. As I said, I love American television. But at first I thought she was talking in a metaphor or something. "What's that?"

"The television show," she said. " 'The Love Boat.' It always stopped in Puerto Vallarta."

I laughed. "Of course it did."

"Do you believe in romance, Gabrielle?"

I turned my head and looked at her. I hadn't thought about the subject really, and yet I felt like I would say something. I actually wondered what would come out of my mouth, like I was sitting in a chair behind me and eavesdropping. This was getting a little strange. "Romance?" I said. "I'm not sure. Not in the easy ways, I don't. Not for anybody over the age of twenty."

"The easy ways." Eileen repeated this phrase thoughtfully and I turned it over in my mind, too. The Love Boat, for instance. And a lot of the other things I could easily get weepy over on television. Reach out and touch someone. I always choked up at the telephone company ads. Pick up the phone and two people could love each other no matter what might've happened between them. The easy ways. I knew it wasn't easy for Eileen and Frank.

"Never in the easy ways," she said and her voice was firm, like the thought was her own now.

But, of course, it was easy to say it was never easy. I kept my mouth shut about that, though. And Eileen said, "Puerto Vallarta is a very romantic place, you know."

"Yes?"

"They made a movie here."

" 'The Night of the Iguana,' " I said. "I know all about it."

"It wasn't easy for them."

"Liz and Dick?"

"Liz and Dick. It wasn't easy for them," Eileen said and she lifted her sunglasses and turned her head and looked me in the eyes.

"You're right," I said.

"The ruins of the movie set are still there. Near Mismaloya Beach." Eileen sat up straight. "Why don't we go down there."

"Just you and me?" I asked, not sure what I wanted to do about that.

Eileen lifted her eyebrows and pinched her mouth tightly shut. She didn't say anything right away. Finally she let her face relax and put her sunglasses back down. "We can try to take them."

"Is that what we want?"

She lay back down and thought this over and I was struck by how odd it was that we were treating the two men like they were somehow the same. This was something that I really didn't see at all. It was why I'd asked Vinh in the dark last night about his impressions of Frank. I'm not the kind of woman who thinks that men are men, all alike in certain basic ways.

Eileen said, "Sure, it's what we want, isn't it? They're our husbands. Wouldn't it be nice to go poke around that place with the men in our life?"

"Sure," I said, though I wasn't convinced. But we let it drop at that. Eileen said no more and we both just soaked up the Mexican sun for a while. A long while. I'd even fallen asleep, because I was suddenly startled by a great red and yellow bird passing before me. I blinked and it was gone and I was twisted on my side on the lounge chair; I'd moved into my natural sleeping position and I sat up and looked in the direction of the great bird and it was one of the parasailors, lifting higher and higher on his tether and veering out to sea. I looked at my watch and saw that nearly two hours had passed.

As if she read my thoughts, Eileen said, "You were sleeping pretty hard."

My head felt oversized, the contents not really fitting inside my skull, threatening to squeeze out my ears. I turned to look at Eileen. The back of her chair was angled up and she was sitting with a straw hat shading her face and she was holding a copy of "People" magazine before her. She said, "You missed an interesting sight."

"What was that?"

"Our two husbands apparently found each other in the lobby. They walked by about half an hour ago and waved at me and they went on down to the beach."

I rubbed at my temples and tried to take this in. Vietnamese people are funny in a few ways. Sometimes they can be very indirect. (Maybe that's the Chinese influence in our culture, though we'd rather think that such an influence does not exist.) But at other times, Vietnamese can be very blunt. This is true. Americans have their own contradictions. All peoples do. Sometimes indirect and sometimes blunt is maybe a little less disturbing to everyone concerned than sometimes tolerant and sometimes intolerant, though I'm not trying to be critical of my new country.

Anyway, my Vietnamese bluntness suddenly made me stop rubbing my temples and lean near to Eileen and say, "Tell me. Do you understand why our husbands seem to be hitting it off so well together? What does Frank say about Vinh?"

Eileen kind of jiggled her head like she was trying to unclog her ears. And her voice got pinched and even a little whiney. "My husband never had anything against Vietnamese people. He hated the Vietcong, of course, but he knew that there was a difference between them and the others."

"Of course," I said firmly, like I knew this all along. And maybe I did. That wasn't really what I was getting at, I decided, though I couldn't quite say what was.

"And how about your husband," Eileen said and her voice was brittle. "What does he say about Frank?"

I leaned closer and smiled my warmest smile. "Like your husband. He knows how to see the individual."

There was no reason for this bit of empty rhetoric to soothe Eileen's hurt feelings and make things right between us again, but that's just what it did. She and I had done a pretty lousy job of understanding any of this, but at least we were smiling at each other again and she said, "Do you want to find them now? Maybe we can get them in a cab and take them away to the movie set."

"Sure," I said and we gathered up our things and walked along the pool and past the hot tub—the rest of the game-show people had not made their appearance yet, much to my relief—and we went down some stone stairs and stepped onto the beach.

Immediately the vendors in white clothes and straw hats surrounded us. They were selling white clothes and straw hats, and somewhere jostled in the crowd I saw the girl with the iguana on her shoulder. Eileen and I no-graciased our way into the clear and we looked around. The men weren't in our immediate view and we both seemed to become distracted by the water at the same moment. Without a word to each other, we trudged through the sucking sands and down to the water's edge.

Down here beside it, the bay seemed enormous. I wondered if the music I'd heard last night would have been more powerful here, too; I wondered what if Vinh and I had been in this spot when the boat passed. Would he have done more than ask what it was? Would he have taken me in his arms and waltzed me over the sand? But that's a vision of romance the easy way, I thought; I should remember the soaps, where everything is hard. There's another contradiction, on the television that I watch. Can we believe both these things? The Love Boat docks and everyone finds what they're looking for; and the next day's installment of "As the World Turns" always brings more disaster.

"I see them," Eileen said.

She was right. The two men were walking along the shore far down to our left. They were walking side by side, heading away from us, and my husband had his hands clasped behind his back, a thing he does when he paces around during business meetings. He was wearing his tan Bermuda shorts and his one purchase for our trip, a rough-weave red cotton shirt from Pakistan. Frank Davies was dressed all in black—I didn't realize until I saw him that they made Bermuda shorts in black—and he was moving his arms, gesturing. We couldn't hear a word, but we saw his hands rise up above his shoulders and flare open and fall.

"I know that story," Eileen said with a sigh. "An ammunition dump has just exploded in Qui Nhon."

"I hope no one was hurt."

"My husband was quite a hero in the aftermath, is the way I understand it." Eileen turned to me. "Listen, Gabrielle, I'm sorry if I seemed upset a little earlier."

"Upset?"

"When you asked about how our husbands were getting on."

I wish I'd been blunt right then and pressed for the two of us to figure out the men in our lives a little better. But I can't imagine that we would have made any sense at that point. We certainly wouldn't have been able to anticipate what happened later on. But for whatever reason, I didn't push it. I just said, "That's okay, Eileen. No problem." And we made off down the beach in pursuit of our husbands.

We caught up with them when they turned around and continued their walking discussion back in our direction. Eileen called out Frank's name and both men looked up at us with a start. At just that moment some young Mexican men shouted at us and motioned us a little farther along the beach. We all followed the Mexicans' gaze high into the air and saw a parasail swinging off the bay and over the beach, and one of the young men blew a whistle and the man hanging beneath the sail reached up and grabbed the rope above and to the right of his head and he pulled. The sail began to veer to the right, angling toward the beach before us, and it was coming down fast. I heard Frank's voice say, "You were airborne, that right?" Vinh grunted in affirmation but I did not look at the two men. I kept my eyes on the parachute, the great red and yellow scoop, tight with air, carrying a man down from the sky. I could do that, I thought.

The whistle blew again and the man let go of the rope and he was coming down fast, and the young men on the ground rushed forward, reached upward, and the parasailor landed with a little run and his chute crumpled behind him.

"Hey, guys," Eileen was saying. "Guys."

I thought for a moment that she was talking to the Mexicans, that she wanted to go up into the air. But I looked and she had pulled the attention of our husbands to her and she said, "Gabrielle and I want to do something. All of us together."

"That's good," Frank said.

Vinh just looked at me with a faint rebuke in his eyes. He hated to be taken off guard like this. I should have talked to him privately first. I understand his feelings, I suppose. An airborne ranger is always prepared. A successful businessman, too. But I just blew his little grimace a kiss and he forced a chuckle to show his good nature. I didn't much care, to tell the truth. I couldn't keep my eyes from slipping back to the Mexicans and their parachute. I knew I would feel disappointed to see anyone get onto that chute right now. It was meant for me. I was just a few moments away from soaring high over the bay, over the whole city, far above all of this.

"Don't you agree, Gabrielle?" Eileen's voice dragged me back to her. She was looking at me meaningfully, like it was time for me to nail this thing down.

"Of course," I declared, not knowing exactly what she had said but sure from the way she was looking at me that this was the right response. She waited, wanting more, and I said to the men, "Let's go. I really want to."

Vinh said, "Is this the place you were telling me about? The iguana thing?"

"Sure," I said. "It'll be fun."

Now I could see Vinh turn up the heat in his eyes. Who were

Liz and Dick to him, after all? Only a product of what he had big trouble tolerating in America. I knew I was supposed to persuade him now. He was persuadable about these little interests of mine, but he always made me work for his approval. Well, I didn't feel like it at the moment. That was for certain. All I knew was that the great red and yellow parachute was lying slack on the beach and I wanted to excite it, wanted it to fill up full of this warm morning air and carry me into the sky.

So without a word I stepped past Frank and Eileen and Vinh, and I asked the young Mexican man holding the harness how much and he told me and I paid it and I turned around and the man put me in the harness, and all of this was so unexpected and it was done so quickly that nobody could react. Frank and Eileen and Vinh just stood there in a row and gawked at me and finally, just before I took off, Vinh choked out a "Gabrielle what are you doing?" and Eileen suddenly smiled and cried something that wasn't quite a word, like "hurrah" or something. And the Mexican was telling me about the whistle and about the rope up there over my right ear and the boat was moving and the tether went taut and there were hands on me briefly, helping me rise, and then there were no hands and I was soaring into the air.

I did not look back. The boat headed straight out into the bay for a time and I looked down at the water and it was calm, it looked as stiff as vinyl, like I'd bounce off it if I fell. But it was very fine being up here. I was very aware of being alone. Off to my right about a hundred meters was a little pack of pelicans heading back toward the beach. They were returning but I was still on the way out. The wind whistled faintly in my ears and it struck me that this was not the ravishing physical experience I'd expected it to be. My feet dangled down, but there was no heaviness in them, like the ride at the carnivals where you sit in a chair and they swing you around. My feet just dangled like I was a child in a tall chair. I was not frightened. The harness held me tight and I gripped the ropes and I looked down at the sea, the green wake of the boat ripping apart the great brown stain from the mountains.

And the boat turned now and headed along the coast and my parachute brought me around and I was as high as the highest hotel, but I pondered the long stretch of Puerto Vallarta along the beach as calmly as if it was a mural on a wall. I was flying but I was very quiet inside. This was more like a certain kind of dream, where you can fly and everything is peaceful. Or it was like I'd left my body, the way some people on the Donahue show had done when everyone thought they were dead. I was separated from my body.

And now I looked back over my shoulder and found the beach and the three tiny figures there, still standing in a row, still gawking, probably. So I turned around and let go of the rope and let my hands dangle like my feet and I felt the air flowing against my face and I drifted there, thinking, Yes, I just died and it's all very nice and I won't have to worry about anything on the planet Earth anymore.

And this feeling lasted for however long it was that I was in the air. It was probably no more than ten minutes, but it seemed much longer, which struck me as odd later, because I enjoyed the experience, I truly did, and usually that makes time go fast. But I floated along and the boat turned and headed back the opposite way and I swung around, too, in a long curve, very graceful, like a gesture I might make with my hand if I was a big movie star. And I was nearer to the shore on the return trip. I was only a little ways out over the sea and I could clearly see the hotel pools passing, the bodies all laid out in the sun.

Then I found myself moving nearer to the shore and nearer still, and I was over the beach. I looked ahead and saw the boat curving out to sea, but it must have slowed because I was starting to come down. That's when I heard the whistle. I looked ahead and I could see the beach where I'd taken off. It was not far away. The whistle blew again, insistent, and I felt a little knot cinch in my stomach. I had something to do now. The rope over my right shoulder. I reached up and grabbed it just as I was supposed to. I pulled it.

It didn't move. It was a heavy rope. Hard to pull. The knot inside me cinched tighter and I pulled as hard as I could. The rope gave a bit, but not nearly as much as it was supposed to. Pull it down by your ear, I remembered the man say. I pulled harder and it budged a bit further and my muscles clamped up in my fist and down my arm and under my arm and down my side all the way to my hip.

I was coming down, down, and I was curving a little, but I could see already I was in trouble. The curve wasn't sharp enough to bring me into the path to the waiting men and the three faces of Frank and Eileen and Vinh, which I could see very clearly for one moment. Their eyes were wide and their jaws were dropping and my arm and side were trembling now and shot full of flames and I didn't know if I could even hold the rope down at all for much longer. The Mexicans were running up the beach and I saw a line of coconut trees at the back of a hotel and I was heading straight for them, I was at about the fourth-floor level and falling fast, like an elevator out of control, the third floor and the trees were dipping like they were afraid of me but they couldn't run, and I fell past the second floor.

I lifted my other arm and grabbed the rope with both hands and I pulled as hard as I could and I closed my eyes and the rope gave some more and I felt myself veer away and a man's voice rushed from beneath me and it said, "Caramba!" and then my feet hit the sand hard and I flexed at the knees and came up standing but I was instantly moving forward again, dragged along the sand, and then there were hands on me, many hands, and I was upright again.

But I was laughing. My eyes were open and I was laughing, though I wished I was back in the sky, especially since everyone was rushing over to me like I'd just fainted or something. Eileen cried, "Are you all right?" as she approached and I looked and I saw Vinh running beside her. His face was sweet. His lower lip was pushed up like he was pouting, like he was a little boy and pouting at some very bad news. Then Frank came from around the other side of Eileen and he was running fast and was the first one to get to me.

"You're one gutsy lady," he said. "Airborne all the way." And he brushed the Mexican boy aside who was taking off my harness and Frank's big hands went flick, flick, and I was free. He took me by the arm and turned me toward Vinh, who finally arrived, puffing.

"I'm fine," I said firmly to them all. "Don't make a fuss."

Vinh pulled up before me and he said, low, "Are you sure you're okay?"

"Yes," I said in a voice as low as his but as sharp as I could make it.

He looked into my eyes and nodded and then he shook his head. "I suppose the only thing to do after an adventure on a parachute is to go to a movie set."

Eileen's face snapped toward Vinh and she said, "Great idea."

I wasn't sure what I thought of the way this all came about. Did he think I went up on a parachute to force his hand on this? Like I was a child threatening to do myself harm if I didn't get my way? It wasn't true, if that's what he thought. At that moment I would've traded the whole trip to Mismaloya for one more flight over the sea. But, of course, that wasn't possible.

Frank said, "Outstanding," and I figured I would at least get a chance to watch these two men together a little more closely.

So Eileen and I went back to our rooms and changed from our bathing suits, both of us reappearing in the hallway almost simultaneously and in record time, for we did not want the men to have a chance to change their minds. We met them in the lobby and we all stepped out the front doors of the hotel together to a chorus of "Hey, taxi" from half a dozen men in sandals and jeans. Vinh stepped a little in front of Frank and motioned for the first man in line and I drew near to the two men because they interested me very much.

"Dodgers," Frank snorted, and I'm sure Vinh did not know what he was talking about, but when the taxi rolled up in front of us and the driver sprung out, he was wearing a Los Angeles Dodgers baseball cap. I knew the cap from television. Many of the actors on television series wear baseball caps and this one was very popular, though I liked the bright red color and the tangle of letters on the cap of the St. Louis Cardinals the best.

The driver saw me looking at his cap, I think, and he did a surprising thing. He tipped it to me, and he opened the back door. He was a man about the same age as Vinh and me, perhaps forty— I could see it around his eyes and in the smudge of gray in his hair— but there was a bounce to him that was very young.

Vinh said, "Why don't you sit in the front, Frank."

"Hey there, Major, you outrank this soldier by quite a lot. You should take the favored place."

"I always rode in the backseat as a major," Vinh said, and there was just a little sharpness in it. But then he added, "Besides, you've got the longer legs by quite a lot."

Frank laughed and so did Vinh. Then Frank turned to us and said, "You watch out for that man back there."

I wanted to hear more of this. Was Frank kidding my husband over some stories they had shared about women? I looked at Vinh and his face was blank and then the taxi driver said, "You are American?" and the conversation moved on.

Vinh motioned first Eileen and then me into the backseat and he climbed in last. Frank was talking to the cab driver as he circled the car and I felt Vinh pressed against me in the crowded backseat. I never thought of my husband as being the kind of man you had to watch out for as a couple of women in the backseat of a car. I was sure it was just a typical male joke, a natural frame of reference for Army men. Vinh had never given me any reason to doubt him. I had always watched those parts of the soap operas about adultery with some detachment. He had always been with me whenever he wasn't working. He wasn't the kind of man to go out on his own. He was a very conservative man. His work was his mistress, I knew, and that was hard enough for me, I guess. But it was odd how my mind kept working at this silly joke Frank made. All the silence between Vinh and me, all the formality, all the waiting for him to take my hand: Would it be better for him if I was someone else? If he was with someone else? Elizabeth Taylor had had a husband and he was a singer. Richard Burton had had a wife, too, though she was less famous. I listened again to the voices bumping around in the taxi.

"Mismaloya Beach?" the driver said, turning his head alarmingly far around, a hundred degrees or more. He looked at Eileen, who I suppose had just told him where we were going. Then he looked at me and I was afraid he would force his head still further, a hundred and forty, a hundred and fifty, until he could see Vinh sitting to my left. But I guess I should have been more worried about the car than about the man's neck snapping. He was rolling down the long drive from the hotel and not watching at all. He said, "You know that you are going to a very special place?"

"We know," Vinh said firmly.

"You know about Liz and Dick?" the cabbie said.

"We know," Vinh said, and I could hear in his voice how little my husband wanted to sit through this story again.

"It all put this town on the map, you know. I was just a teenage delinquent hanging around the beaches all day and trying not to work hard like I do now. We loved it when all the world started looking at our Vallarta." By now, the man's eyes were back on his driving and he turned onto the main road we'd taken in from the airport.

In making the turn, he stopped speaking for a moment and Frank said, "Hell, it must have been nice to be a teenager just goofing around the beaches. Living in a place like this. When I was a teenager all I cared about was turning myself into a goddamn soldier some day. That's *another* kind of teenage dumb."

I was a little startled at how far Frank had to reach to pull the conversation around to his military experience. I wondered if he was doing this for Vinh's benefit, having picked up, too, on how my husband hated all the talk about Burton and Taylor. Vinh said, "When I was a teenager the beaches and the war were all in the same picture."

He said this like he'd topped Frank. He could get wound up about the war, I knew. I'd heard him with our Vietnamese friends. But was this the kind of thing he and Frank had been doing together? Is this what I'd missed? Just the two of them jerking the conversation around to top each other? Or was this a little instinctive game that would keep our cab driver quiet and us two women out of the conversation?

I didn't know. But our driver wasn't picking up on any hints. "The airline, they tried to start it. This was some sleepy godforsaken place when I was a little guy, you know. Then Mexicana Airlines started landing a DC-3 on a dirt strip where the center of town is today."

Frank turned himself half around in his seat. "You ever fly in a DC-3, Vinh?"

"Sure. They were using some DC-3's as troop transports when I was a recruit."

There was only the slightest of pauses after this, like Frank was just taking a little breath before he spoke an answer, but Eileen had wonderful reflexes—probably the key to her success on the buzzer of her game show—and before Frank could open his mouth, she said to the driver, "We know the basic Burton and Taylor story, but tell us something about it we might not know."

Frank rolled his shoulders and turned to the front and I felt Vinh shift a little bit away from me, and the driver said, "Have you seen the house they stayed in?"

"No," Eileen said. "Can we?"

"Sure," the driver said, and to their credit, the men did not protest. "It's in Gringo Gulch. That's where all the rich people came when they found out about us. Leonard Bernstein, you know that man with the orchestra?"

"Yes," Eileen said. "You know about him?"

"Sí, señora. I like good music. I lived in your country three years, in Los Angeles. That's how I speak English like you. I listened to the radio all the time and I liked the good music." The driver raised his hand like a conductor and sang, "Da da da dum," the opening to Beethoven's Fifth Symphony, the Daily Double Audio Clue only last week on "Jeopardy." "But don't worry," the driver added quickly. "I'm just a regular Joe. I liked the bad music, too, in Los Angeles."

"Who else lives in Gringo Gulch?" Eileen asked, afraid, I suspect, that if our driver strayed too far, the men would reclaim the conversation. Not that I would have minded that, really. I wanted to hear them connecting to each other, though it was even very interesting to me just observing this shared silence between them. They were both looking out windows and I'm sure each man was conscious of the other.

The driver said, "There was some lord and lady from England. The Queen even came in her yacht and visited them. And also living in Puerto Vallarta is a very important American I bet you don't know." The cabbie paused for a moment, like we were supposed to guess.

"I bet it ain't Westmoreland," Frank said.

"Any clue?" Eileen said.

The cabbie made an exaggerated nod. "I will tell you his name and it will still be hard for you. Milton Gunzburg."

Frank hooted at this. "The famous Milton Gunzburg is living in Puerto Vallarta? Hell, you remember him, don't you, Vinh? He's the guy who landed his chopper in the middle of Tu Do Street, got him about four bargirls, and took off again for Vung Tau and some Air Cav R and R."

Vinh grunted, Frank laughed, and the driver said, "That must be another Milton Gunzburg."

Eileen leaned forward. "Don't you pay any attention to him, señor," and she dug her knuckle into Frank's shoulder. He flicked at her hand but without any anger, just a casual little flick like a mosquito had buzzed him.

I started feeling disloyal to Eileen. I'd been happy just to sit back and watch all this, but she needed some help. So I asked the driver, "Who is this Milton Gunzburg of Puerto Vallarta?"

The driver turned his face way around to look at Eileen and me. "The inventor of 3-D movies."

I pointed to the street in front of the driver, just to remind him that this was all in 3-D, too. He took my hint and looked to the front just in time to curve around a slow-moving pickup truck full of collapsed and bundled cardboard boxes. He didn't even flinch. "This was a very important invention," he said. "My favorite movie is 'The House of Wax.' You know the movie?"

"Yes," I said, "but I've never seen it in 3-D."

"When I lived in L.A. I saw it there in a theater. Also 'Spacehunter: Adventures in the Forbidden Zone.' These are my favorites in 3-D.

I hope Peter Strauss someday will move to Puerto Vallarta. He starred in 'Spacehunter.' I would like to drive him wherever he wants to go. He is my favorite actor. Did you see him in 'Rich Man, Poor Man'? It was a wonderful thing from American television. Even without 3-D. But Peter Strauss is even better in 3-D."

Vinh's voice was suddenly in my ear, pitched low. "Do we have to go by the house? Isn't the movie set enough?"

I glanced at him and he was looking at me with his head a little bit dipped, like he had glasses on and was peeking over them. This was the position he assumed when he was asking something that he knew he shouldn't.

"It's okay," Eileen said, putting her hand on my arm. "Let's skip it."

I glowered at Vinh and he shrugged. "No, no," he said. "I'm sorry. It's just that we should have plenty of sunlight for the trip to the movie set."

"It's barely noon," I said, not letting him wriggle away.

"Noon," Frank said. "There's a place to eat at this beach, isn't there?"

"Good food at the beach," the driver said. "They sell whole fish roasted on a stick."

"Oh man," Frank said, like he'd just heard about a plane crash.

Eileen leaned forward and said to the driver, "You can skip the Burton-Taylor house."

"No, don't do that, driver," Vinh said.

"I'm Esteban," the driver said.

"You guys hate your C rations as much as we hated ours?" This was Frank broadcasting from another part of the world.

"You can call me Esteban."

"I don't mean to drag you around," Eileen said, leaning a little bit across me to address Vinh.

"It was rude of me to try to overrule your wishes." Vinh spoke with a combination of gentleness and firmness that I have always admired in him.

"It's very close now," Esteban said.

I wanted this for myself, too. I made my voice firm for the driver. "Fine. Drive us past."

"Of course we hated our C rations," Vinh said.

"It figures," Frank said.

"But not as much as we'd hate a fish on a stick," Vinh said, and I wished I had the privilege of digging my knuckle into his arm, even if it was to provoke only a casual flick in response.

Frank laughed. "Roger that."

I was sorry I was sitting in the center in the backseat. I wanted to just put my head out the window and watch the street go by like there was nobody else around. But as it was, I looked across Eileen and watched the shaggy fields and the men talked some more about Army food and we passed a low, whitewashed arena with big cutout signs on top, the silhouettes of bulls. A place for bullfights, I supposed. And then there were palm and coconut trees and then a run of shops and I just kept my mind out the window, as Esteban had finally let himself be shut up by the husbands.

Then we took a curve and there was a statue of a seahorse and we were running along the beach and we passed an artist on the street with his work propped up on display, and the paintings were of tigers and Jesus Christ and Elvis Presley on black velvet, and I hoped Vinh didn't see this, but it all made me smile. Am I somehow perverse this way? Not that I would buy a black-velvet Elvis Presley, much less hang it on a wall in my home. But there is something that makes me smile about it. I have seen Elvis Presley many times as they sell his face and his voice on late-night television—The King, The One and Only, The Idol of Millions, The Loved and the Mourned, just a phone call and a credit-card number away. Why does this make me feel comfortable? Even safe?

The car was on a cobbled street now and we were jiggling and rattling about and the men's voices were cracking and they stopped speaking. And soon we turned into a narrow lane and Esteban said, "Up ahead is where the lovers lived in 1963."

We bounced along and there was a stone wall on one side and an undetached run of houses on the right and Esteban said, "It is where you see the bridge over the street."

A stone pedestrian bridge rose from a roof covered in rosebushes and arched over the cobblestones and landed on the second floor of the house across the way. Esteban stopped the car. "Would you like to get out and take pictures?"

I felt Eileen turn my way, though it was probably Vinh that she looked at. "No," she said. "This is fine."

"There were really two houses," Esteban said. "The one on the left was Elizabeth Taylor's and the one on the right was Richard Burton's, and the whole world watched that bridge for months to see them go back and forth."

I'm sure that Eileen and I were quite a sight to further irritate our husbands—we both leaned forward and strained to look at the two houses. The bridge was tan and had a waist-high rail with a row of little pot-bellied balusters. I'd learned that word, "balusters," some-where—I don't remember where—and if it ever appears on a quiz show, I will probably be the only one to get it right. Why do I go off on this little detail now? Because my mind snagged on it even then, even though I obviously was very interested in the houses before me. And why was I distracted by that detail? Sometimes I can read myself pretty well. It was because the bridge between the two houses made me feel bad. It seemed so empty. It arched there against the blue sky and it cried out for some lover to come across and take his woman in his arms. But it was empty. The rosebushes, which were full of blooms, nodded faintly in a breeze and the bridge stayed empty.

"You like to buy this house?" Esteban said. "It is for sale. Richard Burton bought it for Liz Taylor as a birthday present many years ago and do you know how much he paid?"

"What year?" This was Vinh, whose sense of business was suddenly stimulated.

"I don't know. Maybe 1964. Sometime about then."

"Seventy-five thousand," Vinh said without a pause, and all I could see was that empty bridge. The man who'd crept over it at night so that the world would not notice, he was dead.

"Very close, señor. Sixty thousand dollars American."

Vinh leaned forward next to me and I sat back. He said, "And what are they asking for the house now?"

"One million."

"Ha!" Vinh declared, and I'm not sure what business conclusion this represented. But when Esteban said that the house had been for sale for nearly five years, and no one had bought it yet, Vinh nodded like he wasn't surprised.

It was now that a little voice chirped into the car. We all turned our heads and a young girl was at the back window, right next to Vinh, and she had a basket slung over her shoulder. She lifted a yellow flower that was really very beautiful, with large blossoms and a white center. "You buy?" she said. "Copa de oro."

Esteban turned around in his seat. " 'Copa de oro,' you know what that is?"

"A cup of gold," Eileen said.

"Right, señora. From the movie."

"Yes," Eileen said. "Richard Burton buys it for Sue Lyon at the beginning of 'The Night of the Iguana.' "

I was impressed. This was a detail that I myself had forgotten. I wanted to reach across Vinh and take the flower. I almost did. I had told my arm to rise and move through my husband's space and pluck this beautiful flower from the little girl's hand. I remembered the scene now. Burton, the defrocked and alcoholic priest who could not restrain his desire for the women who reminded him that he was alive, buys this flower, the cup of gold, for the sexy young girl on the bus tour that breaks down here in Puerto Vallarta. Even this ravaged and failed man knew that a woman would love a flower such as this, the copa de oro. I was prepared now to lift my arm, to take action, even as Esteban said, "Would you like to buy a flower?"

But Vinh and Frank in chorus said, "No," and Frank said, "We've got this movie set to get to," and there was nothing more to be done.

Esteban stuck his head out the window and said something to the girl—there was clearly some connection between them, at least a working arrangement for when he brought tourists to this spot. I'm sure Vinh noticed it and I figured he felt smug about it, so as the taxi began to move, I leaned near him and said, "I loved that flower."

I don't say something like this very often, so it must have had a sharp effect, because Vinh turned his face to me and he looked very sad for a moment. It was clearly sadness, to my eye. His mouth sagged and his eyes softened, and I wondered what he would do. But we were going faster now and I turned away to look at the bridge growing larger and then we passed beneath it, the shadow rushing over the car, and Vinh did not say, Wait, let's go back and get a flower. He did not even say, Oh, I'm sorry, Gabrielle; perhaps another time. He said nothing at all, though he may have continued to wear his sad face. I don't know. I didn't look at him.

The taxi was climbing in the hills now, the roads twisting and turning. At first beneath us were the stacked shacks of the poor people, with the baked red mission-tile roofs, and then we were among the villas, the immaculate high walls and the stippled stucco, and then we were rising even above the rich and I watched the ocean and it was very beautiful, very romantic, and I liked being near Vinh, even if he was hardened against all of this.

The roads were very bad, even here, and we had to slow almost to a stop for the big potholes, again and again, but all along the ride there were new hotels going up. We could not go more than half a mile without seeing another hotel with the men barebacked and languorous on the open floors, just the frames of the rooms constructed and the ocean visible through them, and the men were carrying a bucket or smoothing a wall with a trowel or just standing around, happy to be in the shade of a room with its walls open to the sea.

Finally I saw a landmark that the guidebooks had told me about, three huge rocks hunched into the water not far offshore, and one of them had a great arch through it, like a pair of hip boots standing out there with no man in them. Mismaloya was nearby. Then we passed a large hotel, a finished hotel, and we descended a little hill and the road that cut down to the beach ran along a concrete wall that contained the site of still another hotel under construction and the road was rutted and scruffy and instinctively I said to Vinh, "They're still building." It was an apology for the weeds and the ruts and the dog peeing against the wall, and then we stopped at the back edge of the beach.

"Here you are," Esteban said, and he sprang from the cab and circled the car, opening our doors, and even before we could step out, the vendors were swarming around and Esteban was talking to them, waving them away, but not too far. The vendors in white clothes were draped in rugs and silver jewelry and a man was motioning us to a stack of inner tubes for rent. A dog drifted by with skin sores and I concentrated on the beach, the waves coming up, but to our left was another little river running down the mountains, and the surf at this beach, too, was smeared with brown.

I looked around and thought that this had been a big mistake, that I would lose face, as the Chinese say, with Vinh. Of course he was right. This place was not ready for the kind of pleasures that even I had come to expect. Not that if it had all been perfectly beautiful—immaculate—Vinh would have thought any better of it. Then it would have been just like television, slick and irritating to him in a different way. And as I thought these things, a ruckus of men's voices started behind me. I turned and Vinh was holding his hand out as if to brush Frank away. In Vinh's other hand was his wallet and he said, "I'll handle this one."

Frank said, "I'm not a Spec-Five anymore, Major. I make good money."

"I'm sure you do," Vinh said. "But it was I who suggested coming down here."

"We can split it."

Meanwhile Esteban was smiling at them both and smiling at me and smiling at Eileen and in between he was shooting little glances at the vendors, holding them off until he could finally get his own money and leave.

"I'll tell you what," Vinh said. "I'll pay this time and you pay for the cab going back."

Frank flipped Vinh a sort of funny half-salute. "Roger that. You pay the man and I'll secure the beach." At this he turned, and while Vinh was making change, Frank took Eileen by the arm and they moved past me, Eileen hopping a few steps to take her shoes off as she walked.

Vinh joined me and he held my elbow to guide me through the uneven footing of the sands and Esteban called after us, "It's to your left. You must wade across the mouth of the river and then follow the seawall to the old dock."

Vinh turned his face to me. "Did you get that?"

"I'll find it," I said.

We all four of us stopped at the water's edge for a moment and the vendors were orbiting us. Frank and Vinh sort of pulled together near the water and kept their faces out to sea and they flipped their elbows when the silver-plate Indian masks and the VIVA MEXICO throw rugs and the iguana head T-shirts came too close. I myself was tempted by the T-shirts. Why not? They had a large green iguana head, and they made me smile. But then I wondered when Liz and Dick had disappeared from the T-shirts. How many years had it been that the lovers had stopped being an inspiration to the world? I mean "inspiration" in the same way that the late-night television ads would say that Elvis Presley, forever captured on three cassettes or two CDs, is an inspiration. But it was a little sad to me, how things that seem so important can come to an end. Even before Richard Burton was dead, there was no love between these two lovers who had crept over the bridge to each other in Gringo Gulch.

I watched Frank lean near my husband and say, "I wish everybody would just back off." This was spoken in a lowered voice, as if he was trying not to let someone hear who might be offended. This was a surprise, coming from Frank, and it made me wonder who he was talking about. The vendors? They hardly spoke English and their feelings wouldn't be hurt by this anyway. He wasn't talking about Eileen and me, because it would be "they," not "everybody."

I looked at Vinh to see if he was puzzled, but he didn't seem to be. He nodded. It must have been a continuation of some earlier conversation. I suddenly wanted very badly to know what it was all about. I'd been distracted for this whole trip, I realized. These two men had what Sam Donaldson on the news would call their own agenda. I stepped nearer, hoping for more words. Señora, silver. Silver, señora, real silver. I flapped my elbows at this sound and Vinh said something I couldn't catch, casting the words out to sea, and Frank nodded and then Vinh said, "If only one could find a clear betrayer."

"The marchers," Frank said.

"Too many of them. It's like hating a whole race. And if we were winning, no one would have listened to them."

I'd come too near. Frank glanced over his shoulder and he smiled and nudged Vinh and said, "It's time to pull out, Major."

Vinh turned, too, and he said, very deliberately, being a good husband, "This is nice here, Gabrielle. The sun feels good. I'm ready for a walk and some cinema history."

"What's our heading?" Frank said.

Eileen was beside me now and she motioned off to our left, across the narrow river mouth and past a long line of food stands near the shore and down to the end of the beach and then, beyond, along a low seawall running beneath a little hill thick with trees. And in the distance, just before the shore turned, I could see a tall pole in the center of a broken concrete dock and just behind it were two levels of terrace, broad stone walls.

"I see it," Frank said. "Shall the men walk point?"

"Of course," I said, and I heard myself sounding a little bit sharp, though I had not meant it that way. I just wanted them in front of me. I wanted to watch them.

So the two men went ahead and we all took our shoes off and waded across the river, the rocks smooth underfoot and the water rich and thick with its mountain stew, and I tried to stay close to them. We waded around a little gaggle of boys casting nets in the rushing water and Vinh went on about who to blame. "I tried to make it Mr. Thiệu. He was such a grasping fool. But we didn't lose the war because our gold was in some Swiss bank." Frank stumbled a bit and Vinh's hand went out fast to catch his elbow.

"I'm okay," Frank said, snatching his arm away, and then without a pause, "I still think it's the goddamn marchers. They hated our guts."

We came up out of the water and our calves were pasted with leaves. And there was a wonderful smell that I'd smelled when we first got out of the taxi but which only now did I really notice—wood fires, food cooking on wood fires. There were maybe a dozen food stands, permanent-looking ones with frames of timber and tin roofs. A boy came down from one of them with a handful of long pointed sticks, each skewering a whole fish.

Frank was walking on the inside and he recoiled from the boy. "No gracias, kid," and he was very emphatic, obviously bothered by these fish. And they were a pretty grim sight, if you weren't used to such things. There were four fish bobbing there in a row and they all looked rather startled to be dead and cooked and stuck and ready to be eaten. And the roasting over the fire made them look crusty, a little like the lepers on the streets of Saigon.

We moved on and Eileen said, "Aren't you hungry, honey? For something else maybe?"

"Not anymore," Frank said.

Vinh looked at him with a smile that I've seen him use on a particularly stupid customer. "You don't like to see dead fish?"

"Just a slab of their meat on a plate is the only way."

"You never fished as a boy?"

"I was a landlocked kid. Too busy building tree houses and stockpiling dirt-clod hand grenades."

"A boy who does not fish or hunt misses the real life and death," Vinh said, and I could hear what I took to be the little male thing going on again between them.

"Who said anything about hunting?" Frank said. "I could hunt."

"The animals you killed had eyes to stare at you, too, didn't they?"

"I never killed anything slippery. And I always did it with a gun. What's all this worm-on-a-hook shit? What's fishing to a born grunt?"

"Grunt?"

"Grunt. An infantryman. You guys didn't call them that?"

"I heard the word. But I thought you were a mechanic."

It surprised me that Vinh was starting to be hard on Frank. The things that had passed between them that had made them these little vacation-spot buddies so far—was that over now? Had I missed it all? Then it occurred to me that maybe I was myself the reason for Vinh pulling back from Frank. He had not wanted to say anything to me about Frank last night when I asked him. There was something about the man—that was all Vinh would say. Maybe it was just me. He didn't want to show *me* what it was that he and Frank had together.

But Frank didn't seem to pick up on Vinh's mood. He replied quite calmly, not at all defensive, just explanatory, "Anybody who carried a rifle and shot it in anger was a grunt to us. And I did that plenty."

Vinh wouldn't let it drop. "Why were you so anxious to fight, Frank?"

Eileen was probably listening to all of this, too. And it surely bothered her for what were probably some pretty complex reasons. As it was, I had totally forgotten her, I'd become so wrapped up in the men. But now she seemed not to want to hear any more. She said to me, loud, riding over the men's conversation, "It's exciting to be going to this movie set, isn't it? When was the last time you saw 'The Night of the Iguana'?"

As soon as I heard her voice, my face snapped over to her and I grew flushed with shame. I was very sorry that I'd been ignoring her—I'd contrived this trip with her; it was supposed to be mostly for the two of us; we were the ones to enjoy it.

I told her when I'd last seen the film and Eileen and I lagged a little behind as Vinh and Frank talked on, only a background mumble to me as my mouth and part of my brain did their duty to Eileen.

But I was still conscious of the men, the red shirt and the black. And I watched the backs of their legs. They both had really fine, solid calves that clenched and fell, clenched and fell as they walked in the sand.

And we waded another little stream and then climbed some boulders by a beach bar and we went single file down a rocky path, Eileen's voice going on about other Taylor and Burton movies that I loved—"Cleopatra" and "The Comedians" and "The Sandpiper" and even "Who's Afraid of Virginia Woolf?," which I think was really the beginning of the end for Liz and Dick, even though they stayed married for eight years after that. But I was hardly hearing any of this; I was responding over my shoulder and watching the men, Frank out front walking the stones of the path as if they could be booby-trapped and Vinh followed carefully, very quiet, placing his feet, it seemed to me, only where Frank had put his.

And then the path ended and we went even more carefully along the seawall, pretty narrow really, with a shore of boulders just below us on our right and the sharp incline of the weedy bank going up into the trees to our left. Even Eileen stopped talking as we teetered along. The early-afternoon sun was very hot and the sky and water were so bright they hurt my eyes. So when I wanted to glance away from Vinh's heels, which I was carefully following, I would look up the slope into the thick trees. It all felt familiar, up the hill. I don't know why, but it reminded me of Vietnam, even though I was really a city girl. My parents would take me for vacations to Nha Trang and even a few times to Qui Nhon, where we had some relatives and where Frank served, though I hadn't said anything about this to him. But both Nha Trang and Qui Nhon are on the South China Sea, and there must have been some place like this, with the sea so bright and the trees up a slope so thick. Some really special little moment that I'd had as a girl that got buried too deep to remember specifically, but which cleared my eyes and opened me up now to the shine of the water on Banderas Bay off the Pacific Ocean in Puerto Vallarta and to the thick looming of the trees up here near the set of "The Night of the Iguana."

Then we passed a cut in the trees, a groove down the hill, a place where the water runs off, and I could see a brick building up there, crumbling in the woods. But we passed it by and Frank led us farther until we arrived beneath the pole at the dock, rising up maybe forty feet, and it puzzled me what it once was supposed to do. Maybe it was some sort of crane or something to unload supplies. But it kind of gave me the shivers, standing up there so stiff and alone. The dock itself jutted out over the sea here, but its surface was gone; it was just the frame gaping out over the water and I turned around and there were two levels of balconies built into the hillside, fieldstone walls all jagged and irregular.

They had seemed so imposing from the beach, but up close it was clear that they were just facades, illusions, for as walls they contained nothing but the hillside, and as balconies they didn't connect to anything at all. Frank had climbed the broad stone steps beside them and he had run into a dead end. I could even see it from where I was standing. The steps went nowhere, just ending in the weeds and the trunks of the slope trees. "Just a real fine collection of small animal turds up here," Frank declared. Then he glanced down to Eileen at the foot of the stairs and said, "Sorry, honey. At least I didn't say 'shit.' "

Before I had a chance to react to what would have been a slight surprising prudishness in Eileen, she said, "That's right, sweetie. At least you didn't say 'shit.' " And all of a sudden my surprise shifted to this almost tender private joke between them. I was glad for that, but it did take me by surprise.

Frank came down the steps and I looked to Vinh. He was sitting on a pile of stones in the shade and he was watching the sea. I thought to go sit beside him, but Frank passed Eileen by—I was surprised again, expecting the little thing that had happened between them to surely end in an embrace of some sort, or at least a touch, a glancing kiss, something. Frank went past her with his attention already on my husband, and before I could act, it was Frank sitting next to him. This was still all right by me. I wanted to just get close and stay quiet and hope that they would eventually get back in their private mood with each other.

There were more stones piled nearby and I sat down and Eileen came and sat next to me and I was afraid she'd start talking, but she didn't. We all looked out to sea, looked at the big rocks hulking out there and the jagged line of mountains far across at the other side of the bay. Finally Frank said, "This isn't so bad. I figured there'd be people all over us out here selling Liz and Dick stuff."

"Don't you believe in free enterprise?" Vinh said, and I listened for the sound of combat in his voice again. But it wasn't there, exactly. I knew he didn't like all the swarm of vendors either, in spite of his being a businessman. He had too strong a sense of decorum.

Frank kept his face out to sea and he shrugged. "Sure I do. But sometimes it just gets so goddamn silly."

Vinh laughed, and it was a deep, appreciative laugh. I couldn't believe my good luck. All these two men had to do was sit down in the shade for a couple of moments and the first things out of their mouth let me find what I was looking for. "You've got it there, Frank," Vinh said. And I understood that however foolish Frank could appear hanging on so hard to the Vietnam veteran part of himself, however embarrassing it might sometimes be for Eileen, he certainly hadn't given in to the light and lively and less filling and soft as a cloud and reach out and touch someone culture that America had to offer. All the things that I had a sweet tooth for, my husband couldn't stand, not this man who'd been through a war and survived, the man who'd made his way in a strange land. And here was another man as uncomfortable with all that as Vinh was. Sure, these two could be buddies for a week. I fancy myself an observant woman, and there it was at last for me to see, as I sat on a crumbling boat dock at the foot of the set of one of my favorite movies.

Well, that was a relief, I thought. I even turned to Eileen and said, "There's got to be more to the place than this."

"Of course. Through the trees you can see buildings up there on top of the hill." Eileen turned her attention to her husband. "Honey, get us up to the top."

"The stairs lead nowhere."

Then I remembered the water runoff we'd passed. "I saw a place to go up," I said.

Frank and Vinh slapped their knees in acceptance and we all got up and I walked point this time, leading everyone back along the seawall to the cut in the trees and that groove coming down. "We can go up here," I said.

Vinh stepped in front of me and looked up the hill and said, "Okay. If you have to do this."

"There'll be no T-shirts at the top," I said. "I bet I can promise that."

Frank laughed and it looked like he was going to make a move past Vinh to lead the way, but Vinh started up the path too quickly, getting out in front, and Frank hustled to follow. I looked at Eileen and we both watched the men jockeying like this for position, and then she rolled her eyes at me. We both offered the other the opportunity to go next—I wasn't all that eager to be near them, now that I thought I understood. But Eileen finally insisted the hardest, and I went up the rut before her, the hillside squeezing at my hamstrings. I climbed with my face down for a while and the water runoff widened, turned into something more like a path, and there were even a few flat stones along the way, like the cast and crew had used this same way up the hill.

I finally raised my eyes and the two men were about thirty meters ahead, moving pretty fast, Frank still behind. I stopped and watched them and I don't know why I noticed it, but they were remarkably quiet. They were traipsing up among dead leaves and twigs and such and yet I didn't hear them at all. There must have been something in the way they were moving that made me sensitive to this, because somehow I knew it was on their minds as well. They were a little hunched and alert and they moved without any wasted motion, not even bobbing up and down. Then they reached the top of the rise and stopped and Frank came even with Vinh. I followed the turn of their heads and off to their left I could see a small, one-story brick structure without a front wall. They cocked their heads and looked into the gaping concrete rooms.

I put my head down and strained at my tight legs and went on up, conscious now of how much noise I was making, crunching leaves and scraping on the flat stones. I'd always wondered what it was like when Vinh was with his company out patrolling or whatever they did in the jungles. I felt suddenly like I knew. When I got to the top of this rise, I was surprised to find the men gone. The path continued on ahead, through a little open meadow, and then began to climb again. I could see along it far enough to know the men hadn't gone that way.

I flexed my legs to try to stretch out my muscles and I looked around. The two men were nowhere to be seen. The two side-by-side concrete rooms gaped open to me and I glanced down the path and Eileen was struggling up, making a last effort, and then she was beside me. "Where are they?" she asked.

"I don't know."

"Frank?" Eileen's voice quavered into the still, hot air and there was no reply. There was just the sound of the distant surf, coming from over the hill ahead of us, and the buzz of some insect whisking past and then away.

I was curious about this little building. It was too basic to be anything used in the movie, and then as I approached, I noticed an inner wall of tiles and the stubs of old shower heads. This was in the left-hand room, and I stepped into the room to the right as Eileen called out Frank's name again. The walls here were covered with graffiti, the profuse linking of names from floor to ceiling. Ramon and Maria, Ed and Mary, Sigmund and Katherine, on and on, a swarm of lovers touching letters, stuck by arrows, bound in by ragged marker-pen hearts. I saw a flash of color out of the corner of my eye. It was through the back window, beyond a row of low bushes. A red shirt slipping past in the trees, and I looked closer just in time to see the black shirt following.

"They're out in the back," I said to Eileen.

"Frank," she called again.

"Yes, Eileen?"

"Where are you?"

"Here I am." The voice was coming around a corner of the little building now and I looked again at all the names, running my eyes quickly around and around the wall packed with true love, and I wondered how many of these couples were still in love right this moment.

"Vinh and I were exploring out back."

"You having fun, sweetie?" Eileen said, and there was no ridicule or irritation in her voice. It was like she was indulging an active child.

I stepped out of the lovers' room and I thought it was a shame that the front wall was broken down and the place smelled of mildew and stone dust.

Frank did not answer Eileen's little motherly question. Instead he turned to my husband and said, "You keep pretty good noise discipline there, Vinh."

"Perhaps you drowned out my mistakes."

"You weren't hearing any sounds out of this troop either," Frank said, and his voice rasped a bit from Vinh's sharpness.

"Can't we go on?" Eileen said, pretty sharp herself now. "This isn't really part of the set."

Both men looked to the path tracking up and over the hill and I could feel the tension between them. Frank turned first and moved off pretty fast, and I was surprised to see Vinh follow just as fast.

Eileen cried out, "Wait for us," and this did slow Frank down and pull him into an upright position. He glanced over his shoulder and Vinh was coming up on him and it didn't seem fair to me for him to pass Frank while he was just paying attention to his wife.

So I called, "Vinh," and my husband slowed and even stopped and turned to wait for us. Frank stopped as well, just beyond him. Eileen and I looked at each other and I didn't know exactly what was in her mind, but she was obviously noticing the same odd thing going on between the men that I was. She and I took our sweet time about getting ourselves together and strolling up the path and the men were waiting, so I let myself look around.

Things were still pretty wildly overgrown, but we could see some full buildings off to our right, set on higher ground that looked back into the bay. This was the main set, I think, the hotel run by Ava Gardner in the movie.

"Isn't that the place?" I said to Eileen, nodding to the buildings.

"Maybe so. Maybe."

We looked around for a path going off in that direction, but the only one we found didn't go twenty meters before it was overgrown and then just disappeared into a really nasty thicket.

"I don't see a way over there," I said to Eileen, and she was not where I expected her to be. I found her up the hill, at the crest, and she was looking off in the distance and she had her hands folded before her with the wind blowing her hair back and she looked very nice there, very contented. Like a bookplate I once had, a girl standing against a breeze on a hill. Books make you dream, I think it said, just over the place where I wrote my name: This book belongs to Trần Nam Thanh Gabrielle. I miss bookplates. You can't hold a TV show in your hand and put your bookplate inside the cover where a girl stands on a hill dreaming of a wonderful future, just like in this wonderful book.

I glanced at the men and they were shuffling their feet and sniffing the air. I climbed up beside Eileen and the view was very nice; the bay was broad and very blue; the shore over on this side was deserted, a long curve of lacy surf. Very nice. I looked at the path and it wound down the ragged hill to a crumbling two-story brick building, though this one still had its front wall. And closer to the beach was the concrete frame of a foundation, all the walls gone from this one.

"We going over the hill?" Frank said.

It was all lovely but very lonely, too, up here. There was nothing of the movie to recognize, really. No sense of Richard Burton and Elizabeth Taylor ever being here. No ghosts here at all, it seemed. Just wreckage and weeds and silence. I turned my face to the wind coming in from the ocean and I stripped off a scarf that I'd used to tie up my hair and the wind blew my hair behind me, a nice feeling, I guess, though I wouldn't kid myself or anyone else that it had any intensity, this feeling. The wind in your hair is really a thrill only for a girl who hasn't met a man yet.

I don't mean that as cynical as it sounds. I just felt a little let down, I guess. There was a pretty snapshot up here, but no romance. That may sound odd from the woman who found romance in the muddy water spoiling the bay, but this was the mood that had suddenly come over me. I was weary of this vacation. And the men wanted nothing more than to charge over the hill. Frank was waiting for an answer and Eileen apparently wasn't going to give him one. I looked at her and her eyes were closed and I hoped that she was feeling more than I was.

"Over the hill," I said, and Frank flashed past and then Vinh, who gave me a quick glance as he went by. I knew all my husband's gestures, the subtle language of his face, all of that; I knew these things with such certainty and accuracy that it never surprised me when he sometimes seemed uncomfortable around me. But this glance of his as he went over the hill had something to it that I had not seen before and that I did not understand. Like the startled and yet fully comprehending look he might have if he and I had been standing on the edge of a cliff and the ground had just given way and he was hanging out there in the air about to drop straight down and he and I both knew there was nothing to be done about it.

If all this sounds a little odd, well, that's the way it was. I was feeling a little odd, and I sat down. I went to the edge of the hill in a bald spot in the weeds and I sat down and I tucked my legs up to my chest and I looked for a few moments at the breakers all along the shore, but I soon turned my eyes back to the men. They were winding down the path and they were moving, I knew, like they were on some patrol in some real hot battle area in Vietnam. They were just gliding, keeping low, and they were halfway down the hill, heading toward the brick building.

All of a sudden Frank pulled up and raised his hand in the air like he'd heard something. Vinh must have been watching the path at that moment because he ran right into Frank and nearly knocked him over. They were suddenly standing chest to chest and talking fast, both of them, and waving their arms.

I leaned forward and I grunted in frustration, loud enough for Eileen to get alarmed. "Are you going to be sick?" she said.

"No," I said, and I guess she was still looking out to sea, dreaming about whatever it was that made her close her eyes to the breeze. I wondered just for a moment if she was thinking of Frank as he once was, or maybe somebody else altogether. But there was no shifting of my attention, really. The men were arguing and I was out of earshot and that made me angry. A Vietnamese woman never curses, especially aloud and especially in the presence of some other person, but I came very close at that moment.

I wanted to get near the action but I knew I couldn't just run down there. It would stop the words for sure. I wanted this thing to follow its own course. Then I determined to use all of my powers of observation and figure it out. And I did pretty well, I think. I started by keeping in mind the way they'd been going down the hill. Low, silently, like they were on patrol in the war. It had something to do with all that, I figured.

The men had begun to take turns talking and it was Vinh's turn at the moment. I watched his hands. It's hard to ruffle Vinh, but when he does get worked up, he has very expressive hands. His right hand flipped with its palm upturned at Frank as if to say, This is what you did. Then Vinh pointed up the path they'd followed. He quickly traced it down the side of the hill to show the way they had come, and then he squared around to face Frank. He raised both his hands, slowly brought them together, and then flared them out, talking all the while, and it was like I could hear him: You led us down this path and it's the obvious place for the VC to put booby traps; I was watching the path and not you because you put us in danger by doing the obvious thing.

Meanwhile Frank had his arms folded over his chest and when Vinh finished his point, Frank opened his arms and tilted his head like he was being indulgent with a bright child. Frank made a sweeping gesture to indicate the low weeds all along the path down the hill, and I imagined I knew his words, too: That area is no more safe than the other; at least you can see what there is on the path better than in the weeds. Then he turned and pointed at the two-story brick building to remind Vinh of their objective, where they had to be the most watchful. And Frank ended by motioning off to the trees that were tall and thick just behind the building: That's where they are; the enemy's out there in the trees.

Some of this maybe I figured out a little later from what happened, but I was pretty sure right away that this was basically what the argument was about. Who was right? I don't know. Vinh had an answer for Frank, but he crossed his arms on his chest, so I couldn't figure it out. Frank answered that, and he stuck his fists on his hips and I had lost any feeling for the conversation and I whispered, "Damn," very softly.

The two men kept talking and finally they loosened up a little bit. They dropped their hands and they jangled around and Frank even laughed, a friendly, rearing-back kind of laugh. Vinh nodded and nodded again and he looked around.

I have to admit I was disappointed. It struck me as odd even at the time. It wasn't just that I had missed the argument, had only been able to guess at it, though that was certainly part of my disappointment. I'm pretty observant and I felt I'd gotten the pieces right that I'd figured out from the gestures, but there was something else going on, something even beneath the words they were speaking. I needed to hear those words, needed to turn my talent on the words themselves, looking deeper. Then Frank even cuffed Vinh on the shoulder. I said it louder: "Damn." Now they were friends again. I'd missed it all and there didn't even seem to be any hard feelings that I'd be able to observe later. Foolish men. They didn't even know how to hold a grudge.

They were gesturing. I leaned forward. Frank pointed at Vinh and then off to the trees. He touched his own chest and swept his arm toward the sea. Then Vinh pointed at the brick building and they nodded. I didn't figure this out very quickly. It even puzzled me when they both stooped down and studied the path and separated, picking things up off the dirt and stuffing them into their pockets. This was very strange. Then Vinh stood up briefly with one of the things from the ground in his hand. He held it up and it looked like a stone, a rather large stone, and Frank came up behind him and looked, too, and shook his head no. He held something up and it must have been another stone, smaller. Vinh nodded and dropped the large stone and they both kept looking. But when Frank's back was turned, I saw Vinh return and pick up the big one.

I was beginning to understand. They finally had enough stones in their pockets and they approached each other once more and spoke briefly and then they stood back to back, Vinh facing the trees and Frank facing the hillside and the sea. It was like in all the old movies where two men are going to fight a duel. I wondered for a moment if that's what they were going to do, if they'd just go ten paces, turn, and throw rocks at each other.

But they had something else in mind. At some signal between them they began to walk away from each other, but they just kept walking. Frank went over the edge of the hill and disappeared. Vinh kept going until he splashed through a narrow stream and came up to the edge of the woods. I understood now that this was some kind of little war game. They were going to stalk each other or something. Maybe try to capture and control the brick building. When this hit me, I suddenly grew aware of Vinh's red shirt, how it would stand out among the trees. But, as it sometimes happens between husbands and wives, Vinh seemed to have the thought just as I did. Or maybe I sent it to him. I don't know. But he stopped at the trees and looked back, looked briefly for Frank, and when the man was not in sight,

Vinh took off his red shirt and rolled it up and put it under his arm.

My husband's chest and arms are quite strong, really, and I tilted my head at seeing them suddenly like this, across a field, against those trees, the breeze coming off the bay, and I felt a little wiggle of something in me, a snaky little romantic feeling that started in my chest and then, as Vinh moved into the woods and the dark skin of his broad back faded into the shadows, the feeling slithered out of my chest and down inside me real fast and I looked out to the sea and closed my eyes.

Here I was in this little pose and if someone was watching me who knew what to look for in people, she would wonder if I was thinking of Vinh as he once was, or maybe someone else altogether. The answer was that I was thinking of neither of these. As soon as I closed my eyes, I was aware only of myself; I stepped out of myself and saw me, and that was all that was in my mind. The romance was gone right away. I'm sometimes too observant for my own damn good. It should've been Vinh as he once was who I was thinking about. That would have been nice, that moment.

But instead I remembered Eileen sitting in this same way nearby, and I opened my eyes. The hillside and the brick building and the woods were deserted. I glanced over to Eileen and she was lying on her back, her forearm over her face. She seemed to be asleep.

I looked back down the hill and that feeling of being let down that I'd had earlier came back. The whole scene in front of me kind of blurred. Even all the things that my mind knew were beautiful seemed flat all of a sudden, like a postcard you'd buy in a hurry at the airport.

But I did wonder where the men were. So I looked harder. Frank had claimed the shore and the hillside, and I figured it would be easier to spot him at this point. The slope went down and then rolled over a crest and into another slope I couldn't see, and beyond, there was the meadow with the naked foundation in the center. Farther on was another crest and another invisible slope, this one dropping down to the shore and the sea. I figured Frank was on one of the far slopes and I waited for a few moments and he was staying out of sight and so I peered into the woods where Vinh had gone.

It seemed like a pretty silly game to me. I wasn't sure what they were doing. They weren't exactly stalking each other, or they probably would've both gone into the woods. But maybe they were stalking. Frank had to defend his earlier actions out here in the open, going down the path and all. Maybe he was the force that had taken the beach—like those first Marines coming ashore in Đà Nẵng or something. And Vinh was the other side—would he actually play the part of the Vietcong, who he hated? Perhaps. Perhaps if this American had given him no choice, he would play the Vietnamese no matter what the politics. I didn't know. And I guess it's important to realize that I didn't know what Vinh would do in this situation. The man in the woods was hidden from me, too.

Then I saw Frank. His black shirt and shorts would have been good camouflage in the shade of the trees, but against the meadow he was very clearly visible. He was moving in that low glide of his and he crouched behind the stone foundation. He peeked up and looked in the direction of the brick building, which was maybe a hundred and fifty meters across the meadow and up a roll of the hill. I didn't know what he was waiting for, if the point was to go take the building. Vinh was nowhere in sight, and I didn't know what Vinh was waiting for either.

The truth be told, my husband was in the airborne, but I think he was mostly back at the base camp giving orders and organizing supplies and looking after paperwork. He is a businessman, always has been and I guess he always will be. And Frank said himself he was a helicopter mechanic. These men weren't fighters, in spite of their nearness to a war.

I scanned the tree line and then I saw Vinh. He was sliding around a tree, and it struck me that I was watching this old movie. These men were crouching and hiding and sneaking around like all the old movie actors in all the old war and spy and detective movies ever made, all those wonderful old unreal movies that made my hours after midnight so peaceful. Vinh was a heavy sleeper and I had good hearing and so I could watch these films in my bed. I would pull the sheet up to my nose and lie there on my Posturepedic mattress and I was in the United States of America in an era of peace and prosperity in spite of the deficits and I could hear the wind outside as a Louisiana summer storm blew in and I was safe and I was cozy and I was watching a whole world of men with steel pots or fedoras on their heads and they were in the middle of big trouble, but boy, could they sneak around and glide around, and they were never going to get hurt by anything, you knew that for sure.

Vinh slipped out of the woods and I realized that Frank didn't see him because the brick building was between the two of them. Vinh stood by the little stream and he looked up to the top of the second floor of the building and sighted from there down to his feet on the bank of the stream. Then he laid his rolled red shirt next to a rock and he crouched low and stepped over the flowing water.

I looked at Frank and he was moving. He was going around the far side of the foundation in his low crouch and he was heading, I guessed, for the building. Meanwhile, Vinh was edging his way around the near end, his neck craned hard to his left so he could catch early sight of Frank if he should suddenly appear. But Frank was circling wide now to approach from the other direction, and so the men were still unaware of each other.

Vinh made it to the side staircase that led to the upper floor. He climbed it quickly but he slowed abruptly and ducked down as he neared the top. Then he peeked over to make sure that Frank wasn't already there, and when he saw that the place was deserted, I swear

I could see his body actually ripple in delight. He scrambled up on top of the building, went to the back edge so he could view his red shirt by the stream, and he dug into his pocket and placed some of his stones beside him.

Frank was high-stepping down a slope and he disappeared as soon as I saw this. I waited, and then a few moments later, his head popped up at the crest of the hill at the far side of the brick building. The head disappeared again and then popped up once more.

"Aren't they lovely?" This was Eileen's voice. Needless to say, the sentiment surprised me. I turned to her and she was still on her back but she had moved her forearm off her eyes. She was looking up into the sky. I followed her gaze. There were some high, white clouds.

"That one is the head of a pony," she said. The head of a pony. Do I sound like that sometimes? I bet I do. Eileen and I probably respond to the same things. Not even the head of a *horse*. She saw a sweet little pony. Of course. A lonesome little pony, and the little girl makes a long-distance phone call to the pony and it isn't lonesome anymore. If they filmed that and put it on between the soaps, I'd weep at that one, too. The little pony shaking its forelock in delight as someone holds the phone up to its ear. I'm a sucker for any of that. But at this moment the pony struck me as pretty uninspired. Dumb, even, seeing a pony in the cloud and getting dreamy-voiced over it.

But I said, "It sure does" as sincerely as I could and I turned to see Frank spank across the grass and throw himself—out of my sight now—against the far wall of the building. Vinh raised his head and looked over his shoulder. He had probably heard the impact. I waited and I expected to see Frank ease his way around the corner and come along the front wall. But he was apparently suspicious of the front, because I waited and waited and so did Vinh, though he eventually turned his face back to his shirt at the stream.

Finally I saw Frank. Vinh tipped me off by suddenly lowering his head. A moment later I saw Frank slip up and press himself against a tree at the back of the building. He was looking toward the woods now, and I wondered if he saw the shirt. Even as I thought this, Frank did a double take. A real double take, a little bit like the cartoon characters, though Frank's eyes didn't bug out. His face extended forward and he looked at the red color, and connections were going off in his head.

He looked all around and he studied the tree line carefully and then he dug into his pocket and armed himself with a rock—I could imagine him whispering to himself, "Lock and load, troop." And Vinh was all this time sneaking little glances over the edge of the roof, his rock already in his hand. I wondered if it was the big rock that Frank had made him throw down. I figured it wasn't, however. Not at this point. Vinh even held the stone up briefly, perhaps to see if it was the roundest one, the one he could throw most accurately, and it didn't look from this distance like the big one. I was glad. I was sure if he used the big one that Frank would get very angry.

Frank was slung low and creeping up to the stream, eyeing the red shirt very carefully. He stopped just across the stream and he looked at it and he cocked his head and finally he even straightened up. I don't know what he was thinking. So it was Vinh's shirt. Did he expect that to help him find the man? Obviously Vinh wasn't in the shirt. But I think Frank was very pleased with himself for finding it. It seemed meaningful to him. Then Vinh's stone hit him right on the point of his left shoulder.

Frank spun around and I could hear his curse even from this distance. Vinh immediately jumped up and raised his arms in the air in victory. Frank rubbed his shoulder and then he darted away, behind a tree, and then to another, and then he ran to the near side of the building and pulled up and pressed himself against the wall. Vinh was clearly agitated. He thought he had already won. He flapped his arms in exasperation and I could see Frank was ready for more war. He had a stone in his hand as if to throw it. He looked up above him and dashed to the foot of the steps and again pressed back against the wall. Vinh called out something that I could not hear. Probably Frank's name. Probably telling him that the little game was over.

But Frank was creeping up the steps and obviously wasn't answering my husband, and finally Vinh dug in his pocket for more stones and moved into the center of the roof. He figured that Frank was on the way up. This time Vinh looked very carefully at the contents of his pocket and I knew even before he held it up that he had the big stone.

I stood up, afraid for them both. But there was nothing I could do, of course. Frank figured he was just wounded, since Vinh had only hit him in the shoulder. Vinh figured the war was over and was really angry when it turned out that it wasn't. I wanted to call out to them, but I could find no words. This was a distant event, farther from me even than the Hollywood studio-set wars I watched from under the covers. It was as far from me as my husband was far from me; as far as that secret, silent part of him that was so difficult a thing between us.

Frank stopped just before his head was ready to show itself to Vinh. My husband was now poised in the center of the roof with the big rock in his right hand and cocked back over his shoulder, ready to throw. Frank waited and I could feel him mustering his strength, focusing on one leap into the open, his own rocks flying. Just like in the movies. But for a moment I wondered if Vinh would kill him, if Vinh would fire at the first sight of the man's head and hit him in the temple with the big rock and that would be the end. I could not draw a breath. "How lovely," Eileen sighed.

Then Frank clambered up the final few steps, very slowly, it seemed to me, although his legs and arms were obviously straining to make this a lightning strike. Hold, hold, I cried in my mind to Vinh's arm. Don't aim at the head.

Frank's first stone or two flew wildly past Vinh and Vinh did wait, he waited and set himself and he threw the large stone and it hit Frank in the pit of the stomach. I knew this because Frank doubled over and then there was a moment of suspension. Frank's knees bent and he put one hand on the surface of the roof so he didn't fall over, and Vinh stayed in the crouch he'd assumed after the throw. The two men were suddenly frozen there, like props left over from the movie.

"How truly lovely," Eileen said.

Then Frank lifted his face a little and I guess he saw the stone that Vinh had used. It must have been lying there before him. He looked up at Vinh and I think he said something, probably some angry name, and then he lunged forward and Vinh tried to sidestep him but only got partly out of the way and Frank glanced off him, scooping wide with his arms, but Vinh was turning away and slipped Frank's grasp, although he did fall backward, even as Frank spun and hurtled on and also fell on the rooftop.

I hoped that that was the end of it, but both men bounced to their feet very quickly and there seemed to be no question of what to do now. They rushed at each other immediately and Vinh, being smaller, got under Frank's grasp and he butted Frank in his stomach with his head. Frank fell backward and Vinh fell on top of him and they rolled over immediately, first Frank on top and then Vinh, and arms were flailing and legs and the two men were fighting hard.

"A great white duck," Eileen said. "I had one just like it when I was a child."

I looked into the sky and sure enough, there was a white cloud passing overhead that looked like a duck. You could see its bill and its long neck and even its wings.

I sat down and chose curtain number three—the sea. I glanced at the men, still rolling around on the roof, and I chose the sea. The sea was bright and flat and it crumpled along the shore and I just watched that for now. How silly it had been for me to think I'd understood them. Neither of them could stomach the feel-good culture. But that was hardly all of the feeling between them. They had shared something once, something important—rage, fear, the urge to violence, just causes, life and death. They'd both felt those things in service of the same war. And neither of them wanted to let go of all that. But even finding *this* connection between them didn't really explain everything.

Don't ask me what did. I watched mostly the sea for the next few minutes, and when I finally peeked back in the direction of the brick building, I saw them sitting about ten feet apart, their backs to each other, their legs spread and their arms lolling in exhaustion. Frank was facing the woods and my husband was facing the sea. He seemed to be looking very intently out to sea. Just like I was.

We took separate cabs, the two couples, back to the beautiful Fiesta Vallarta Hotel. Vinh had come up the hill first and he was a mess. He had forgotten his red shirt, but he wouldn't have been comfortable wearing it over all the abrasions anyway. Eileen screamed when she saw him. "It's all right," I told her. "They're both all right." I didn't say any more. I just went with Vinh along the path and left Eileen on the hilltop ready to kill Frank, I think. She was already assuming the worst.

I didn't say anything to Vinh as we walked back to the beach or rode in the taxicab or crossed our hotel lobby and entered the elevator or even when we first stepped into the room. Nor did he say anything to me. When our door clicked shut and we were out of the eye of the public, I turned to him, but he averted his face and dipped his head and I knew he could say nothing about this anyway. Still, I yearned to know what it was that he felt, what he may have learned.

He said, "I'm going to wash up."

"Do you need some help?"

"No," he said. "Thank you."

I nodded and he stepped into the bathroom and closed the door.

I crossed the room and the curtains ruffled before the open balcony doors. It was getting on to late afternoon now and the light looked very nice on the floor beneath the curtains and so I opened them. The sunlight was suddenly thrown against the wall and the shadow of a potted plant on the balcony was pressed there, too, like it was trying to sneak in without anyone noticing. A silly impression, a hangover from the scene I'd witnessed at Mismaloya. I sat on the end of the bed and looked at the wall. The light was really very nice. A pale, buttery yellow, and the plant dipped and rose there, the broad, shapely leaves of a croton.

I'm not sure why all this was occupying my mind. Maybe because of Vinh's silence. Maybe it was the weariness that had come over me again. All this fresh air, hilltops and beaches—I wasn't used to it. It made me want to sleep. I thought to lie down on the bed, but I heard the water running in the bathroom and I waited. I sat on the end of the bed and I waited, and the shadow of the croton crept across the wall and then at last the bathroom door opened and Vinh stepped out.

He was dressed in gray slacks and sneakers and one of the short-sleeved dress shirts that he usually wears to work in the hot Louisiana summers. His hair was wet and combed down neatly and the battle showed on his face only in a dull red abrasion the size of a silver dollar on his cheek. He looked at me for a moment and I strained to see some clue there of something, anything. His mouth was relaxed but unsmiling. His eyes were steady on me and all I could sense was that whatever he had felt this afternoon was not yet put aside. Then he moved to me and stood over me where I sat on the bed. I felt I should stand up before him; perhaps he would take me in his arms.

I was about to do that, but before I could, his hand came out and
brushed a lock of hair off my face.

That was all. Was he trying to say that since he was cleaned up
now, I should pull myself together as well? I didn't know. Then I
thought there was something nice about his hand, but before I could
identify it, he took the hand back and said, "I'm going out."

I nodded and he turned and he was across the room and out the
door quickly, closing it behind him with the softest of clicks. I lay
back on the bed and looked at the ceiling and I wished it was a sky
full of clouds, full of ponies and ducks, and I put my forearm over
my eyes. But the thinking did not stop. Where was he going? I had
lived with my husband for nearly twenty years, and I should have
been able to guess where he was going after the events of this day.
At first I thought he was going to Frank's room to make up with
him. But that didn't feel right. Perhaps tomorrow, running into them
as if by accident in the lobby. That would be the time to shake hands.
My husband would not seek the man out at this moment.

Then the thought struck me that from all of this purging of the
war, he was now free to do something special. There had been
tenderness in his hand when it scolded my stray lock of hair. I thought
that perhaps Vinh was going down to get into a taxi and go to Liz
and Dick's bridge and buy me a copa de oro, a cup of gold. He had
denied me a flower earlier and all of sudden he realized it; he had
even denied me that flower in chorus with the man who he went on
to fight to some resolution on this day. I tried to imagine Vinh coming
through the door and bringing the flower and putting it into my hair,
the very hair that he had arranged before he left.

But this was the thought of a woman who could weep over
television commercials. I realized that very quickly, lying there alone
on the bed in the Fiesta Vallarta Hotel. And then I thought that Vinh
would never return. He had walked out of this room and he had
decided never to come back to me. He had put his passport and his

ticket into the pocket of his gray slacks and he had walked out forever.

This I believed for perhaps ten minutes, and they were the worst ten minutes of my life in America. I suddenly knew that it was I who had withdrawn from Vinh. I had embraced this culture with such intensity that it isolated me from him, made it impossible for him to find a way to touch me anymore. Even Frank, this poor American living in the past, knew enough to pull away from the excesses of the empty-headed culture around him. That must have been terrible for Vinh, that even this man who he would fight was more accessible than his own wife. I was, for about ten minutes, as black and still as the water that ran beneath the river shacks of Saigon. My skin felt like it could be wiped away with the slightest touch, like the skin of the leper beggars who did not even have a river shack. Could I not remember these things?

But then something in me said, Wait. It's not just me. Vinh, too, has been distracted by the American culture. He is a seller of Swedish meatballs and cocktail franks, after all. He wears his dark gray suit and he studies his spreadsheets and he flies here and there carrying a leather briefcase with all the other Americans and he makes much money from food that people eat with toothpicks. But in Vietnam, in the war, there was passion. And there is a passion still inside him. He did fight with this man today.

I lay there for a few minutes more and I don't know what it was, exactly, that moved me to think about stepping onto the balcony. The sunlight on the wall had darkened into peach and I stood up and faced the breeze from the bay. It was lovely out there, with the sun nearing the horizon. A tight little family of pelicans drifted past and I moved through the sliding doors and leaned on the balustrade. I watched the pelicans wheel off to their right and head out to sea.

But my eyes stayed with the shore and a parasail rising there. I sent my body out to float with the sailor. I didn't need to be on the parachute myself; I could stand here and let myself separate from my body, from all the strangeness that had come upon me, that made up my life, and I could glide in the long angle of this sun and feel at peace. And so I watched the parasail swing around and head this way. The chute was red and yellow and it was as high as my balcony now and I closed my eyes briefly, remembering the green wake of the boat far below me, and I rode over those waves smoother than any ship.

I opened my eyes and the parasailor was drawing almost even with my hotel, right at my eye level, and I, of course, expected to see the dangling bare legs of someone in a bathing suit. But these legs were clothed in long gray slacks. And my eyes went instantly to the face and it was Vinh. He was holding the ropes and at first I wondered if he was being an airborne soldier again. But it was very much different from that. I had failed to understand his face when he was standing before me, but this much I could tell now as he glided past me strapped to a parachute. He was looking down with the calmest of pleasures. The angle of his head, lolled to the side like I was scratching his neck up under his ear like I used to; the loose hold of his hands on the ropes with one elbow even tucked comfortably into his side; the slight boyish kick in his legs: all this told me he was enjoying himself. He was high above Puerto Vallarta and the sea and he was happy now.

And finally he was eye to eye with me. The boat went on down the coast, into the glare of the sun, but then it swung around, and when Vinh came past once more, he turned his face to the Fiesta Vallarta Hotel and he saw me on the balcony and he smiled. I could see the smile very clearly, and when I waved at him, he raised his hand and threw me a kiss. He drifted past and I looked out to the setting sun. Just like in the movies. A beautiful sunset at the end of this very strange day. Night was coming on and my husband was about to return to earth. And so was I.

A GOOD
SCENT FROM
A STRANGE
MOUNTAIN

Hồ Chí Minh came to me again last night, his hands covered with confectioners' sugar. This was something of a surprise to me, the first time I saw him beside my bed, in the dim light from the open shade. My oldest daughter leaves my shades open, I think so that I will not forget that the sun has risen again in the morning. I am a very old man. She seems to expect that one morning I will simply forget to keep living. This is very foolish. I will one night rise up from my bed and slip into her room and open the shade there. Let *her* see the sun in the morning. She is sixty-four years old and she should worry for herself. I could never die from forgetting.

But the light from the street was enough to let me recognize Hồ when I woke, and he said to me, "Đạo, my old friend, I have heard it is time to visit you." Already on that first night there was a sweet smell about him, very strong in the dark, even before I could see his hands. I said nothing, but I stretched to the nightstand beside me and I turned on the light to see if he would go away. And he did not. He stood there beside the bed—I could even see him reflected in the window—and I knew it was real because he did not appear as he was when I'd known him but as he was when he'd died. This was Uncle Hô before me, the thin old man with the dewlap beard wearing the dark clothes of a peasant and the rubber sandals, just like in the news pictures I studied with such a strange feeling for all those years. Strange because when I knew him, he was not yet Hô Chí Minh. It was 1917 and he was Nguyễn Aí Quốc and we were both young men with clean-shaven faces, the best of friends, and we worked at the Carlton Hotel in London, where I was a dishwasher and he was a pastry cook under the great Escoffier. We were the best of friends and we saw snow for the first time together. This was before we began to work at the hotel. We shoveled snow and Hô would stop for a moment and blow his breath out before him and it would make him smile, to see what was inside him, as if it was the casting of bones to tell the future.

On that first night when he came to me in my house in New Orleans, I finally saw what it was that smelled so sweet and I said to him, "Your hands are covered with sugar."

He looked at them with a kind of sadness.

I have received that look myself in the past week. It is time now for me to see my family, and the friends I have made who are still alive. This is our custom from Vietnam. When you are very old, you put aside a week or two to receive the people of your life so that you can tell one another your feelings, or try at last to understand one another, or simply say good-bye. It is a formal leave-taking, and with good luck you can do this before you have your final illness. I have lived almost a century and perhaps I should have called them all to me sooner, but at last I felt a deep weariness and I said to my oldest daughter that it was time.

They look at me with sadness, some of them. Usually the dull-witted ones, or the insincere ones. But Hô's look was, of course, not dull-witted or insincere. He considered his hands and said, "The glaze. Maestro's glaze."

There was the soft edge of yearning in his voice and I had the thought that perhaps he had come to me for some sort of help. I said to him, "I don't remember. I only washed dishes." As soon as the words were out of my mouth, I decided it was foolish for me to think he had come to ask me about the glaze.

But Hô did not treat me as foolish. He looked at me and shook his head. "It's all right," he said. "I remember the temperature now. Two hundred and thirty degrees, when the sugar is between the large thread stage and the small orb stage. The Maestro was very clear about that and I remember." I knew from his eyes, however, that there was much more that still eluded him. His eyes did not seem to move at all from my face, but there was some little shifting of them, a restlessness that perhaps only I could see, since I was his close friend from the days when the world did not know him.

I am nearly one hundred years old, but I can still read a man's face. Perhaps better than I ever have. I sit in the overstuffed chair in my living room and I receive my visitors and I want these people, even the dull-witted and insincere ones—please excuse an old man's ill temper for calling them that—I want them all to be good with one another. A Vietnamese family is extended as far as the bloodline strings us together, like so many paper lanterns around a village square. And we all give off light together. That's the way it has always been in our culture. But these people who come to visit me have been in America for a long time and there are very strange things going on that I can see in their faces.

None stranger than this morning. I was in my overstuffed chair and with me there were four of the many members of my family: my son-in-law Thắng, a former colonel in the Army of the Republic of Vietnam and one of the insincere ones, sitting on my Castro convertible couch; his youngest son, Lợi, who had come in late, just a few minutes earlier, and had thrown himself down on the couch as well, youngest but a man old enough to have served as a lieutenant under his father as our country fell to the communists more than a decade ago; my daughter Lâm, who is Thắng's wife, hovering behind the both of them and refusing all invitations to sit down; and my oldest daughter, leaning against the door frame, having no doubt just returned from my room, where she had opened the shade that I had closed when I awoke.

It was Thắng who gave me the sad look I have grown accustomed to, and I perhaps seemed to him at that moment a little weak, a little distant. I had stopped listening to the small talk of these people and I had let my eyes half close, though I could still see them clearly and I was very alert. Thắng has a steady face and the quick eyes of a man who is ready to come under fire, but I have always read much more there, in spite of his efforts to show nothing. So after he thought I'd faded from the room, it was with slow eyes, not quick, that he moved to his son and began to speak of the killing.

You should understand that Mr. Nguyễn Bích Lê had been shot dead in our community here in New Orleans just last week. There are many of us Vietnamese living in New Orleans and one man, Mr. Lê, published a little newspaper for all of us. He had recently made the fatal error—though it should not be that in America—of writing that it was time to accept the reality of the communist government in Vietnam and begin to talk with them. We had to work now with those who controlled our country. He said that he remained a patriot to the Republic of Vietnam, and I believed him. If anyone had asked an old man's opinion on this whole matter, I would not have been afraid to say that Mr. Lê was right.

But he was shot dead last week. He was forty-five years old and he had a wife and three children and he was shot as he sat behind the wheel of his Chevrolet pickup truck. I find a detail like that especially moving, that this man was killed in his Chevrolet, which I understand is a strongly American thing. We knew this in Saigon.

In Saigon it was very American to own a Chevrolet, just as it was French to own a Citroën.

And Mr. Lê had taken one more step in his trusting embrace of this new culture. He had bought not only a Chevrolet but a Chevrolet pickup truck, which made him not only American but also a man of Louisiana, where there are many pickup trucks. He did not, however, also purchase a gun rack for the back window, another sign of this place. Perhaps it would have been well if he had, for it was through the back window that the bullet was fired. Someone had hidden in the bed of his truck and had killed him from behind in his Chevrolet and the reason for this act was made very clear in a phone call to the newspaper office by a nameless representative of the Vietnamese Party for the Annihilation of Communism and for the National Restoration.

And Thắng, my son-in-law, said to his youngest son, Lợi, "There is no murder weapon." What I saw was a faint lift of his eyebrows as he said this, like he was inviting his son to listen beneath his words. Then he said it again, more slowly, like it was code. "There is *no weapon.*" My grandson nodded his head once, a crisp little snap. Then my daughter Lâm said in a very loud voice, with her eyes on me, "That was a terrible thing, the death of Mr. Lê." She nudged her husband and son, and both men turned their faces sharply to me and they looked at me squarely and said, also in very loud voices, "Yes, it was terrible."

I am not deaf, and I closed my eyes further, having seen enough and wanting them to think that their loud talk had not only failed to awake me but had put me more completely to sleep. I did not like to deceive them, however, even though I have already spoken critically of these members of my family. I am a Hòa Hảo Buddhist and I believe in harmony among all living things, especially the members of a Vietnamese family.

After Hồ had reassured me, on that first visit, about the temperature needed to heat Maestro Escoffier's glaze, he said, "Đạo, my old friend, do you still follow the path you chose in Paris?"

He meant by this my religion. It was in Paris that I embraced the Buddha and disappointed Hồ. We went to France in early 1918, with the war still on, and we lived in the poorest street of the poorest part of the Seventeenth Arrondissement. Number nine, Impasse Compoint, a blind alley with a few crumbling houses, all but ours rented out for storage. The cobblestones were littered with fallen roof tiles and Quốc and I each had a tiny single room with only an iron bedstead and a crate to sit on. I could see my friend Quốc in the light of the tallow candle and he was dressed in a dark suit and a bowler hat and he looked very foolish. I did not say so, but he knew it himself and he kept seating and reseating the hat and shaking his head very slowly, with a loudly silent anger. This was near the end of our time together, for I was visiting daily with a Buddhist monk and he was drawing me back to the religion of my father. I had run from my father, gone to sea, and that was where I had met Nguyễn Aí Quốc and we had gone to London and to Paris and now my father was calling me back, through a Vietnamese monk I met in the Tuileries.

Quốc, on the other hand, was being called not from his past but from his future. He had rented the dark suit and bowler and he would spend the following weeks in Versailles, walking up and down the mirrored corridors of the Palace trying to gain an audience with Woodrow Wilson. Quốc had eight requests for the Western world concerning Indochina. Simple things. Equal rights, freedom of assembly, freedom of the press. The essential things that he knew Wilson would understand, based as they were on Wilson's own Fourteen Points. And Quốc did not even intend to ask for independence. He wanted Vietnamese representatives in the French Parliament. That was all he would ask. But his bowler made him angry. He wrenched out of the puddle of candlelight, both his hands clutching the bowler, and I heard him muttering in the darkness and I felt that this was a bad sign already, even before he had set foot in Versailles. And as it turned out, he never saw Wilson, or Lloyd George either, or even Clemenceau. But somehow his frustration with his hat was what made me sad, even now, and I reached out from my bedside and said, "Uncle Hồ, it's all right."

He was still beside me. This was not an awakening, as you might expect, this was not a dream ending with the bowler in Paris and me awaking to find that Hồ was never there. He was still beside my bed, though he was just beyond my outstretched hand and he did not move to me. He smiled on one side of his mouth, a smile full of irony, as if he, too, was thinking about the night he'd tried on his rented clothes. He said, "Do you remember how I worked in Paris?"

I thought about this and I did remember, with the words of his advertisement in the newspaper "La Vie Ouvrière": "If you would like a lifelong memento of your family, have your photos retouched at Nguyễn Aí Quốc's." This was his work in Paris; he retouched photos with a very delicate hand, the same fine hand that Monsieur Escoffier had admired in London. I said, "Yes, I remember."

Hồ nodded gravely. "I painted the blush into the cheeks of Frenchmen."

I said, "A lovely portrait in a lovely frame for forty francs," another phrase from his advertisement.

"Forty-five," Hồ said.

I thought now of his question that I had not answered. I motioned to the far corner of the room where the prayer table stood. "I still follow the path."

He looked and said, "At least you became a Hòa Hảo."

He could tell this from the simplicity of the table. There was only a red cloth upon it and four Chinese characters: Bảo Sơn Kỳ Hương. This is the saying of the Hòa Hảo. We follow the teachings of a monk who broke away from the fancy rituals of the other Buddhists. We do not need elaborate pagodas or rituals. The Hòa Hảo believes that the maintenance of our spirits is very simple, and the mystery of joy is simple, too. The four characters mean "A good scent from a strange mountain."

I had always admired the sense of humor of my friend Quốc, so I said, "You never did stop painting the blush into the faces of Westerners."

Hồ looked back to me but he did not smile. I was surprised at this but more surprised at my little joke seeming to remind him of his hands. He raised them and studied them and said, "After the heating, what was the surface for the glaze?"

"My old friend," I said, "you worry me now."

But Hồ did not seem to hear. He turned away and crossed the room and I knew he was real because he did not vanish from my sight but opened the door and went out and closed the door behind him with a loud click.

I rang for my daughter. She had given me a porcelain bell, and after allowing Hồ enough time to go down the stairs and out the front door, if that was where he was headed, I rang the bell, and my daughter, who is a very light sleeper, soon appeared.

"What is it, Father?" she asked with great patience in her voice. She is a good girl. She understands about Vietnamese families and she is a smart girl.

"Please feel the doorknob," I said.

She did so without the slightest hesitation and this was a lovely gesture on her part, a thing that made me wish to rise up and embrace her, though I was very tired and did not move.

"Yes?" she asked after touching the knob.

"Is it sticky?"

She touched it again. "Ever so slightly," she said. "Would you like me to clean it?"

"In the morning," I said.

She smiled and crossed the room and kissed me on the forehead. She smelled of lavender and fresh bedclothes and there are so many who have gone on before me into the world of spirits and I yearn for them all, yearn to find them all together in a village square, my wife there smelling of lavender and our own sweat, like on a night in Saigon soon after the terrible fighting in 1968 when we finally opened the windows onto the night and there were sounds of bombs falling on the horizon and there was no breeze at all, just the heavy stillness of the time between the dry season and the wet, and Saigon smelled of tar and motorcycle exhaust and cordite but when I opened the window and turned to my wife, the room was full of a wonderful scent, a sweet smell that made her sit up, for she sensed it, too. This was a smell that had nothing to do with flowers but instead reminded us that flowers were always ready to fall into dust, while this smell was as if a gemstone had begun to give off a scent, as if a mountain of emerald had found its own scent. I crossed the room to my wife and we were already old, we had already buried children and grand-children that we prayed waited for us in that village square at the foot of the strange mountain, but when I came near the bed, she lifted her silk gown and threw it aside and I pressed close to her and our own sweat smelled sweet on that night. I want to be with her in that square and with the rest of those we'd buried, the tiny limbs and the sullen eyes and the gray faces of the puzzled children and the surprised adults and the weary old people who have gone before us, who know the secrets now. And the sweet smell of the glaze on Hô's hands reminds me of others that I would want in the square, the people from the ship, too, the Vietnamese boy from a village near my own who died of a fever in the Indian Ocean and the natives in Dakar who were forced by colonial officials to swim out to our ship in shark-infested waters to secure the moorings and two were killed before our eyes without a French regret. Hô was very moved by this, and I want those men in our square and I want the Frenchman, too, who called Hô "monsieur" for the first time. A man on the dock in Marseilles. Hô spoke of him twice more during our years together and I want that Frenchman there. And, of course, Hô. Was he in the village square even now, waiting? Heating his glaze fondant? My daughter was smoothing my covers around me and the smell of lavender on her was still strong.

"He was in this room," I said to her to explain the sticky door-knob.

"Who was?"

But I was very sleepy and I could say no more, though perhaps she would not have understood anyway, in spite of being the smart girl that she is.

The next night I left my light on to watch for Hô's arrival, but I dozed off and he had to wake me. He was sitting in a chair that he'd brought from across the room. He said to me, "Đạo. Wake up, my old friend."

I must have awakened when he pulled the chair near to me, for I heard each of these words. "I am awake," I said. "I was thinking of the poor men who had to swim out to our ship."

"They are already among those I have served," Hô said. "Before I forgot." And he raised his hands and they were still covered with sugar.

I said, "Wasn't it a marble slab?" I had a memory, strangely clear after these many years, as strange as my memory of Hô's Paris business card.

"A marble slab," Hô repeated, puzzled.

"That you poured the heated sugar on."

"Yes." Hô's sweet-smelling hands came forward but they did not quite touch me. I thought to reach out from beneath the covers and take them in my own hands, but Hô leaped up and paced about the room. "The marble slab, moderately oiled. Of course. I am to let the sugar half cool and then use the spatula to move it about in all directions, every bit of it, so that it doesn't harden and form lumps."

I asked, "Have you seen my wife?"

Hô had wandered to the far side of the room, but he turned and crossed back to me at this. "I'm sorry, my friend. I never knew her."

I must have shown some disappointment in my face, for Hô sat down and brought his own face near mine. "I'm sorry," he said. "There are many other people that I must find here."

"Are you very disappointed in me?" I asked. "For not having traveled the road with you?"

"It's very complicated," Hô said softly. "You felt that you'd taken action. I am no longer in a position to question another soul's choice."

"Are you at peace, where you are?" I asked this knowing of his worry over the recipe for the glaze, but I hoped that this was only a minor difficulty in the afterlife, like the natural anticipation of the good cook expecting guests when everything always turns out fine in the end.

But Hô said, "I am not at peace."

"Is Monsieur Escoffier over there?"

"I have not seen him. This has nothing to do with him, directly."

"What is it about?"

"I don't know."

"You won the country. You know that, don't you?"

Hô shrugged. "There are no countries here."

I should have remembered Hô's shrug when I began to see things in the faces of my son-in-law and grandson this morning. But something quickened in me, a suspicion. I kept my eyes shut and laid my head to the side, as if I was fast asleep, encouraging them to talk more.

My daughter said, "This is not the place to speak."

But the men did not regard her. "How?" Lợi asked his father, referring to the missing murder weapon.

"It's best not to know too much," Thắng said.

Then there was a silence. For all the quickness I'd felt at the first suspicion, I was very slow now. In fact, I did think of Hồ from that second night. Not his shrug. He had fallen silent for a long time and I had closed my eyes, for the light seemed very bright. I listened to his silence just as I listened to the silence of these two conspirators before me.

And then Hồ said, "They were fools, but I can't bring myself to grow angry anymore."

I opened my eyes in the bedroom and the light was off. Hồ had turned it off, knowing that it was bothering me. "Who were fools?" I asked.

"We had fought together to throw out the Japanese. I had very good friends among them. I smoked their lovely Salem cigarettes. They had been repressed by colonialists themselves. Did they not know their own history?"

"Do you mean the Americans?"

"There are a million souls here with me, the young men of our country, and they are all dressed in black suits and bowler hats. In the mirrors they are made ten million, a hundred million."

"I chose my path, my dear friend Quốc, so that there might be harmony."

And even with that yearning for harmony I could not overlook what my mind made of what my ears had heard this morning. Thắng was telling Lợi that the murder weapon had been disposed of. Thắng and Lợi both knew the killers, were in sympathy with them, perhaps were part of the killing. The father and son had been airborne rangers and I had several times heard them talk bitterly of the exile of our people. We were fools for trusting the Americans all along, they said.

We should have taken matters forward and disposed of the infinitely corrupt Thiệu and done what needed to be done. Whenever they spoke like this in front of me, there was soon a quick exhange of sideways glances at me and then a turn and an apology. "We're sorry, Grandfather. Old times often bring old anger. We are happy our family is living a new life."

I would wave my hand at this, glad to have the peace of the family restored. Glad to turn my face and smell the dogwood tree or even smell the coffee plant across the highway. These things had come to be the new smells of our family. But then a weakness often came upon me. The others would drift away, the men, and perhaps one of my daughters would come to me and stroke my head and not say a word and none of them ever would ask why I was weeping. I would smell the rich blood smells of the afterbirth and I would hold our first son, still slippery in my arms, and there was the smell of dust from the square and the smell of the South China Sea just over the rise of the hill and there was the smell of the blood and of the inner flesh from my wife as my son's own private sea flowed from this woman that I loved, flowed and carried him into the life that would disappear from him so soon. In the afterlife would he stand before me on unsteady child's legs? Would I have to bend low to greet him or would he be a man now?

My grandson said, after the silence had nearly carried me into real sleep, troubled sleep, my grandson Lợi said to his father, "I would be a coward not to know."

Thắng laughed and said, "You have proved yourself no coward."

And I wished then to sleep, I wished to fall asleep and let go of life somewhere in my dreams and seek my village square. I have lived too long, I thought. My daughter was saying, "Are you both mad?" And then she changed her voice, making the words very precise. "Let Grandfather sleep."

So when Hồ came tonight for the third time, I wanted to ask his advice. His hands were still covered with sugar and his mind was, as it had been for the past two nights, very much distracted. "There's something still wrong with the glaze," he said to me in the dark, and I pulled back the covers and swung my legs around to get up. He did not try to stop me, but he did draw back quietly into the shadows.

"I want to pace the room with you," I said. "As we did in Paris, those tiny rooms of ours. We would talk about Marx and about Buddha and I must pace with you now."

"Very well," he said. "Perhaps it will help me remember."

I slipped on my sandals and I stood up and Hồ's shadow moved past me, through the spill of streetlight and into the dark near the door. I followed him, smelling the sugar on his hands, first before me and then moving past me as I went on into the darkness he'd just left. I stopped as I turned and I could see Hồ outlined before the window and I said, "I believe my son-in-law and grandson are involved in the killing of a man. A political killing."

Hồ stayed where he was, a dark shape against the light, and he said nothing and I could not smell his hands from across the room and I smelled only the sourness of Lợi as he laid his head on my shoulder. He was a baby and my daughter Lâm retreated to our balcony window after handing him to me and the boy turned his head and I turned mine to him and I could smell his mother's milk, sour on his breath, he had a sour smell and there was incense burning in the room, jasmine, the smoke of souls, and the boy sighed on my shoulder, and I turned my face away from the smell of him. Thắng was across the room and his eyes were quick to find his wife and he was waiting for her to take the child from me.

"You have never done the political thing," Hồ said.

"Is this true?"

"Of course."

I asked, "Are there politics where you are now, my friend?"

I did not see him moving toward me, but the smell of the sugar on his hands grew stronger, very strong, and I felt Hồ Chí Minh very close to me, though I could not see him. He was very close and the smell was strong and sweet and it was filling my lungs as if from the inside, as if Hồ was passing through my very body, and I heard the door open behind me and then close softly shut.

I moved across the room to the bed. I turned to sit down but I was facing the window, the scattering of a streetlamp on the window like a nova in some far part of the universe. I stepped to the window and touched the reflected light there, wondering if there was a great smell when a star explodes, a great burning smell of gas and dust. Then I closed the shade and slipped into bed, quite gracefully, I felt, I was quite wonderfully graceful, and I lie here now waiting for sleep. Hồ is right, of course. I will never say a word about my grandson. And perhaps I will be as restless as Hồ when I join him. But that will be all right. He and I will be together again and perhaps we can help each other. I know now what it is that he has forgotten. He has used confectioners' sugar for his glaze fondant and he should be using granulated sugar. I was only a washer of dishes but I did listen carefully when Monsieur Escoffier spoke. I wanted to understand everything. His kitchen was full of such smells that you knew you had to understand everything or you would be incomplete forever.

SALEM

I have always been obedient to these true leaders of my country, even for their sake curling myself against a banyan root and holding my head and quaking like a child, letting my manhood go as we all did sooner or later beneath the bellow of fire from the B-52s. I said yes to my leaders and I went into the jungle and gave them even my manhood, but I sit now with a twenty-four-year-old pack of Salem cigarettes before me and a small photo trimmed unevenly with scissors and I whisper softly no. I whisper and I raise my eyes at once, to see if anyone has heard. No one has. I am alone. I look through my window and there is a deep-rutted road, bright now with sunlight, leading into the jungle and we are at peace in Vietnam, hard stuck with the same blunt plows and surly water buffaloes but it is our own poverty now, one country, and I turn my face from the closing of trees a hundred meters down the path. I know too much of myself from there, and I look at the objects before me on the table.

     He was alone and I don't know why, this particular American, and I killed him with a grenade I'd made from a Coca-Cola can. Some powder, a hemp fuse and a blasting cap, some scraps of iron and this soda can that I stole from the trash of the village: I was in a tree and I killed him. I could have shot him but I had made this thing and I saw him in the clearing, coming in slow but noisy, and he was very nervous, he was separated and lost and I had plenty of time and I lobbed the can and it landed softly at his feet and he looked down and stared at it as if it was a gift from his American gods, as if he was thinking to pick up this Coca-Cola and drink and refresh himself.

I had killed many men by that time and would kill many more before I came out of the jungle. This one was no different. There was a sharp pop and he went down and there was, in this case, as there often was, a sound that followed, a sound that we would all make sooner or later in such a circumstance as that. But the sound from this particular American did not last long. He was soon gone and I waited to see if there would be more Americans. But I was right about him. I'd known he was separated from his comrades from just the way he'd picked up one foot and put it ahead of the other, the way he'd moved his face to look around the clearing, saying to himself, Oh no, no one is here either. Not that I imagined these words going through his head when I first saw him—it is only this morning that I've gone that far. At the time, I just looked at him and knew he was lost and after the grenade I'd made with my own hands had killed him, I waited, from the caution that I'd learned, but I knew already that I'd been right about him. And I was. No one appeared.

And then I came down from the tree and moved to this dead body and I could see the wounds but they did not affect me. I'd seen many wounds by then and though I thought often of the betrayal of my manhood beneath the bombs of the B-52s, I could still be in the midst of blood and broken bodies and not lose my nerve. I went to this dead body and there were many jagged places and there was much blood and I dug into each of the pockets of the pants, the shirt, and I hoped for documents, for something to take back to my leaders, and all that I found was a pack of Salem cigarettes.

I do not remember if the irony of this struck me at the time. I was a young man and ardent and at turns full of fury and of shame and these are not the conditions for irony. But we all knew, even at that time, that one of the favorite pleasures of the dear father of Vietnam, Hồ Chí Minh, was to smoke a Salem cigarette. A captain in our popular forces had a personal note from father Hồ that thanked him for capturing and sending north a case of Salem cigarettes. This was all common knowledge. But I, too, liked American cigarettes, encouraged in this by the example of our leader, and I think that when I took this pack of Salem from the body, I was thinking only of myself.

Like now. I am, it seems, a selfish man. Hồ Chí Minh died that same year and we all went through six more years of fighting before our country was united and I owe my obedience to those who have brought us through to our great victory, but they have asked something now that makes me sit and hesitate and wait and think in ways that surprise me, after all this time, after all that I have been through with my country. The word has come down to everyone that we are to find any objects that belong to dead American soldiers and bring them forth so that the American government can name its remaining unnamed dead and then our two countries can become friends. It's like my wife's old beliefs and her mother's. These two women live in my home and they love me and they care for me but they do not change what they deeply believe, in spite of what I've been through for them, and they would understand this in their Buddhist way. It is as if we had all died and now we were being reborn in strange new bodies, destined to atone in this particular new incarnation for the errors of our past. The young VC and U.S. soldier reborn as middle-aged friends doing business together, creating soda cans and cigarettes.

Is it this that makes me hesitate to obey? I only have to ask the question to know that it is not. In the clearing, I put the pack of Salem cigarettes in my pocket and then I slipped back into the jungle and I smoked one cigarette later in the afternoon, shaking it out of the pack with my mind elsewhere as I sat beside a stream, a little ways apart from my own comrades. I did not wish to share these cigarettes with them and when I lit one and drew the smoke into my body, there was that familiar letting go from a desire both created and fulfilled by this thing I did, and I looked down the stream away from the others and in a few hundred meters the jungle closed in, black in the twilight, and I blew the smoke out and my nostrils flared from an odd coolness. I had never before smoked this favorite cigarette of Hồ Chí Minh and for a moment I thought this soft chill in my head was somehow a sign of him. Such a thought—the vague mysticism of it—came easily to me and I never questioned it, though I think Hồ himself would have been disappointed in me because of it. This was not the impulse of a mature communist, and much later, when I learned that there was a thing called menthol in some American cigarettes, I remembered my thoughts by the stream and I felt ashamed.

But at the time, I let this notion linger, that the spirit of Hồ was inside me, and I took the pack of cigarettes out of my pocket and now I looked at it more carefully: the blue-tinted green bands of color at the top and bottom, the American words, long and meaningless to my eyes except for the large SALEM in a central band of white—this name I'd known to recognize. And there was a clear cellophane wrapper around the pack, which I ruffled a little with my thumb and almost stripped off, but I stopped myself. This was protection from the dampness. Then I turned the pack over and there was a leaping inside me as if a twig had just snapped in the jungle nearby. A face smiled up at me from my hand, a woman's face, and I stopped my breath so that she would not hear me. I suppose that this reflex ran on even into my hands where I was ready to draw my weapon and kill her.

And she is before me now. The pack of Salem is in the center of the oak table that I made with my own hands, breaking down a French cabi-

net from an old provincial office building to make a surface of my own.
The cigarette pack lies in the center of this table and the photo looks up
from behind the cellophane, just where he put it, the man from the clearing. I have never taken the photo out of its place and I have never smoked
another cigarette from the pack and these are things that I knew right
away to do, even before my hands calmed and the beating of my heart
slowed again beside the stream, and I did not ask myself why, I just knew
to look once more at the woman—she had an almond-shaped face and
colorless hair and a vast smile with many teeth—and then to put the cigarette pack into my deepest pocket with the amber Buddha pendant my
wife had slipped into my hand when I went away from her.

I expect her soon, my wife. I look through my window and down
the path and she and her mother will come walking from out of the
closing of the trees and she will be bearing water and her sudden appearance there along this jungle path will make my hands go soft and I
am wrong to say that the hair of this woman in the picture has no color,
there are times of the day when the sunlight falls with this color on our
village and her hair has no color only against the jungle shadow of my
wife's hair.

I wish I had the reflexes of the days when I was a freedom fighter.
Instantly I could decide to kill or to run or to curl down and quake or
to rob a dead man's pockets or I could even make such a strange and
complicated decision as to put this pack of cigarettes into my pocket
with the secret resolve—secret even from myself—to preserve it for
decades. Now I sit and sit and I can decide nothing. Something tells
me that my leaders will betray all that they have ever believed in and
fought for, that they will make us into Japanese. But even shaping that
thought, I do not have a reflex, my hands do not go hard, they just lie
without moving on the tabletop before the smile of an American
woman, and perhaps what began beneath the bombs of the B-52s is now
complete. Perhaps I am no longer a man.

Still, I will not act in haste about this. That is the way of a twenty-year-old boy. I am no longer a boy, either. And even the boy knew to put this thing away and not to touch it. Why? I bend near and I wait and I watch as if I am hidden in a tree and watching the face of the jungle across a clearing. The photo has three sharp, even edges, top and bottom and down the left side, but the right side is very slightly crooked, angling in as it comes down through a pale blue sky and a dark field and past the woman's shoulder, and then it seems as if this angle will touch her at the elbow, cut into her, and the edge veers off, conscious of this, leaving the arm intact. I speak of the edge as if it created itself. It is of course the man who made the cut, who was careful not to lose even the thinnest slice of the image of this woman he clearly loved. He trimmed the photo to fit in the cellophane around a pack of cigarettes and I understand things with a rush: he placed her there so that every time his unit stopped and sat sweating and afraid by a jungle stream and he took out his cigarettes to smoke, she would be there to smile at him.

Is this not a surprising thing? A sentimental gesture like that from an American soldier who has come across an ocean to do the imperialist work of his country? Perhaps that is why I kept the pack of cigarettes. I am baffled by such an act from this man. Even my wife has such ways. We still have an ancestor shrine in our house. A little altar table with an incense holder and an alcohol pot and a teakwood tabernacle that has been in her family for many years and there is a table of names there, written on rice paper, with the names of four generations, and she believes that the souls of the dead need the prayers of the living or they will never rest and I tell her that this is not clear thinking in a world that has thrown off the tyrannies of the past, but she turns her face away and I know that I hurt her. This altar and the prayers for the dead do not even fit her Buddhism, they are from the Confucianism of the Chinese who oppressed us for centuries. But she does not hear me. It is something that lives apart from any religion or any politics. It is something that comes from our weakness, our fearful hopes for a life beyond the one that we can see and touch, and it is this that allows governments to oppress the poor and create the very evils I helped fight against.

But as I look more closely at these objects and think more clearly, I realize I should not have been surprised at the sentimentality of this American soldier. I am confused in my thinking. His wife was alive. This was the picture of a living person, not a dead ancestor. And whatever excess of sentiment there was in his wanting to see his wife in the jungle each time he stopped to smoke a cigarette, his government had bred such a thing in him—it was their power over him—and I look beyond this smiling woman and there is a sward of blue-green nearby but then the land goes dark and I bend nearer, straining to see, and the darkness becomes earth turned for planting, plowed into even furrows, and I know his family is a family of farmers, his wife smiles at him and her hair is the color of the sunlight that falls on farmers in the early haze of morning and he must have taken as much pleasure from that color as I take from the long drape of night-shadow that my wife combs down for me and the earth must smell strong and sweet, turned like that to grow whatever it is that Americans eat, wheat I think instead of rice, corn perhaps. I am short of breath now and I place my hand on this cigarette pack, covering the woman's face, and I think the right thing to do is to give these objects over to my government. I have no need for them. And thinking this, I know that I am trying to lie to myself, and I withdraw my hand but I do not look at the face of the wife of the man I killed. I sit back instead and look out my window and I wait.

Perhaps I am waiting for my wife: her approach down the jungle path will make it necessary to put these things away and not consider them again and then I will have no choice but to take them into the authorities in Đà Nẵng when I go, as I do four times a year to report on the continued education of my village. If my wife were to appear right now, even as a pale blue cloud-shadow passes over the path and a dragonfly hovers in the window, if she were to appear in this moment, it would be done, for I have never spoken to my wife about what happened in those years in the jungle and she is a good wife and has never asked me and I would not tempt her by letting her see these objects. But she does not appear. Not in the moment of the blue shadow and the dragonfly and not in the moment afterward as the sunlight returns and the dragonfly rises and hesitates and then dashes away. And I know I am not waiting for my wife, after all. It is something else.

I look again at the face of this woman. The body of her husband was never found. I left him in the clearing and he was far from his comrades and he was far from my thoughts, even after I put his cigarettes in a place to keep them safe. Perhaps she has his name written on a shrine in her home and she lights incense to him and she prays for his spirit. She is the wife of a farmer. Perhaps there is some belief she has that is like the belief of my own wife. But she does not know if her husband is dead or he is not dead. It is difficult to pray in such a circumstance.

And am I myself sentimental now, like the American soldier? I am not. I have earned the right to these thoughts. For instance, there is already something I know of that is inside the cigarette pack. I understood it in a certain way even by the stream. I think on it now and I understand even more. When I shook the cigarette into my hand from the pack, the first one out was small, half-smoked, ragged at the end where he had brushed the burnt ash away to save the half cigarette, and I sensed then and I realize clearly now that this man was a poor man, like me. He could not finish his cigarette, but he did not throw it away. He saved it. There were many half-smoked cigarettes scattered in the jungles of Vietnam by Americans—it was one of the signs of them. American soldiers always had as many cigarettes as they wanted. But this man had the habit of wasting nothing. And I can understand this about him and I can sit and think on it and I can hesitate to give these signs of him away to my government without thinking myself sentimental. After all, this was a man I killed. No thought I have about him, no attachment, however odd, is sentimental if I have killed him. It is earned.

Objects can be very important. We have our flag, red for the revolution, a yellow star for the wholeness of our nation. We have the face of the father of our country, Hồ Chí Minh, his kindly beard, his steady eyes. And he himself smoked these cigarettes. I turn the pack of Salem over and there is something to understand here. The two bands of color, top and bottom, are color like I sometimes have seen on the South China Sea when the air is still and the water is calm. And the sea is parted here and held within is a band of pure white and this word *Salem,* and now at last I can see clearly—how thin the line is between ignorance and wisdom—I understand all at once that there is a secret space in the word, not Salem but *sa* and *lem,* Vietnamese words, the one meaning to fall and the other to blur, and this is the moment that comes to all of us and this is the moment that I brought to the man who that very morning looked into the face of his wife and smoked and then had to move on and he carefully brushed the burning ash away to save half his cigarette because this farm of his was not a rich farm, he was a poor man who loved his wife and was sent far away by his government, and I was sent by my own government to sit in a tree and watch him move beneath me, frightened, and I brought him to that moment of falling and blurring.

And I turn the pack of cigarettes over again and I take it into my hand and I gently pull open the cellophane and draw the picture out and she smiles at me now, waiting for some word. I turn the photo over and the back is blank. There is no name here, no words at all. I have nothing but a pack of cigarettes and this nameless face, and I think that they will be of no use anyway, I think that I am a fool of a very mysterious sort either way—to consider saving these things or to consider giving them up—and then I stop thinking altogether and I let my hands move on their own, even as they did on that morning in the clearing, and I shake out the half cigarette into my hand and I put it to my lips and I strike a match and I lift it to the end that he has prepared and I light the cigarette and I draw the smoke inside me. It chills me. I do not believe in ghosts. But I know at once that his wife will go to a place and she will look through many pictures and she will at last see her own face and then she will know what she must know. But I will keep the cigarettes. I will smoke another someday, when I know it is time.

MISSING

It was me you saw in that photo across a sugarcane field. I was smoking by the edge of the jungle and some French journalist, I think it was, took that photo with a long lens, and you couldn't even see the cigarette in my hand but you could see my blond hair, even blonder now than when I leaned my rifle against a star apple tree with my unit on up the road in a terrible fight and I put my pack and steel pot beside it and I walked into the trees. My hair got blonder from the sun that even up here in the highlands crouches on us like a mama-san with her feet flat and going nowhere. Though my hair should've gone black, by rights. It should have gone as black as the hair of my wife.

Somebody from the village went into Đà Lạt and came back with an American newspaper that found its way there from Saigon, probably, brought by some Aussie businessman or maybe even an American GI come back to figure out what it was he left over here in Vietnam. There are lots of them come these days, I'm told, the GIs, and it makes things hard for me, worrying about keeping out of their sight. I've got nothing to do with them, and that's why the photo pissed me off. As soon as I saw it, I knew it was me. I knew the field. I knew my own head of hair.

And because you can't see the cigarette, my hand coming down from my face looks like some puny little wave, like I'm saying come help me. And that's the last goddam thing I want.

I grew the tobacco myself. That's what we do in my village. And up here we grow coffee, too. The first time I saw the girl who would be my wife she was by the side of a road spreading the coffee beans out to dry. Spreading them with her bare feet. And when her family finally let me marry her and we lay down at last in our little house—with wood walls and a wood ceiling in this place in Vietnam where there are hardwood trees and cool nights—she rubbed her hands through my hair, calling it sunlight, and I held her feet in my hands and kissed them and they tasted of coffee.

I'm not missing. I'm here. I know the smell of the wood fires and the incense my wife burns for the dead father and mother who gave her to me and the smell of my daughter's hair washed from the big pot in our backyard to catch the rainwater, and instead, the "USA Today" has got me on the run, waving pitifully across a field at a photographer to put the word out to the world, but they don't wonder why I'm apparently not smart enough to walk on across that field and say, Take me back to my mama and my papa and my brothers and my sisters who are living ruined lives in America because I'm missing in action. I don't even have the sense to get close enough to the road so I can be identified, so I'm the lost child of every family in the country with someone whose body was never found.

But I walked away. I just walked away. And there were a thousand of them like me. Two thousand. More, I heard, a lot more. In the back alleys of Saigon, in the little villages in the highlands and along the sea, trying to keep out of the way of the killing just like these people who took us in and didn't ask any questions.

Though I could see the questions all come back in the faces of my people when the newspaper showed up. We all went out to see it. It's the way here. The village is small and our elder is Binh and he knew me from the first, he was the first man I saw when I walked in here in 1970 unarmed and bareheaded and I said in the little bit of Vietnamese I had that I was a friend, I wanted to lie down and sleep. He knew what I was doing.

It was yesterday that we sat on mats in front of Tiên's house and she brought us tea and we looked at the paper.

"It's you, I think," Binh said, and he curved his lower lip upward, lifting the little wisp of a Hồ Chí Minh beard, a beard that he wore not from approval of the man but with a kind of irony.

Tri, who had brought the paper, put it before me again now, and the dozen faces around watched me for the final word. I nodded. Thảo, my wife, touched my shoulder. She could see it, too. "Yes," I said.

"What does it say about you?" Binh asked.

"Nothing," I said. "They don't know who I am."

Binh nodded and he did it slow enough that I knew he wanted me to say more. I waited, though, looking away beyond the circle, across the dirt street to the tobacco-drying racks, and some kids were there, two of Tiên's boys squatting and looking back at me and Tri's little girl, who stood staring at a dragon head set on a table in the sun. Tiên had been working on the head, repainting the green and red ridges in its face, getting it ready for Tết, the new year. When I looked away from Binh, I thought my daughter, Hoa, might be there, but she wasn't. And I didn't want to cast my gaze farther with Binh waiting for me to say more.

But I'd waited a little too long already. Binh asked, "Does it speak of some other man?"

"Not one particular man. No. It says some people in America have seen the photo and think it's proof that Americans are still alive over here, men being held by the communists."

"MIA," Binh said, pronouncing each letter with a flat American inflection that he'd picked up from me long ago.

"Yes," I said.

At this, Binh turned his face, in respect, away from Quang who sat next to him. Quang was almost as old as Binh, clean-shaven, with skin the color of this dirt street moments after a rain. But I glanced at him briefly, and there were others from our little circle who did, too. He was holding the newspaper spread tight in his two hands as if trying to stretch any wrinkles out of it. He was looking at my image there, and I think his mind now was on his own lost son. Most of the people of a certain age in my village have dead children from the war. But Quang's boy is missing, still, after more than twenty years, and he worries about where the body might be, the spirit lost and hovering around it waiting for rites that would never come.

My village believes in spirits. Last night we all burned incense in our kitchens for the god of the hearth. Such a god lives in each of our houses, and seven days before Tết he goes up to heaven to report on the family. A family is very important in Vietnam. We work and we care for each other and we live under one roof and there is no ending for such a thing. My wife's mother and father slept on straw mats in our house until the day that each of them died. I will sleep on a straw mat in the house of my daughter until I die. That is my wish.

Perhaps that's why I'm so frightened now to see this image of myself in an American newspaper. Why I looked again across to where the children were, more of them now, gathering to watch us and wonder, and I looked for my daughter and I wanted to see her in that moment, a brief glance even. We are meant to protect our families in all their linked parts like we protect our bodies. And the god of the hearth takes special note in his report of how careful we are about that. And how we respect the spirits, the spirits of our family gone to the afterlife before us and the spirits of all the others in the air around us. And we must respect the gods, as well. The minds and wills that animate the universe. Look where they have brought me.

And Hoa appeared. My daughter is tall now, her body changing from a girl to a woman, and her hair is the brown of the dried tobacco, not black but the color of what we grow and prepare here, and I don't know why I was caught by her hair at that moment but it is long and it has this color that belongs to no one else here, not my wife, not me. And she stepped behind Tri's daughter and she looked to me, briefly, and then at the little girl staring at the dragon.

Binh still had something on his mind. "Do you think some people in America will look at this picture and remember?"

"There will be many who do that," I said, and my eyes moved to Quang, and I was thinking of the grief he was drawing from the paper in his hands even then, and Binh knew what I was saying. But I also understood him. He meant: Do you have other people in that past life of yours who will recognize this son or husband or brother of theirs and suffer from this?

I felt my wife stir beside me. She heard this beneath Binh's words as well, and grew angry at him, I think. It made her fear another woman. I should speak, I knew. But I looked again at Hoa and she was bending to the table and she picked up the dragon head and turned to face Tri's daughter and I could see Hoa's face for a moment there, caught full in the sunlight, and in this light the parts of her body that she had because of me seemed very clear, the highness of her brow, the half-expressed roundness of the lids of her eyes, the length of her nose, the wideness of her mouth, her hair neither dark nor light. And I had a twist of sadness for her, as if she had gotten from me imperfect cells that had made a club foot or an open spine or a weak heart.

She lifted the dragon high with both hands and raised it over her, and she slowly brought it down: her hair, her brow disappeared into the dragon, her eyes and her nose and her mouth, my daughter's face disappeared into great bright eyes, flared nostrils, cheeks of blood red and a brow of green. And Tri's daughter clapped her hands and laughed and the dragon head angled down and opened its mouth to her as if to cry out.

I looked at Binh and he was waiting for me to speak and I looked at the others and then at Thảo. Her face was slightly turned to me but her eyes were lowered. I thought, It's been nearly twenty years since I first lay down with you and touched those places on your body that were smooth and soft and that are coarser now, and I love them still, I love them more for their very coarseness. I do not wish to open the past either, my wife. But this is my village and I was seen across a field by millions and the eyes of that other country turn this way.

I let a little of the past back into me then, and I did not know what to say. A house with a wraparound porch and maple trees and a grass yard cut close and edged each week in a perfect line along a sidewalk: things unknown in this place. Things that I could see without pain only when they sat unpeopled in my head. Things of a family that were worth keeping only from a summer day when the maple leaves did not stir and when no one from inside this house was visible, no sounds could be heard from inside. How to say that for these Vietnamese who sensed— always—even the dead spirits of a family? Who in this circle could imagine that only this was good in that past life of mine: a maple tree and the smell of fresh paint on the porch, just dried into a Victorian green and smelling like something new, and the creak of a chain on a swing there, my feet touching and pushing, lifting me as if I was flying away.

And these thoughts frightened me. I was thinking about these Vietnamese now from a distance, how they could not know me, and I wanted to blame this distance on that other self that was creeping back in, but it was hard now entirely to do that. After all, this was my past and the haunches it crept on could find strength only from me. And Tri's daughter shrieked and laughed across the way and there was a faint, muffled roaring that I recognized as my daughter's voice and I knew not to look. I could not look at that.

And I rose up from where I crouched and I said, "I'm sorry," and I stepped out of the circle and I did not look at my wife and I did not look at my daughter and I hesitated only for a moment and I knew that no one here would ask me again to speak of this and that was their way and I looked along our village street, down a little slope to a closing of the trees, the road I had followed when Binh first saw me weary and ready to sleep. And I took one step now in that direction, toward the trees, and another step, and I walked away.

I walked for a long time and went up, into a piney wood, and this was an American smell, as American as it was Vietnamese. There were two tall pine trees in the yard behind the house with the wraparound porch and it smelled just like this and there was a chill that made me tremble briefly, tremble in the chest, in the heart, right then, passing through the shadow of a great isolated pine in a little clearing and open to the wind, and the nights in the highlands could be American, too, it could be cold at times here in Vietnam, even in this country of rice paddies and water buffalo.

And I stopped and I sat on a knoll and I looked at my hands darkened by the sun, not as dark as my wife's skin or Binh's or any of the others in the circle I'd broken but as dark as the skin of a Vietnamese child, that dark. This could be the skin of a Vietnamese child. Except for the blond hairs on my knuckles, and I looked at my arms and there was a forest of blond hair on this dark arm, and I was on the porch swing, in the very center, and my arms were taut, my legs were just long enough now to touch and push and lift and my arms were rigid grasping the lip of the seat, and for a moment there was only the cry of the chain above me: I pushed and the chain cried out, over and over, and it seemed painful to this thing for it to carry me, and I rose but always came down again and I never did move from the porch, and I stopped and I sat and still there was silence from the house but I knew I would go in. Against all that I desperately desired, I would go in.

Binh was asking me to go in. They all asked me that now. Just to have me speak. I was to walk into the great bland jaws of that house and what I feared was this: perhaps a family scattered even to the other side of the earth did not truly cease. Once I went in again, perhaps I could never return to Vietnam. I sat now and waited and trembled and nothing came to me to do.

But I could not sit in the woods and I rose and I went back down to the path and I walked again into the village and I went past the vegetable garden and there were three women there in conical straw hats and I knew their names and I knew their children and I passed the house of Tri and the house of Quang and the houses of others whose names I knew, whose children I knew, and I stopped in front of Tiên's house and there was the smell of wood fire from her kitchen and the smell of incense and the dragon's head was sitting in her doorway now and smelling of paint. There was the smell of fresh paint in her doorway and they all came, gradually. Tiên first and then Binh and then the others, all of them came, and my wife came and Hoa was with her and about to go away and I shook my head no and then nodded her to the circle that was forming.

Hoa crouched beside me and Thào next to her, anxious still, I knew, and my daughter turned her face up to me and then away and I leaned near and her hair smelled of the rain, smelled of the water that we gathered in a great stone pot, as is our way here, and we believe that the spirits of our ancestors come close to us and need our prayers, the prayers in our houses with the smoke of incense rising, and I understood how odd and wonderful the air of this village was now because I came here and married and made this child. The air here was filled with the spirits of Thào's coffee farmers and tobacco farmers and woodcutters but also filled with the spirits of my clothiers and newspapermen and bankers, all drawn into this place, into my house, by our incense and our prayers, all brought together by my child, the confluence of families who were, in that invisible realm, astonished to find themselves together.

And I said, "Each new year when I was a child, the god of the hearth went to heaven from my house in America. He came to the council of the gods and he said, There are children in this house and they sleep each night in great fear and they have places on their bodies that are the color of the sky in the highlands of Vietnam just after the sun has disappeared. And they pray, even the youngest of them, a boy, for escape and when they love each other, these children, it is to pray that each of the others escapes. And they know that this will happen for them, if at all, one at a time. And this house is empty of incense. And this house sees no spirits in the world."

And I stopped speaking and the faces in the circle lowered their eyes in deference to me and they understood and they said no more and we all rose and we went away and that night I lay in the dark on a straw mat and my wife lay awake next to me. I could hear her faintly jagged breath and I said, "There was no woman in that life." And my wife sighed softly and her breathing grew as smooth as her body when I first touched her and I closed my eyes.

And I thought of this place in Vietnam where I lay and how it grows coffee and it grows tobacco, and in that other life there was a time in the morning when I could slip out of the house and there was no one around but me and I knew that one day I would escape, and inside they drank coffee and smoked cigarettes and read the newspaper.

Robert Olen Butler served in Vietnam in 1971 as a Vietnamese linguist. He is the author of nine novels and two collections of stories. The short stories in this collection have appeared in such places as *The Hudson Review*, *The Sewanee Review*, *The Virginia Quarterly Review*, and have been anthologized in *The Best American Short Stories* and *New Stories from the South*. *A Good Scent from a Strange Mountain* was awarded the 1993 Pulitzer Prize for Fiction and was nominated for the PEN/Faulkner Award. He is also the winner of a Guggenheim Fellowship for Fiction and the Richard and Hinda Rosenthal Award from the American Academy of Arts and Letters. He is the Francis Eppes Professor of English holding the Michael Shaara Chair in Creative Writing at Florida State University.